Ryan,

They say a book is a dream you can hold. Thank you for letting me share my dream with you!

[illegible]

White Noise Stories

Volume One

White Noise Stories

Volume One

By
Tammy Vreeland

E-BookTime, LLC
Montgomery, Alabama

White Noise Stories
Volume One

Library of Congress Control Number: 2017943430

ISBN: 978-1-60862-693-9

First Edition
Published June 2017
E-BookTime, LLC
6598 Pumpkin Road
Montgomery, AL 36108
www.e-booktime.com

Dedicated To:

The ones who will never know the true story.

White Noise Stories

Lauren looks around at her cluttered new apartment. Sighing, she tries to ignore the mess and walks over to the window.

Looking out Lauren sees the city below her. Her new apartment is located on the second floor of a very tall, old apartment building.

Her view is dismal but each floor up not only increases your view but your rent as well. Unfortunately, for now this was the best she could do.

It is her first day staying in the apartment so she tries to be optimistic. At least her new job doesn't start for a month, which gives her plenty of time to get organized.

Lauren is a little surprised at how much noise seems to be coming into the apartment from down below. Horns honking, people yelling. Surely there must be an open window somewhere for her to hear so much. Lauren looks around the tiny apartment and realizes all the windows are securely shut. Sighing, she reminds herself she needs to take the good with the bad.

Lauren begins to unpack and thinks to herself that eventually she will be able to tune the noise out. Until then, she would have to be content with listening to her music through her headphones as she worked. Yes, this is all going to work out!

As the days go by in the new apartment, Lauren realizes tuning the noise out is far more difficult than she thought it would be!

Lauren is exhausted. She has not had a good night's sleep since she moved in. Not only is she dealing with the noises outside, but inside too. There is a neighbor next door with a crying baby, and on the other side, a barking dog. She can't quite believe it could be possible, but Lauren swears she hears people through her duct vents from several floors up!

Lauren tries every idea she can come up with. First, she tries falling asleep with her headphones on but she can never seem to get comfortable and the music itself seems to keep her awake. Then she tries every ear plug she can find, but most of them fall out. Frustrated, Lauren finally does some research on good ol' Amazon and finds something called a white noise sound machine. It is not very expensive with free shipping so she decides to give it a try. Until it arrives, Lauren forces herself to concentrate on making her new little apartment her home.

After the first week, the apartment is completely finished. Now it is time to acclimate herself to her new location. For her second week, Lauren starts waking up at the time she thinks she will need to get ready for work.

Once dressed, she leaves the apartment as if she is going to work. This gives her an estimate of how much time she will need to give herself each day.

With everyone else in the apartment leaving for work in the morning, she quickly realizes waiting for the elevator is a waste of time. Fortunately, Lauren will only have to walk down two flights of stairs each day to avoid the elevator.

Once in the lobby, she is amazed by the intricate hustle and bustle of the city. People coming and going. Deliveries being made. Kids going to school. Soon, Lauren will be in the middle of it all, but for now she is an outsider.

A doorman holds the door open for people. He notices Lauren standing in awe and calls over to her, "You must be Ms. Styles!"

Lauren is shocked that the old man knows her name. Not interfering with his job, Lauren walks over to the side of him and asks, "Yes, how did you know?"

The doorman continues to greet each person as he holds the door. Lauren is amazed that he knows everyone's name. In between the people coming and going the doorman answers her, "They told me we had a new girl moving in and they also told me your name. I take great pride in knowing all of our tenants."

Lauren watches for a break and then quickly puts her hand out. "You can call me Lauren. What is your name?"

The doorman shakes her hand warmly, "I am Mr. Akeru."

Lauren is not at all surprised, given his age, that he would prefer to be called Mister. "Mr. Akeru, it is a pleasure to meet you. Quick question. I have a box coming from Amazon… how do they deliver it here?"

Mr. Akeru replies, "They hold them at the front desk."

Lauren looks relieved. "I bought a white noise sound machine to help me get used to all of this noise."

Mr. Akeru smiles, "In time, you will get used to it."

Lauren is enjoying their conversation. "I am going on a quick walk to where my new job is, and then I will get a cup of coffee. Would you like a cup?"

Mr. Akeru is a little surprised, "That would be mighty nice of you, Ms. Lauren. Nothing fancy, just straight black coffee."

Lauren is happy, "Not a problem, I should be back within the hour."

Lauren finds her new job easily and fortunately a Starbucks is on the way. With so many people on the street and in line, Lauren realizes she will have to allow more time than she thought to get to work.

Lauren decides to give the people who need to get to work a chance to get coffee first. Looking around, Lauren is happy to find an empty park bench. Pulling out her phone, she gives her mom a call.

Her mother answers the phone happily, "There's my little girl! How are things going?"

Lauren smiles, "Got my big girl panties on today and testing out the waters."

Her mother laughs, "How do you think it will be?"

Lauren sighs, "May have to get up a little earlier than I thought but for the most part I think I will do ok."

Her mother is frustrated because she is stuck in traffic. "Although I would never want to live in the city, I can understand why you do! This traffic is unbelievable!"

Lauren agrees, "I know, and yet foot traffic looks like it may be just as aggravating. I have watched this one poor businessman try and get around these two heavyset women three times!" Lauren laughed. "Every time he goes to make his move, one of them throws their hand out gesturing to whatever they are talking about. And by the looks of it, they are in no hurry to get where they are going."

Lauren's mom sympathizes, "That sucks. Go figure... even walking to work you can get behind the wrong people!" Her mom changes the subject, "Have you been able to sleep any better in the apartment?"

Lauren sighs, "No, not yet. However, there is hope. I ordered a sound machine from Amazon and am hoping for it to come today."

Her mom is curious, "Let me know how it works. Maybe after all these years it will be the key to me getting a good night's sleep too. Lord knows, I have tried everything when it comes to your father's snoring!"

Lauren looks at her watch and realizes her mother must be getting close to work. "I will. I know I used to tease you all those years that it could not be that bad with Dad, but as tired as I am now, you have my full sympathy!"

Lauren's mom chuckles, "Ah well, the things we do for love."

Before saying goodbye Lauren's mom is curious, "Real quick, I was wondering if you have been afraid in the apartment?"

Lauren is not surprised by the question. "You know I thought I would, it certainly is different than college. In college, I was never alone in the apartment; people were coming and going at all times." Lauren enjoys the sunlight beaming down on her. "And yet, I can honestly say I have not once been afraid. For that matter, I have been enjoying the alone time," Lauren admits and chuckles, "although I do find myself having conversations with myself."

Lauren's mom pulls into the parking lot for where she worked. "I am so happy for you, being afraid can be crippling. I still have a hard time at the house when no one is there."

Lauren understands. "Mom, you are out in the middle of the country with the nearest neighbor two miles down the road. I only have to walk a few feet in either direction and I have neighbors."

Lauren's mom parks her car, "I finally made it to work! Enjoy your day sweetie, we will talk later. Love you."

Lauren smiles, "Love you too Mom."

Lauren's timing is perfect, hardly anyone is waiting in line for coffee now. Amazing how much of a difference a couple of minutes before the work day can make, the streets are now almost empty.

Walking back with both coffees, Lauren is pleased with herself. The location of her new apartment is perfect. It is close to work, plenty of places to eat, even a nice market for groceries.

With most people already at work, Lauren sees Mr. Akeru standing alone. He opens the door with a smile, "Find everything Ms. Lauren?"

Lauren nods, "I did Mr. Akeru and here is your coffee. It's still pretty hot so be careful."

Mr. Akeru takes the cup gratefully. "A man could get used to such treatment."

Lauren agrees, "I have three more weeks of freedom before I disappear into the rat race. So, until then you will probably see me more than you would like."

Mr. Akeru disagrees, "No, that is perfect! Gives me time to get to know you! There are far too many people here who are too busy to even know I exist."

Lauren looks around and lowers her voice, "I will not be getting you in trouble will I?"

Mr. Akeru laughs out loud, "Ms. Lauren, I have been here forever. To be honest, I am not even sure the front desk remembers I am here. Nah, they are good people, they leave me be."

Lauren is happy to have met her first friend. "Very well, I will probably see you at lunch. What little food I had in the apartment is gone. Might pick your brain on some good places to eat."

Mr. Akeru smiles, "Not a problem, I know them all."

Lauren says her goodbyes and goes to the front desk. Sure enough, her package had been delivered. Happily she rides the elevator to her apartment.

Once inside, Lauren opens the box. She is a little disappointed when she holds up a square black box the size of her hand. Not impressed, she frowns, fearing yet another disappointment.

The only nice thing about it is that it is portable enough to take with her anywhere in the apartment. Sitting in the living room, Lauren puts the batteries in and clicks through the many sounds it offers.

Finally settling on one sound, Lauren turns it up and sits back in her chair. Amazingly, all the sounds around her are gone! Replaced by a soothing hiss of white noise. A noise that pleasantly reminds Lauren of being young at her grandmother's house and staying up so late that only a white noise came from the TV.

Curious, she reaches for her headphones and turns on the TV. Yes! It even allows her to watch her TV with the headphones on at a normal level. This is going to work!

Lauren can't wait until evening to finally get a good night of sleep, she so desperately needs it! In fact, as she yawns Lauren thinks, screw it! Why not take a nap until lunch? She will be rested to do some exploring and grocery shopping afterwards.

Lauren takes the sound box into the bedroom and turns it on. She undresses and gets into bed, listening to the white noise. Her ears strain to hear something. She realizes there is nothing to hear but the constant hiss of the white noise.

Her body relaxes and she finally falls asleep. At the beginning, her sleep is a deep and gratifying one. However, as the nap proceeds she becomes restless and starts to dream one of the most realistic dreams she has ever had.

The
Ferry

The Ferry

Joyce has been driving all night and is completely exhausted. She picks up her coffee cup only to find it empty. Sighing, she puts it back into the cup holder.

The music streaming from her phone to the radio is not bringing any relief either. If anything, even the fast beat songs seem as if they are trying to lull her to sleep.

Suddenly the music stops in mid song. Confused, Joyce looks down at the seat and realizes she did not plug her phone in while she listened to the music. Now her phone is dead, damn!

Joyce looks up at the dark foggy road ahead of her while she blindly tries to find the cord for her phone with her hand. Frustrated, she looks down at the seat and in the console but can't seem to find the damn cord!

Joyce feels the car lurch. In a moment's time, she has veered off the road. With no shoulder and the uneven terrain, Joyce finds herself and the car rolling over. The car flips only once and lands upright. Dazed, Joyce's only thought is, can she still drive the car back up the embankment and make it to the ferry on time?

Adrenaline running high throughout her, Joyce drives the car back onto the road while ignoring the sharp pain in her neck.

As Joyce races down the road, she tries to reassure herself that her neck had been hurting before the accident. The stress of her job and living in the city was taking a toll on her.

Her greatest desire is to get to her home on the island. Joyce will worry about the damage to either her or the car once she gets on the ferry.

Joyce glances at the clock on the radio and speeds up even more. Where had the time gone? The accident could have only taken a few moments. Unless she had passed out. Joyce refuses to think about that either. Joyce has to make the ferry! There is no other option.

Joyce is encouraged when she sees the sign for the dock, but the fog has rolled in so heavily that it is hard for her to see the ferry. Ahead, she thinks she sees a figure waving her forward. Awesome! She must have made the last ferry.

A nagging thought comes to her as she looks at the clock and sees how late it is. The ferry never leaves this late but, Joyce reasons to herself; they must have been delayed due to the fog. Joyce slowly pulls the car forward. She always hates this part even in the bright sunlight; however, now is much worse. She has no idea how far to pull forward.

Joyce can barely see the figure motioning her on. Wow! There are no other cars on the ferry! As long as she had been doing this, never had she been the only car on the ferry, especially this late on a Friday night.

Exhausted but relieved, Joyce turns her car off. She rests her head gently against the head rest and closes her eyes. Her neck feels extremely sore. In fact, Joyce can barely keep her head up.

Loudly someone knocks at her window, scaring the shit out of her! Trying to regain her composure, Joyce slowly rolls the window down.

A distraught older woman looks at her worrisomely, “Ma’am what are you doing here?”

Joyce shrugs her shoulders, “I am riding the ferry over.”

The woman looks around, frightened, “No, this ferry is…” she stumbles for the right words “under repair. You missed the last ferry.”

Pissed, Joyce raises her voice, “Damn it! Some guy waved me on, so I simply followed him!”

Joyce leans forward to turn her car on when suddenly she feels the familiar lurch of the boat moving. She looks back at the woman. “We are moving!”

The old woman closes her eyes and answers simply, “I was afraid this would happen.”

Joyce’s heart races a little, “Where are we going to?”

The old woman looks around but it is very hard to see in the heavy fog. “I am not sure, just stay in your car. I know the Captain, maybe she can find something out for me.”

Before Joyce can thank her, the old woman is gone. Joyce sighs and rolls her window back up. She sits quietly in her car looking forward; she sees nothing but heavy fog. Heavy fog is an understatement! In fact, Joyce has never seen fog like this before!

With the fog being so heavy, it makes her eyelids even heavier. Joyce can't believe how tired she is. She closes her eyes a second time. This time, Joyce finds herself dreaming about falling. How she hated dreams like this! Strangely, for the first time in her life, Joyce actually feels herself hit the ground. The pain is intense, but only for a moment. Then a complete nothingness comes over her. Startled, Joyce forces herself to wake up.

Joyce opens her eyes abruptly and finds herself back in her car. Sighing, she rubs her eyes and tries to calm herself from the dream. Joyce carefully moves her head and is relieved that she no longer feels any pain.

Joyce looks around and sees what a mess the accident made of her car. She can only imagine what the outside must look like. She begins to look for her phone but remembers it is dead. In fact, it was the reason for the accident. Joyce realizes now, she must have left her cord back in the apartment. Finally, she finds her iPad back between the seats. If she can get a signal she can go ahead and contact her insurance company.

Joyce gets out of the car in hopes of finding someone to tell her what is going on. The old woman did not seem trustworthy. Carrying her iPad with her, Joyce cautiously walks blindly towards where she thinks the cabin of the ferry is. It must have rained recently because everything she touches is soaking wet.

Finally, Joyce finds a door and cautiously opens it. "Hello? Anyone in here?"

The cabin is dimly lit with what seems to be emergency lighting. At least she can see better than outside.

Joyce hears someone walking down the stairs. Good! Maybe it will be someone that can tell her what is going on. Walking over to the stairs Joyce looks up and sees it is the old woman. "Did you find out anything for me?"

Winded, the old lady stops and nods. "I spoke to the captain. She did not realize the men had allowed you on. However, not to worry, they plan on taking you to your destination."

Joyce can't help feeling responsible for the old woman being stuck on the boat as well. "What about you? Were you planning on staying on the boat?"

The old woman sighs, "Yes, I suppose it is time."

Shadows at the top of the stairs dance strangely around. The old woman turns and starts walking back up the stairs. "Go ahead and have a seat. It may take longer with all of this fog."

Joyce nods, "I understand and thank you! It was very kind of you to take care of me."

The old woman simply nods her head and continues up the stairs. Joyce finds a seat, but when she sits down she suddenly stands back up. The seat is completely wet! Even though it is hard to see in the dim light, she can tell the cabin is soaked with water. This is strange!

Joyce sighs and sits back down. Obviously someone had sprayed down the whole cabin. She turns on her iPad as she thinks; a wet butt is a lot better than having to wait for the next ferry in the morning!

Quickly, Joyce realizes she has no Wi-Fi connection. Not a big surprise. Joyce pulls up a game to play to pass the time. Lost in her game she doesn't realize there is a man sitting in the shadows. He quietly clears his throat to get her attention. Startled, Joyce laughs out nervously, "Oh! You scared me!"

The man in the shadows answers sympathetically, "I am sorry."

Joyce makes small talk, "Are you a passenger or a worker?"

The man becomes a little defiant, "Does it matter?"

Joyce is taken back a little, "Not at all, just making conversation." She smiles and continues, "This has not been a good day for me. First I leave late from the city, and then I forget my phone charger."

Embarrassed, Joyce admits, "Worst of all, while looking for the phone charger I flip my car!" Joyce can't help but chuckle a little, "Does that deter me? No! I race like an idiot to get here on time. You would have thought I learned my lesson after the accident!"

Surprised the man has not said a word, Joyce finishes, "I did not realize this ferry was not the original ferry."

The man nods, "And yet, you ended up getting your way."

A little defensively Joyce responds, "Well yea, but I tried to move the car when the old woman told me. Unfortunately, we had already started moving."

The man sneers a little, "That old woman has her own worries!"

Not knowing what else to say, Joyce asks, "And what worries would that be?"

The man points toward the windows, "Have you seen how thick the fog is out there? Being the Captain, she has more concerns than you right now!" Before Joyce can reply he adds, "We should have never left the port in this fog, especially for a routine check. This could have easily been done tomorrow!"

Joyce agrees but is still shocked, "Forgive me, but that old woman is the Captain?"

The guy nods. "Yup, I remember the day she came to us all young like you and so proud to be a woman Captain. Me and the guys were not too sure about her. Boats and women tend to have a bad history."

Joyce sighs. She can't believe in this day and age there are still such thoughts. Defending the woman, Joyce replies, "Apparently she did alright for herself, to be that old and still doing it!"

The guy shrugs his shoulders and asks, "What do you do for a living?"

Joyce hates it when someone asks that question, it is never an easy answer. "I am a writer."

"What do you write?" the guy asks, curious.

Joyce sighs, "Horror stories."

The guy laughs out loud and answers, "Really? Did not see you as the type. Though I admit, I give you credit for being here alone talking to a stranger."

Joyce looks around at the desolate cabin with the heavy fog pressing in on the windows. She supposed most women would be terrified of the situation she was in. Being on the wrong boat, scary looking fog, cell phone dead, no Wi-Fi; however, she can't help but laugh along with the guy, "I know right? I should be sobbing hysterically, but I have never been that kind of woman."

Surprised at her candor, he wonders, "Why is that?"

Joyce thinks about it before she answers, "As a kid, I used to love anything that scared me. I would take it as a challenge. The more it scared me, the more I would go back and try to conquer it."

The man can't help but smile, "Impressive."

Joyce shakes her head, "Not really. Unfortunately, the thing I enjoyed most, being scared, seems no longer an option for me. Nothing I read or see gives me that thrill I first had when I was a kid."

The man answers, "You have conquered fear, most have not."

Joyce has to know, "Are you the man who waved me onto the ferry?"

The man shakes his head, "No, that would have been Johnny. Poor kid still doesn't know any better."

Joyce smiles a little, "Ah, so you are a worker?"

The man nods, "Yes, I am one of the work hands on this vessel."

Joyce is curious, "Then why didn't you say that when I first asked?"

The man shrugs his shoulders, "I have found that once passengers know I am a worker they tend to not want to have a conversation with me."

Joyce tries to look straight at him but it is still hard to see him in the shadows. "It would not have mattered to me. I love talking to people, no matter who they are. I have found that everyone has a story to tell, and that fascinates me."

The man points to her iPad, "Do you keep your stories in there?"

Joyce looks at her iPad. "Yes, I usually write down any new thoughts here and when I get home I write on my computer."

The man clears his throat, "I have a story for you. Do you want to hear it?"

Excited, Joyce asks, "Do you mind if I type while you talk?"

The man shakes his head, "Not at all, in fact, I would be honored if you would write this story down."

Joyce quickly gets situated and nods, "Ok, I am ready when you are."

The man looks out the window at the fog and begins. "Several years ago on a night like this, a captain decided one passenger was more important than the safety of the boat and crew. These boats are not made for open sea. Unfortunately, that night the captain completely lost their way to the island and they found themselves heading out to the open sea."

The man sighs, "Of course none of them knew before it was too late. Running low on fuel was the only clue they had because none of their equipment was working. Even the radio had failed them."

The stranger sits in silence as he thinks about it and then goes on, "When morning came they had no idea where they were and there was no land in sight."

Joyce interrupts, "Surely there were people who knew the boat was missing?"

The man shakes his head, "No, the boat was to go into the service bay for the weekend. The crew was going to be given the weekend off." The man explains, "The crew were nothing but misfits and were their own family. The captain had plans to be alone."

Joyce is curious, "And what of the passenger, surely he had family?"

The man can't help but laugh, "Come to find out the passenger was on the run, he did not want to be found. In fact, that was why he paid the captain so handsomely. He was in dire need to travel to the island."

Fascinated, Joyce quickly writes down some notes. "Did the crew not have other ways of communicating with someone?"

The man looks disgusted, "The boat had been stripped previously, readying it to be retired."

Joyce is in disbelief, "You are telling me there was not even a flare gun on the boat?"

The man shakes his head, "No, everything useable had been taken off to use on the other boats."

The man hesitates, "You don't like holes in a story, do you?"

Joyce laughs, "It is a pet peeve of mine, no holes allowed. I want the story to be believable."

The man laughs, "Well, this next part will be a little hard for you but it did happen."

Joyce waits anxiously, "Go ahead."

The man continues solemnly, "A full day goes by with the entire crew, captain and passenger trying to figure a way to the island." Disgusted, he explains, "The only thing they had on the boat was the passenger's car and trailer which happened to have a Jet Ski loaded on it."

Joyce smiles, "Ah, let me guess. The passenger insisted on taking the Jet Ski because he did not want to be on the boat when they were rescued?"

The man nods, "What a nightmare it was for the crew to lower the damn thing into the sea, let alone trying to tell the man he had no way of knowing where to go. Nevertheless, he was not about to listen. The captain, trying to secure payment, assured the passenger that together, he and the captain would find the island."

Joyce adds, "Somehow they did get to the island, right?"

The man nods sadly, "Yes, but once on the island the captain refused to say anything to anyone for fear of being found out helping the fugitive. The captain, in disguise, left the island with the money and never looked back."

Joyce is shocked, "This was the captain's crew. Surely there would be some sort of loyalty?"

The man agrees but answers, "The crew never really respected that captain. They should have, but they did not."

Joyce is confused, "Once the boat was found, the crew would tell everything. Then the captain would become a fugitive. That was an awfully big gamble."

The man sighs, "For the money that was at play, the gamble was worth it to both the captain and the passenger."

The man finishes his story, "The gamble paid off. The boat was lost at sea and thought to have claimed all lives. Part of the trailer was found with the license plate still on it, placing the refugee as a passenger on the boat. He was pronounced dead which was exactly what he wanted."

Joyce is saddened by the story. "What happened to the boat?"

The man speculates, “It is believed that a rogue wave came upon them. With no power they had no chance and the ship went under.”

Joyce feels the boat lurch and a bit of terror creeps up on her, something she had not felt for a very long time.

The man stands up, “It seems as if you have reached your destination. I think it is time for you to return to your car.”

Joyce closes her iPad and gets up, “The story you told me… fact or fiction?”

As the man turns he mumbles, “Is that not for the reader to decide?”

Joyce smiles, “Spoken like a true author. Thank you Sir, I enjoyed your company.”

Joyce walks back to the car carefully; the heavy presence of fog still surrounds the ferry. Once inside her car, Joyce is overwhelmed again at how tired she is. As her eyelids get heavier, Joyce begins to see ghostly figures surrounding her car. Her heart races as she watches watery looking men pass her car.

Although it felt good to feel the old throb of her heart being terrified, for some reason the ghostly figures pass her by. Joyce hears distant screams coming from what sounds like the old lady.

Knowing she should try to get out and help the old lady, Joyce is more concerned that when she reached for the car door her own hand passes through it. Terrified more than she has ever been, Joyce looks down and realizes she is not quite inside her own body. In fact, her own body is slumped with her neck twisted at a strange angle.

Defeated, Joyce’s only thought is, at least soon she will be home.

****

Everyone gathers around the strange sight on the dock. No one bothers it, for obviously this is a police matter and they had not yet arrived. However, everyone’s big question is, how the hell did it get there?

Finally, a siren and a police car comes rolling up. One of the dock hands approaches the car, "Hi, Sheriff, glad you are here. Strangest thing we have ever seen!"

The sheriff gets out of his car and walks with the dock hand. "When did you find it, Todd?"

Todd scratches his head. "Right at sunrise. Fog was so bad last night you could not see anything until the sun rose."

The sheriff walks around inspecting it, "Did you talk to the ferry people? They know anything about it?"

Todd nods, "Called them right after I called you. They said they did their last run last night on time, but the fog was following them. Once they docked and let the passengers off, they could tell the fog was not going to let up so they decided not to chance it and stayed on the island for the night."

The sheriff has to ask, "And they did not deliver this car?"

Todd looks at the beat up car, "No, not something they would have delivered anyway. The policy is that all cars have to be running and drivable to bring to the island. Unless, of course, it is salvage."

The sheriff nods, "By chance did you talk to Frank? Maybe he brought it without knowing. You know, I've heard of people transporting cars and not even realizing someone is still in them."

Todd shakes his head, "Nah, ol' Frank is on the mainland visiting his grandchildren for the week. His boat has been docked over there all week."

Just then the ambulance comes rolling up and two paramedics casually walk over. "We were told not to rush."

The sheriff nods, "You can tell she has been dead a while. Load her up so I can go through her things."

Once the body has been removed the sheriff looks inside the car. The car itself looked as if it had gone over an embankment and even rolled. Yet, there was still a possibility the car could run and be driven. In fact, the inside of the car is not as horrendous as you may think. No blood anywhere.

When they pulled the woman's body out it looked like not only did she have a concussion, but the way her head rolled, it was quite obvious her neck was broken.

The sheriff gets in and tries to start the car up. Sure enough, the car starts with no problem. He then tentatively puts it in drive and is surprised to feel the car move forward. Although the car looks totaled, it is still capable of driving. The sheriff turns the car off and looks around the inside.

He can tell from the inside of the car it is fairly new and had been maintained well. Yet, everything in the car had been thrown all over. An empty coffee cup in the back seat. Coins and papers strewn all over. However, laying perfectly flat and upright is an iPad on the passenger seat. The sheriff opens the iPad and is surprised to see a story titled "The Ferry". Quickly reading the story, chills come over him and he can no longer stand to be in the car. Hanging on to the iPad, he walks back to his car.

Todd calls out to him, "What do you want us to do with the car?"

The sheriff answers, "Call Roy and have him take it to the salvage yard."

The sheriff slowly drives back to the station as he thinks about the story on the iPad. Unfortunately, too many things were adding up to be coincidences. For example, just yesterday he received a call from a woman who claimed she was his sister. You see, his sister had been a captain of a ferry that had been lost at sea. This woman on the phone claimed she was her. Now that her life was almost at an end she wanted to make her peace.

Was she the old woman Joyce had met on the ferry? Joyce had put a question mark when the man mentioned the captain in the story. To the side was a note wondering if the old woman she herself had met tonight on the ferry was the captain the man was talking about.

In Joyce's notes she also had wondered, why was the ferry's cabin soaked in water? Joyce went as far as to question, am I on the ferry that this shadowy strange man is talking about?

The sheriff thinks about Joyce. Was it possible that after the crash Joyce had continued to drive to the dock in hopes of making her destination on time? After missing the main ferry had Joyce ended up on the ferry that was lost at sea? Had the fog brought the ferry in to pick up his sister, the captain, who was thought to have originally been lost at sea with the ferry?

The sheriff sighs as he looks over at the iPad and tries to think logically. Perhaps Joyce had written this story before getting on the ferry? A fictional story he was trying to make fit the facts. The sheriff quickly looks at the time stamp on the last entry and feels chills course through him. The time would have had Joyce writing the story while she was on the ferry.

What if Joyce had to be dead to be able to interact with the shadowy man? The sheriff is no betting man; however, he would bet everything he has that this woman's time of death will be before the time stamp on the iPad.

Joyce's strong desire to make it home had enabled her to not even realize her own death. As for his sister, the sheriff is surprised that she would choose a watery grave as her punishment. Then again, it was only appropriate.

The captain's place is to go down with their boat, even if it is several years later.

White Noise Stories Continued

After the dream Lauren wakes with a start. Unsure of her surroundings, it takes a minute for her heart to stop racing.

Lauren quickly turns off the sound machine, annoyed with a pounding headache; only to be more annoyed by a damn dog barking and a baby screaming at the same time! Frustrated, she turns the sound machine back on. The white noise begins to calm her down. She closes her eyes and takes in a deep breath.

Flashes of the dream Lauren had comes back into her mind. Strange, she has always been one where when she wakes up she can never remember her dreams. And yet, she can remember this dream in full detail.

At first the dream felt like a memory and then it was as if the dream continued from the memory in hopes of finding an explanation for the memory.

Lauren had dreams of her own memories and then found herself dreaming of a "what if" scenario. It was as if her subconscious played out what might have happened after the memory.

Throughout this dream, Lauren felt like the main character; however, as a slight shiver comes over her, in no way did the dream feel like it was hers! She scolds herself; of course it was your dream! A strange one, but yours all the same!

Lauren stumbles to the bathroom and looks sleepily into the mirror. Surprised, she notices some gray hair coming up. In fact, quite a lot gray! Frustrated, she makes a mental note to stop at the drug store during lunch to get some coloring. Her mother had gray hair at an early age; however, unlike her mother, she plans on covering that little secret right up!

When she finishes up in the bathroom, Lauren reaches to turn the light off, but before she flips the switch she notices water beside her tub. Even though she had taken a shower earlier this morning, there should not have been any water on the floor. She always prided herself in being very clean and efficient. It was not like her to have so much water by the tub.

Curious, she opens the shower curtain to peer in, hoping that it is something simple she can fix. Lauren looks inside the tub and is confused, little puddles of water are in random parts of her tub, almost as if several people had been standing in her tub, soaking wet. Even more bizarre, the puddles had not pooled together. The hair on her arms begins to rise up as she thinks about the watery men from the dream. Quickly, she closes the curtain and exits the bathroom, shaking her head.

No! She was not going to scare herself. Just this morning, she had been bragging to her mother about not being afraid in her apartment. For God's sake, it is in the middle of the afternoon! Was it not an unwritten rule that ghosts could not bother you unless it was during the dark of night?

Lauren gets dressed and refuses to think any more about the stupid dream. Feeling better, she heads down to the lobby.

Mr. Akeru has not left his spot from this morning. He smiles warmly at Lauren, "You look refreshed!"

Lauren blushes, "You caught me, I took a nap. My white noise sound machine came in and I could not wait until this evening to finally get some sleep."

Mr. Akeru raises an eyebrow, "White noise you say? Might want to be careful with that, you never know…" before he can finish someone comes off the street. Mr. Akeru greets them as he holds the door for them. After they leave, Mr. Akeru stands there just smiling.

Lauren asks, "You were saying?"

Mr. Akeru looks a little confused, "I don't know, lost my thought. Any interesting dreams during your nap?"

Lauren is a little surprised at the change in topic, "Actually, yes. I had this vivid dream of a woman writer. She was taking the ferry home but…" Lauren stumbles for the right words, "She never quite made it."

Mr. Akeru hesitates for a moment, "You know, we had a woman writer live here years ago. Kept the apartment for work during the week and took the ferry home on the weekends."

Lauren's curiosity perks up, "What happened to her?"

Mr. Akeru shrugs his shoulders, "I think I heard she died in a car accident."

Chills come over Lauren, "Please tell me she did not live in my apartment!"

Mr. Akeru starts laughing, "Oh goodness no! She lived on the sixth floor."

Lauren is unnerved, "Still, what a coincidence!"

Mr. Akeru shakes his head, "Now Ms. Lauren, don't you worry! Any story you tell me, I can guarantee you I will know one that is similar. This is the city, with so many people and stories. Plus, I have been here a mighty long time!"

Lauren realizes he is right. After getting a good recommendation for lunch she leaves and explores her new location. Not once does she give another thought to her dream after she left the apartment complex.

Lauren returns several hours later and is a little disappointed not to see Mr. Akeru. Feeling more tired than she realized, she is happy to see the elevator is patiently waiting for her. Once in the apartment, she gets to work putting all the groceries away.

Reluctantly, Lauren heads to the bathroom to tackle the messy chore of coloring her hair. She is relieved to see that all of the water she saw earlier is completely gone; making her wonder if it was even there to begin with.

Afterwards, Lauren makes a light dinner and watches TV. Her eyes become heavy and she decides to make it an early night.

The
Pound

The Pound

I can remember the first time I came to this place. I was young and had no idea what was going on. I think the hardest part of it all is being able to hear their excuses for why they are leaving you. Even the attendant was a little surprised by how young I was the first time.

"She is so young and you have had her since she was a baby." The attendant hesitates, "Are you sure you want to do this?"

The man and woman nod, "We have decided to keep her brother. We chose him over her."

It is strange how when you leave you forget about this place until you find yourself here once again.

The next times were several brief times, where relatives of the family would come and go. Even friends of the family would come and go. However, every one of them would say the same thing, "We have chosen another."

I then tried to be different; hoping that perhaps, if I tried hard enough to be what they wanted, they would keep me. It worked, but not well enough.

"Sir, are you sure you want to do this? You had her for quite a long time. If I understand correctly, you even had a family with her." The attendant implores, "Surely, she is part of your family by now."

The man arrogantly shakes his head, "I am quite sure! You see, she never fit in with my lifestyle. My parents never liked her when they came to visit. Though she was good around the children, I have chosen another."

He was right I suppose, I was only happiest when the children were around. Soon they grew older and as they continued with their lives, I became less to them.

At one point I had hopes when one of the children came by with what looked like a child of his own in a stroller. He brought the mother of the child over to look at me but instantly she shook her head no. "I really don't like the idea of her being around my child, she will not do. We have chosen another."

By now I was battered and bruised; it was hard to believe there was anyone out there that would want me; however, I was given one last chance. I jumped through all the regular hoops to make it work. The parents and family of the new owner did not like the idea that I had previous owners. What was wrong with me for so many to abandon me?

My fear of coming back to this place inevitably made the new owner frustrated and tired of me and he too finally chose a life without me.

The attendant comes to the door and shakes her head, "I am sorry old girl, but I am afraid that was your last chance. You know what we have to do. Follow me."

As I walk down the long corridor I see so many like me; hopeful that their next chance will be there shortly. In a way, I am relieved there will be no more chances. The hope, the excitement, the work, the heartache had become too much.

I look up above the large furnace doors and read the sign, "Souls Retired".

My soul indeed was tired. As I step into the furnace and hear the human screams around me, I realize this must be what it feels like for a dog at a pound.

White Noise Stories Continued

Waking up from her dream, Lauren finds herself wiping tears from her eyes. She tries to figure out what the dream could mean. This was a dream a person would have who has endured heartache after heartache in their life. It was not something even close to what she has ever experienced. She is young and hopeful. She comes from a loving family and is content with where she is at in this moment of her life.

Perhaps this is a deep rooted seed of fear of what the future may have in store for her? She shakes her head no, that doesn't seem right either.

Similar to her previous dream, it feels like it is someone else's dream. Lauren forces that thought from her mind. She had always believed dreams could mean anything. Suddenly, Mr. Akeru's words come to mind, it is no different than what he said about the stories he knew.

Lauren takes a deep breath and gets up to get dressed. Once dressed she begins to feel better. She heads to the lobby once again, looking forward to a nice cup of hot coffee. She is surprised to see Mr. Akeru standing off to the side as paramedics take a covered body out to an ambulance.

Lauren sees a distraught older man follow the paramedics. Her heart aches for him. She could see the man is devastated. Realizing that Mr. Akeru will not be able to talk about it now, she leaves the building.

Lauren purchases her cup of coffee and goes back to the park bench she had sat at yesterday. Another beautiful, sunny day. This time Lauren decides to call her friend Roxi. Roxi should be on the train for her commute to work and should have a couple of minutes to talk.

Roxi answers the phone, "Hi, stranger! How are the rich and famous doing?"

Lauren smiles, "I don't know, perhaps I should stop that woman walking the little poodle over there. She looks like she might know!"

Roxi laughs, “That, my friend, will be you in only a couple of years.”

Lauren pretends shock, “My dear, do you know something I don’t? Are you going to finally introduce me to a rich uncle you never talked about? I can guarantee you, my career will most likely top out in the middle class comfort zone.”

Roxi teases, “Honey, have you not heard? Middle class is the new poor!”

Lauren sighs, “Ah yes, we have been brought up hearing that from our parents all our life. I suppose we will find out soon enough for ourselves.”

Roxi shakes her head, “I did not go to college to set myself up for a career. I went to set myself up for a job to rub against those rich guys and hopefully land me one!”

Lauren laughs, “Money well spent!”

Roxi smiles, “That is exactly what I keep telling my dad! For some reason though, he shakes his head and looks disappointed. However, I guarantee you when I come home with a lawyer he will be singing a different tune!”

Roxi changes the subject, “How is the new place coming along?”

Lauren sighs, “I think there may be an opening, if you are interested. This morning they took someone out on a stretcher.”

Roxi is intrigued, “Oh, do tell! Murder, suicide or unexplained?”

Lauren shrugs her shoulders, “Unexplained for now, but I am thinking health reasons. An older man was in tears as they rolled the body out. I assume it was the husband.”

Roxi softens her voice, “Aw, that is sad.”

Lauren agrees, “I know, that is kind of why I needed to hear your sweet and upbeat voice.”

Roxi understands, “It is crazy how certain things can affect you that are not even related to you. I would offer for us to go out tonight but it is going to have to wait until this weekend. I am on overload at work right now.”

Lauren smiles, “This weekend is fine. Still some things around the apartment I want to finish up. Plus, I have not caught up on my sleep.”

Roxi is curious, "Is all the noise keeping you up?"

Lauren shakes her head, "No, actually that new sound machine I bought is awesome! Last night I slept soundly, but for some reason it is not enough."

Lauren is not aware that she has not mentioned the two strange dreams she has had. In fact, she has completely forgotten about them, although, a part of her feels as if she is forgetting to tell Roxi something. Any other time, Lauren would have gone on about her dreams. Especially the incident that happened in the bathroom with the watery footprints. However, being away from the apartment complex it is as if out of sight out of mind.

Roxi sighs, "My stop is coming up, I have to let you go. Enjoy your day off, you bum!"

Lauren laughs, "I will be sure to think of you working hard as I stroll around checking out my new environment."

Roxi snarls, "Keep it up girlfriend. By the time my next vacation is over you will wish you never mentioned your time off to me!"

Lauren smiles, "Oh, you are so right, you are way better at bragging than I am!"

Both laughing, the girls say their goodbyes.

Finishing up her coffee, Lauren decides to explore a little before going back to the apartment. Surprised at how tired she still is, she cuts her exploring time short and heads back to the apartment, craving another nap.

Mr. Akeru holds the door open, more somber than usual. "Ms. Lauren, how are you today?"

It is not until Lauren is back in the building that she remembers she wanted to find out what happened this morning. She lowers her voice in respect, "I am fine thank you. What about you? Looked like you had an eventful morning."

Mr. Akeru looks sad, "That I did, Ms. Lauren."

Lauren's curiosity is killing her, "Mind if I ask what happened?"

Mr. Akeru somberly replies, "Not at all. That was poor Mrs. Anderson from 1B. Remember, I told you the first day I met you that she moved in the same time as you."

Lauren tries to remember but shakes her head, "No, I don't think you did."

Mr. Akeru persists, "I am sure I did. I told you how sad she was, no family, her kids not around and she had just separated from her husband." Mr. Akeru sighs, "That poor woman had a lifetime of sorrow."

Lauren is sympathetic, "I saw what must have been her husband. He looked devastated."

Mr. Akeru nods, "The ironic thing was, he had come by early this morning to ask her to come back to him. Did not realize how much she meant to him. Unfortunately, she had already passed during the night."

Realizing Mr. Akeru was in no mood to talk, Lauren finishes up, "I am so sorry to hear about all of this, she will be in my thoughts."

Lauren leaves and while riding the elevator up the dream she had last night comes flooding back to her. It seems as if it might have been a dream like something Mrs. Anderson would have dreamed before she died.

An irrational thought comes over her, or perhaps while Mrs. Anderson was dying? Or, even after she died? Lauren has an even stranger thought, can the dead dream?

The elevator opens up startling her back to reality. Once inside the apartment, Lauren finds herself extremely tired. What is wrong with her? She never took naps, but now it is like she needs one.

Not fighting it, Lauren goes to bed. Turning her sound machine on, she finds her body is relaxed but her mind is racing into the next dream.

Sissy

Sissy

Angela looks nervously around her apartment. This is where she will know once and for all if it is her, or if it had been the house she lived in. She had lived with her parents while going to college. This apartment would be the first time she had ever lived alone.

Growing up Angela had a strange relationship with her dead sister. Sissy died tragically when Angela was only three. Both of her parents were so distraught over losing their favorite, they embraced the idea that Angela could see and interact with her sister. Not only did they embrace it, they encouraged it; however, Angela was not as happy with the idea as they were. In fact, she was terrified!

Many nights she would scream in terror that Sissy was in her room. Sissy would steal the blankets. Sissy wanted to play.

When Sissy was alive, she had often accused Angela of any wrong doing that happened in the house. If something got broken, it was all too easy to blame a three year old. Once Sissy died, it seemed as if the roles reversed. Anything that happened now became Sissy's fault.

The day Angela cut a big chunk out of her pretty long hair it was Sissy's idea. Of course, mother then had to cut all of her hair off to make it look even. While doing so, she scolded Angela that Sissy would have never done this, she had been a perfect child. How mother wished Angela would be more like Sissy.

Toys were suddenly getting destroyed, only for Angela to blame Sissy. Father was extremely angry with Angela, siding with mother on how Sissy would have never done such a thing. Meanwhile, when mother and father packed up Sissy's belongings after she died, they found many toys violently destroyed. Neither parent would admit to themselves that Sissy could have done such a thing. In fact, it was all too easy to think that Angela must have done it even though Angela was far too young to cause the damage. Faulting Angela, rather than scarring their memories of the perfect daughter they had lost, was the route they chose.

Sissy was only four years older than Angela. Their parents had tried for many years to have a child. When Sissy was conceived they were older and ready to spoil their only child. Angela was a surprise and their parents tried to prepare Sissy for the major change that was about to come. Sissy became her nickname. Her parents wanted her to feel important that she was going to be the big sister. Instead of feeling proud, Sissy felt nothing more than abject jealousy. Sissy liked being the only child and she intended to be the only child.

The accidents that occurred to poor Angela over the next three years led her parents to believe she was simply accident prone. They grew tired of the bumps and bruises that occurred on Angela and the trips to the doctor's for a broken bone here or there. She became much more of a handful than Sissy had ever been. They began to resent Angela. They missed the days of having only one child. The luxury of spoiling her without feeling guilty.

Poor Angela had no one but herself to depend on. Even at such an early age her instinct to survive kicked in.

One day, Sissy was playing with matches in her closet. Angela, realizing this may be a new way for Sissy to hurt her, quickly closed the door on Sissy. Startled, Sissy dropped a lit match and it set the small closet on fire. Terrified, Sissy tried to open the door but Angela leaned against it until it was too hot. She then ran down to her mother, who was watching TV, and told her that Sissy was in danger. By then it was too late.

That night Sissy visited Angela in her room; however, she was no longer the cute little girl that Angela's parents knew. No, this was a monster burned beyond recognition.

Her parents reassured Angela that Sissy was there to protect her and she never had to be afraid. Sissy was her big sister and loved her.

Angela's young mind learned to cope with the sightings of her burned sister; however, the things Sissy did were another matter. Eventually Angela learned to keep her mouth shut about Sissy and deal with the consequences.

Her parent's resentment towards her only grew. In fact, once while cleaning up a mess Sissy had caused, Angela's mother had screamed at her saying she wished it had been her in that dreadful closet!

While in high school, Angela looked forward to going to college and escaping that dreadful house. Many times she had begged her parents to move away. Neither one of them had a desire to leave the house that once had their precious Sissy alive and well in it. If there was any chance Sissy was still around, even after death, they were not going to leave her.

You would think her parents would have been just as anxious for Angela to leave for college as she was to go, but instead they forced her to stay home, almost as if it was a punishment for Sissy's death.

Not that they knew the truth. In fact, Angela could barely remember that day. Did she really hold the door or had she wanted to hold the door but became too scared and ran to tell her mother?

The fireman said the flames went up so quickly and burned so hot that Sissy would have perished immediately. The small area would not have given Sissy much time to escape.

Angela takes a deep breath and tries to clear her mind and focus on the present. No more thoughts about Sissy. Sissy had tried ruining her life for far too long. It was time for Angela to be free.

A couple of weeks pass and Angela begins to relax in her apartment. No sightings of Sissy whatsoever.

Her parents had not even bothered to come and see her in her new apartment. It was as if they had completed their job of raising her and now no longer had any interest in her. Angela was fine with that; she was more than capable of living on her own.

Then one night she gets a phone call from an old neighbor. "Is this Angela?"

Angela answers the person on the phone groggily, "Yes, it is and who is this?"

The man's voice hesitates, "It's uh, Mr. Nelson. I lived next door to your parents."

Even not fully awake, Angela catches the mistake the man makes, "Lived? Has something happened?"

The man stumbles, "Yes, I am afraid there has been an awful fire. The house is completely gone."

Angela is wide awake now, "And my parents?"

Mr. Nelson sighs, "I am afraid they were in the house when it happened."

Angela becomes completely silent. Mr. Nelson continues, "The police are here and would like to know your address so they can come over to talk to you."

Angela manages to whisper out her address before she drops the phone in fear of what she is seeing in front of her.

Sissy stands in front of her bed smiling. The evil looking burnt child actually looks happy to see Angela.

Angela screams out, "What are you doing here?"

Sissy speaks in a raspy harsh whisper, "I missed you. Unfortunately, so did mother and father."

Angela is confused, "What do you mean?"

Sissy becomes defiant, "I got tired of hearing how much they missed you! I started doing things so they would remember me, pay attention to me, but they turned on me!" Sissy looks confused, "They began to realize you had been right all along and how bad they had treated you. You were their favorite now. They were going to sell the house and try to make things up to you."

Angela begins to smell a strong odor of gas flooding the apartment. Terrified, she asks, "Sissy, what have you done?"

Sissy looks quite pleased, "I forced them to stay at that house. In the fire they burned like me."

Sissy looks directly at Angela, "And now I have come for you because I can't find them. They are gone and I need someone." She smiles sinisterly as she lights a match, "Even if it is my baby sister."

White Noise Stories Continued

Lauren wakes up soaked in sweat. This dream, by far, had to be the worst dream she had ever had. As if that was not bad enough, it was even worse to actually feel the heat from the explosion in her dream wash over her!

Lauren quickly checks herself over. Her night gown is soaked in sweat and her face feels hot to the touch, as if she is sunburned! She rushes to the bathroom to check her face. Her face is indeed flushed, but more than likely just a result from her blood pressure being so high from the intensity of the dream.

Lauren is also shocked to see a large section of hair is still gray! What the hell? She just colored her hair last night! Could this be due to the dream too? She takes a deep breath and tries to concentrate on her hair instead of that God awful dream. The only thing she can think of is that she simply missed a whole section when she colored her hair.

Lauren pulls her hair up into a bun and gets dressed. She plans on going back to the drug store she went to yesterday.

On the way down in the elevator thoughts of the dream are still with her, haunting her. How could a person ever deal with such a situation? Granted, the girl in her dream had been very young the first time she saw her sister in such a monstrous form. The mind does seem to have a way to accept things when there is no other choice.

Lauren chuckles slightly to herself. You are acting as if this dream was an actual account of real events! Get a hold of yourself! First of all, there is no such thing as a ghost! Second of all, do you really think this girl could have lived a normal life with that God awful apparition constantly being a nuisance? No way! That girl would have been institutionalized in a heartbeat!

And yet, something deep inside Lauren disagrees. In fact, she is terrified when she hears a girl's voice inside her head answering her, "I believe I did lose my sanity when I was very young; however, it was replaced by a need to survive."

Lauren speaks out loudly into the empty elevator, "This is not happening!"

The girl's voice assures her it is, "That is the first part of losing your sanity. Denial. You will continue to deny it until it is impossible for you to ignore the facts." Slowly the voice begins to fade out as she finishes, "Then you will have to embrace the need to survive or the insanity will take you over."

Lauren hears another voice, an older woman's voice, speak up, "Listen to the girl; she was wise before her years. Our desire to continue to make things fit into a reality we are used to only denies us of the inevitable truth."

As this woman's voice begins to fade out, Lauren quickly realizes this was the woman from the ferry dream! And the first voice was from the girl in her dream from last night! Lauren is shocked! People from her dreams are now speaking to her inside her mind. What the hell!

Lauren shakes her head violently as if to get the voices out. Like everyone, she has had her fair share of nightmares in the past, some of them quite terrifying. However, she would have the nightmare, realize it was a nightmare, vow to not watch any more scary movies, then go back to sleep. By the next day, she would have completely forgotten about the nightmare.

Never had Lauren experienced what she is experiencing now. These nightmares are not only staying with her, for God's sake, they are interacting with her! This is unacceptable! Subconsciously, Lauren makes a deal with herself to no longer think about the dreams. Isn't there a saying that if you give something your attention you are giving it power? Well, Lauren is turning off the power right now!

Lauren begins to reason with herself again. The move must have been more stressful than she thought. Plus, not seeing her friends or having any interaction from work probably has not helped.

Ever since she moved into the apartment, Lauren has found herself having deep conversations with herself. Now, perhaps her mind is compensating for the lack of interaction with real people by inventing different voices to add spice to her conversations. She feels she may be giving herself way too much credit for being that creative but the alternative is simply ludicrous. Perhaps by ignoring the dreams the voices will never come back. However, she has to admit she has never felt fear like this before! As the elevator opens she sees Mr. Akeru.

Mr. Akeru is surprised at her disheveled appearance, "Good day, Ms. Lauren. Is everything okay?"

Lauren blushes, "Yes, did not do as great a job on my hair color as I thought. Heading back to the store to get what I need to fix it."

Mr. Akeru rolls his eyes and compliments her, "I am sure it still looks beautiful."

Lauren cringes a little at the word beautiful due to a flash of the evil burnt child from her dream the night before. Before going through the door Lauren has an impulse to ask, "Were the stoves in this apartment complex always electric?"

Mr. Akeru shakes his head, "No, back in the 80's there was an explosion. The complex was forced to evacuate everyone."

Lauren's heart begins to race a little, "How many were killed?"

Mr. Akeru answers, "Quite a few. After the explosion a raging fire erupted. It took out several floors before they could get it under control. No worries though, there has not been anything like that since. After the fire, the city forced everyone to vacate the premises."

Lauren is a little surprised, "Permanently?"

Mr. Akeru nods, "Yes. The apartment complex went under and a woman doctor purchased it which is lucky for you because she made it into a clinic and basically gutted the whole complex." Mr. Akeru looks around proudly, "It is still considered one of the safest places to live in the city because of her."

Lauren can't visualize this building being a clinic. "It doesn't look much like a clinic."

Mr. Akeru agrees, "No, the doctor wanted to have a normal apartment complex living atmosphere for the type of research she was doing."

Lauren is curious, "Does she still own the building?"

Mr. Akeru sighs, "I am afraid she was several owners back. This place seems to have a revolving door when it comes to owners."

Lauren thinks about her dream and wonders if yet again there is a connection. Obviously, the dream was about an explosion and fire. Was the dream a memory, or even a dream, from the girl whose dead sister may have caused the explosion and fire? Chills run up and down her arms. She is becoming more convinced that her dreams are no longer random; however, she doesn't want to sound crazy.

Lauren shrugs her shoulders and tries to dismiss the story as not a big deal, "Sometimes history can be quite horrifying."

Mr. Akeru thinks about it, "True, but by learning from the past are we not able to improve the future?"

Lauren smiles, "You are right."

Lauren says goodbye as she walks through the door. What is going on? Why did her dreams seem to be tied to real events that happened to people in her apartment complex?

As soon as Lauren steps into the sunlight all thoughts of dreams disappear. She walks happily to the drug store without a care in the world. Once inside she grabs what she needs and goes to the cash register. The cash register girl remembers her from the day before, "Were you here yesterday?"

Lauren blushes, "Yea, I guess I am not so good at coloring my own hair. I missed a whole section."

The girl can't help but look at Lauren's hair and finally sees what she is talking about. "Ah yes, white hair. Don't be surprised if the color doesn't take again. Sometimes white hair will just not color, almost like it's dead or something."

Lauren nervously chuckles, "Well, that is a comforting thought!"

The girl realizes what she said and apologizes, "I am sorry. I just know my mother has tried for years to cover a streak of white and has always been unsuccessful."

Lauren tries to defend herself, "Honestly, I am probably not much older than you. I am sure it is just my technique and I think it is more gray than white."

The girl shakes her head, "My mother has had her streak since she was very young. She was in a terrible car crash with three of her friends. She was the only one that survived."

Lauren is shocked, "How awful, I am so sorry!"

The girl agrees, "She woke up from a coma and the streak of white was there. She says she can't remember anything from that terrible night. She says she is fortunate her mind has blocked it out."

The girl hands the bag to Lauren after she pays for it. "I guess though, her body told a different story. Not only did her hair turn white, but she felt years older. I suppose the mind can make you forget but fear will still rob the body."

Lauren walks away troubled as if there is something she should remember but has forgotten. Quickly, she runs through a mental list of the items she may need at the apartment but can't think of anything else she needs. Lauren's phone rings, interrupting her thoughts, "Hi Mom, how are you?"

Her mother answers, sounding a little worrisome, "The question is, how are you? Why won't you pick up your damn phone?"

Lauren is confused as she looks at her phone, "Mom, I have no missed calls from you. When did you call?"

Her mom answers sarcastically, "When haven't I? I even called Roxi and she said she had tried to get a hold of you too but had no luck."

Lauren apologizes, "Seriously Mom, I did not do it intentionally. I wish you could see my phone, it is showing no missed calls!"

Her mother softens her tone, "Perhaps there is something wrong with your service. Have you tried using your phone since you have been in the apartment?"

Lauren thinks back and is surprised with the answer, "Uh, no, I don't think I have."

Her mother sighs, "This is why I wanted you to get a land line. I will even pay for it if you don't have enough in your budget."

Lauren becomes defensive, "No Mom, that won't be necessary. When have I ever asked for your help? You know I can take care of myself!"

A little hurt, her mother tries to defend herself, "I did not mean it like that. I just worry about you."

Lauren understands, "I am sorry. Was there a reason you needed to call? Nothing has happened has it?"

Her mother reassures her, "No, we are all fine. I was just curious how you were doing with the new sound machine."

Lauren smiles, "I love it! In fact, all I want to do is sleep for some reason. Either I am playing catch up or I might be coming down with something."

Her mother understands, "Moving can be so stressful. It tends to take a toll on you more than you know; fortunately you still have a couple of weeks to shake it off."

Lauren feels there is more, but for the life of her she can't think what. "That is what I thought too. I have been taking naps when I need them."

Her mother sighs, "I envy you! Work has been so crazy; I would kill for a nap!"

Lauren laughs, "You and Roxi both are jealous. Roxi says she is going to brag while she is on vacation as payback."

Her mom smiles, "That is our Roxi! You might let her know I finally got a hold of you, wouldn't want her to keep worrying too."

Lauren agrees, "I will, but I think I will wait until after I am in the apartment and checked to see if there is a problem with my service. God, I hope not! You know what a pain it would be to not have cell phone service?"

Her mother is a little skeptical, "I can't imagine a complex that big not having service for you. You know how many upset people there would be. Hopefully it is nothing more than just your phone."

Lauren sighs, "True, but oh how I hate figuring anything out when it comes to my phone!"

Her mother laughs, "It is crazy, your generation is supposed to know more than mine when it comes to that stuff!"

Lauren sighs, "I know and that is what makes it even worse!"

Her mother suggests, "Isn't it time for a new phone anyway?"

Lauren nods, "It is, and I should get one before I go back to work so I know how to use the damn thing."

Her mother shakes her head, "Let Roxi figure out the new phone for you. I would love to see some new selfies of you two!"

Her mother looks at the clock, "Let me getting going, I have a late meeting. I am just so relieved I got to talk to you, you know how I worry."

Lauren appreciates her concern, "I know Mom, but I will be fine."

They say their goodbyes as Lauren approaches the apartment complex. She shields her eyes as she looks up at the building. A little proud, Lauren has to admit the building is prettier than most of the apartment complexes she had looked at.

The minute Lauren steps into the lobby; however, the conversation with the cashier floods over her. Her mind acts as if it has been un-paused and continues with its line of thinking. What if a person experiences fear while sleeping due to dreams? And yet, the mind protects you by forgetting about the dream or making the dream not feel as intense when you are awake.

A slight chill comes over Lauren as she continues with her thinking; but the fear you endured in the dream still robs the body? That could explain normal aging; however, she takes it a step further. What if you start remembering your dreams, even interact with your dreams, during the day? When would your body ever have the chance to rest? What if, once you have experienced a dream that intense, your body allows you to continue experiencing dreams in that manner? How would you ever break the cycle?

Since Lauren started having these weird dreams, her hair started getting greyer. What about not having the desire to take the stairs this morning? Was perhaps her body aging faster because of these dreams? What had changed in her life at the time she started having these dreams? The white noise sound machine! It was when Lauren started using the machine that the dreams had begun. What is unusual about white noise? She thinks and quickly realizes, isn't white noise what they use on those gadgets to hear ghosts?

Meanwhile, Lauren doesn't find it odd that once she is outside the apartment complex nothing she experienced inside the complex comes to mind.

Most people don't put much thought to when they actually think of something. You sort of group it all together and in Lauren's mind she figures she has done nothing but think about it all day. How could she not? For God's sake, didn't she hear different voices inside her head when she was in the elevator this morning? That certainly is not something one would forget!

Lauren looks around for Mr. Akeru. She wanted to ask him about white noise, he had never finished his sentence about it the other day. Unfortunately, Mr. Akeru's shift must be over because he is nowhere to be found.

In the elevator, Lauren decides it is time to do some investigating on the white noise phenomenon. Once inside the apartment, she curls up on her couch and grabs her iPad to start her research. From what she can figure out, white noise is a random signal with different frequencies. Compared to the rest of the scientific terms, this is the best way for her to describe it. Frustrated, she tries researching "paranormal white noise" which only leads to a lot of speculation. She rubs her eyes and closes her iPad.

Lauren sits there thinking about what she just read. From what she can tell, anything paranormal involving white noise is nothing more than personal speculation. What few examples that are out there can easily be explained as random frequencies coming from nearby radio transmissions. Or, simple misinterpretations of forcing random frequencies to fit a word or words that are familiar to you. Bottom line, none of it fits into a theory of complete dreams or stories that would be transmitted to her via her sound machine.

Another thought comes across Lauren; she quickly grabs her iPad and looks up what causes white or gray hair. She is surprised to see that not only stress but anemia or thyroid issues could cause it.

Lauren wonders if she should look up why she is hearing voices but decides against it. What's the point? It only happened once after a crazy ass dream. She simply reasons that the stress from the dream also caused the voices.

Lauren slowly closes the iPad again. It has been a while since she had a checkup. Definitely something she should do in the next couple of weeks before she starts her new job.

She can't help but smile as she thinks how silly this all is. Completely relaxed in knowing nothing sinister is going on in her new little apartment, she decides to re-color her hair.

Lauren lets her hair down and looks at herself critically in the mirror. The gray in her hair doesn't seem as noticeable. In fact, she is beginning to like how the gray gives her hair dimension. It's a new unique look for her, one that may even help her in the new job. Perhaps looking older is not such a bad thing.

Lauren puts the box of color away; it will still be there if she changes her mind. Proud of herself for accepting her new appearance and not allowing herself to think silly ideas about her new sound machine, Lauren gets ready for bed, not even realizing it is several hours before her normal bed time.

Shadow
People

Shadow People

Chapter One

Jordan is a bit nervous at the thought of Steven moving into her apartment. It is a big step for them both and yet it is the next logical step. Steven sleeps over more often than not. With them both only paying half of the rent, money will loosen up for them to do other things they enjoy. The only thing Jordan hates about it is that it doesn't seem like a romantic move. More like a necessity move. Had romance died?

Jordan approaches her apartment a little hesitantly. Steven had insisted she stay the weekend at her parents while he moved his stuff in. It would give him a chance to move in without shocking her too much. It helped that she had a two bedroom apartment.

Before she left, Jordan cleaned the little bedroom she used as an office to give Steven a place to put his belongings in. Some might say losing her office may be the thing that is bothering her. But, to be honest with herself, she hardly used it, opting for the laptop while sitting watching TV instead.

Jordan takes a deep breath and puts her key in the lock. Before she can open the door, Steven swings it wide open and smiles, "Oh no you don't!"

He picks her up and carries her through the threshold. Jordan is shocked and giggles, "What do you think you are doing?"

Steven closes the door with his foot and takes her into the bedroom, "Trying to make things special."

Jordan quickly looks around and is surprised to see how nice the apartment looks. "Are you all moved in?"

Steven plops her down on a bed sprinkled with rose petals. Candles are lit around the room. "Yes my dear, and tonight will be all about you!"

Jordan is wide eyed, "What has gotten into you?"

Steven sits on the bed with her, "I know this move seems more like a chore. I just wanted you to see we can also have fun living together."

Jordan is deeply moved and leans over to kiss him, "Thank you, you have no idea what this means to me!"

After kissing for several moments Steven pulls back and stands up. "You get undressed while I pour you a bath. When you are completely relaxed, come out and we will have dinner together."

Jordan feels guilty, "This is all so very nice and yet I feel bad, I haven't done anything for you!"

Steven winks at her, "Oh you will, later tonight!"

Jordan starts unbuttoning her top, "Fair enough."

After a wonderful bubble bath, Jordan puts on one of her sexiest nighties and a silk robe. Walking into the kitchen she admires the way Steven has integrated his stuff with hers, "I can't believe what a great job you did in here! Seriously, I thought there would be hockey sticks and basketballs everywhere."

Steven laughs, "You haven't gone into the second bedroom yet, have you?"

Jordan has a seat at the lovely prepared table, "That is quite ok, we can always close the door when company comes."

Steven brings her a glass of wine. "Exactly what I was thinking!"

Steven lays the food out on the table. Even though it is take out from their favorite restaurant, Jordan appreciates the effort he has put into making everything nice.

Raising her glass, Jordan makes a toast, "To us and our new living arrangement. If the first night is any indication of how it will go, life will be wonderful!"

Steven clinks his glass with hers and takes a sip, "Now you do know this is not an everyday occasion, you won't appreciate it as much if it were."

Jordan giggles, "I understand, but for now you have won big time points!"

Steven leers at her outfit lustily, "I just hope I can make it through dinner before I ravish you!"

Jordan gets up and walks over to him seductively, “Who says we can’t have an appetizer first?”

Steven smiles as he thanks his sister over and over in his mind. It had been Shelly’s idea for the romantic touches. At first Steven thought it was stupid, but now he realizes romance may be underrated by men.

Chapter Two

Both of them are spent from a long evening of activities so Steven and Jordan get ready for bed. As Jordan brushes her teeth, Steven closes the curtains.

After Jordan is done she comes into the bedroom and is a little surprised, "Why did you close the curtains? You know no one can see us, for that matter, there's nothing more to see than what we did earlier!"

Steven laughs, "I know right? I just like sleeping in a very dark room."

Becoming a little concerned, Jordan says, "I didn't think you minded sleeping with the light on."

Steven shrugs his shoulders, "What was I supposed to say? I was sleeping in your apartment and I didn't want to blow any chances!"

She teases him, "Oh, I see. Now that you have moved in, you figure it's a done deal?"

Steven laughs and pats the bed, "Of course, now come to bed sweetie."

Jordan slowly crawls into bed, "Is it too much to ask to keep the light on?"

He sighs, "Honey, you don't have to be afraid anymore. I will be right here to protect you!"

A little defiantly Jordan replies, "It's not because I am afraid!"

Steven rolls his eyes, "Then what is it?"

Jordan takes a deep breath, "You are going to think I am crazy if I tell you."

Steven sits up and gives her his full attention, "We are in this together, I promise not to judge."

Jordan thinks back to the first time it happened, "My family and I moved into this old house. My mother absolutely fell in love with the place and had to have it. I never understood why, to me it was a beaten down old house. However, she wanted to take her time and repair it back to the spender it supposedly had at one time."

Steven is curious, “How old were you?”

Jordan answers, “Around sixteen.”

“So, you were older,” Steven said, surprised.

Jordan nods, “Old enough to know better. You know me, I’m a bit of a tomboy. Things really didn’t scare me when I was younger; it was more like it made me curious about why it scared me.”

She sees the confusion in Steven’s eyes, “You had to have seen this house, Steven. The local kids were terrified of it!”

Steven understands, “I’m sure that didn’t help you sleep at night either.”

Jordan agrees, “No, it did not. Let alone the folklore that went with it.”

Interested, Steven perks up, “What kind of folklore?”

Jordan thinks back, “A really strange tale. A cult-like group lived in the house.”

Steven is surprised, “A devil worship cult?”

Jordan laughs, “No, actually like 60’s hippies. A kind of true love cult.”

He was not expecting that, “You are kidding me, right?”

Jordan shakes her head, “Oh no, it was a big deal. All these hippies living in this house, doing their drugs, having their free love. Quite a big deal back then for a small town.”

Steven can’t help but laugh, “So, what did they do? Love people to death?”

Jordan becomes serious, “No one knows, they all disappeared.”

Chapter Three

Finally Jordan breaks the awkward silence, "The guy that owned the house at the time was rumored to have worked for the government." Shrugging her shoulders, she continued, "Some sort of super genius who not only was a chemist but was also into astrophysics. His name was Ethan."

Steven looks a little confused, "Tell me again what astrophysics is?"

Jordan smiles, "Don't worry, I had to look it up myself. Astrophysics is astronomy that employs aspects of physics and chemistry. They try to figure out if there are black holes, time travel and multi-universes. You know, really far out things."

Steven can only imagine, "Add drugs to that way of thinking and I am sure there were some crazy conversations going on in that house!"

"Exactly!" Jordan agrees.

Steven is confused, "Honestly, how are a bunch of free loving intelligent hippies scary?"

"Maybe, because they all went missing?" she reminds him.

Steven is not convinced, "Who is to say the townspeople did not get fed up and run them out of town?"

Jordan shakes her head, "They were not squatters. Ethan owned the house legitimately and paid taxes. For the most part, they kept to themselves."

Steven counters, "Honey, those were different times back then. God fearing people got rid of you if they didn't like who or what you did!"

Jordan sighs, "I know, but I seriously don't think that is what happened."

"What do you think happened?" Steven asked curiously.

Jordan hesitates, "I think they are still in the house."

He doesn't follow her, "What, buried in the basement or something?"

Jordan shakes her head, "No, trapped somehow in a parallel universe." Before Steven can ask anything she explains, "From the first night we slept in the house, whenever we would turn the lights off to go to sleep…" She searches for the right words… "When we closed our eyes we would see shadows."

Frustrated, Steven wonders, "If your eyes are closed, how can you see shadows?"

Jordan is trying not to become defensive, "Close your eyes!" Steven closes his eyes. Jordan waves her hand back and forth. "What do you see?"

Steven answers, "Ok, shadows going back and forth."

Jordan smiles, "Exactly! This is what we would see when we would go to sleep at night."

Steven is surprised, "All of you?"

Jordan nods, "Yes, Mom and Dad admitted to me that they saw them as well."

Steven admits, "Ok, I'll give you that. It must have been scary. So, I take it you and your family started sleeping with the lights on."

She begins to get chills thinking about it, "We did, until of course one night I could not stand not knowing what the shadows were."

Anxious to know, Steven asks, "What did you do?"

Jordan rubs her arms as she tries to make the goose bumps go away, "I slept one night with my light off. I was determined to find out what the shadows were. Did you ever have a spot in your eye or a floater where you would try to follow the spot but you could never really focus on it?"

Steven nods, "Yes."

Jordan sighs, "That's what I did while my eyes were closed. I tried to track the shadows that seemed to dance in front of my eyes." Jordan thinks back, "The more I focused, the more I felt drawn in."

Steven lowers his voice, "What happened?"

Jordan shakes her head, "Fortunately, my mother felt a need to check on me that night. She said even though it was dark in the room, it looked as if I was fading into the darkness. I'm not sure if I had self-hypnotized myself or put myself in some sort of a trance, but that's exactly how it felt to me. Like I was fading into the dark. It felt as if all these arms were around me and encouraging me to come with them."

Now it is Steven's turn to have goose bumps rise up, "What happened after your mom came in?"

Jordan thinks about it, "Mom turned on the lights and came over to the bed to check on me. She said it was like I was only half there. Terrified, she wrapped her arms around me and demanded that I come back to her."

Jordan looks at Steven, "I heard her voice and cried for them to let me go. I could hear whispers all around me telling me they would for now but one day they would be back. We left the house that night and I never set foot in it again. Mom and Dad paid for movers to get our things."

Chapter Four

Steven tries to reassure her, "Ok, I admit that after dealing with something like that I would sleep with the lights on for a while too." He reaches out and moves a strand of hair from her face. "However, you are no longer in that house. We are in a nice safe apartment, high up in an apartment complex." Steven playfully flexes his muscles. "You have a big strong guy like me sleeping right next to you. What could possibly go wrong?"

Jordan is not convinced, "What is the big deal if we sleep with the lights on?"

"Because I really like having a dark room at night. For that matter, I wake up better in the morning if the room is still dark. Gives my body a chance to adjust."

Jordan thinks about it, "Ok, I guess. However, promise me if I start to call out or do anything in my sleep you will automatically turn the light on and do just like my mother did. Hold me and call out to me. Ok?"

Steven smiles, "Honey, it is not going to come to that, but I promise you."

Jordan takes a deep breath and turns the light off. She turns on her side making herself comfortable and then lies there terrified of what might happen.

Sensing her fear, Steven spoons up next to her. Placing his big arm around her waist, he whispers in her ear, "I am right here."

Jordan begins to relax, "It's not until you are in a dream-like state that you see them."

Steven tries to be logical, "Then perhaps it was nothing more than a dream."

Jordan would love to think that and has tried to convince herself of that very idea. But no matter how much she tries to assure herself it was a dream, what her and her mother dealt with that night was real! Besides, her mother had not been sleeping when she saved her from the dark.

Jordan finds herself falling asleep and can't help smiling. How nice it is to have Steven right beside her. To be nestled up to him while he protects her.

Finally, she allows herself to fall asleep. At first Jordan thinks she is dreaming. Then suddenly she realizes this is the time in your sleep that is between dreaming and sleeping. The time when the shadows appear! She first tries to open her eyes but they feel too heavy to open. She then tries to moan or call out but her voice is lost. Jordan strains to hear Steven beside her and finally she hears the rhythmic sound of his snoring. Trying to move to get his attention, she is trapped under his arm.

The shadows reach out to her, touching her, caressing her. They whisper that it will be ok. Since she had almost crossed the doorway the last time, it should be no problem to cross over to them. They will help pull her through.

Jordan shakes her head and tears begin to fall. She screams in her mind, "I don't want to go, don't make me go!"

In unison the shadows answer her, "We will bring Steven with you. Will that make you happy?"

Jordan shakes her head, "No, we need to stay here!"

The shadows disagree, "No, we need you and him here more. I am sorry, but there is no other choice."

Jordan feels her body being pulled into the darkness, the only comfort she has is that Steven is beside her.

****

Several days pass and Jordan's mother, Alice, becomes concerned that she has not heard from her daughter. The apartment complex superintendent, police, and Alice walk into Jordan's apartment.

Neither Jordan nor Steven are anywhere to be found. The police try to convince Alice that the two of them may have ran off, not wanting anyone to know.

Alice goes into the bedroom and notices the lights are turned off and the bed looked as if the two of them had been sleeping in it.

No matter what anyone says, Alice is convinced that Jordan and Steven were taken by those damn hippies! Every parent's worst fear.

White Noise Stories Continued

Lauren shuffles to the kitchen to make coffee. Her energy is at an all-time low. As she makes her coffee she wonders if perhaps she is getting too much sleep.

Lauren sighs as she fights the desire to go back to sleep. She pours her cup of coffee and looks at the calendar on the fridge. The days until she goes back to work are dwindling. Trying to encourage herself, she reminds herself that everything she wanted to get accomplished before she started working is finished. In fact, the remaining days were to be a form of relaxation.

She yawns and wonders if she really is coming down with something. If that is the case, she ponders on taking the next couple of days easy. The weekend will be here and by then Lauren will be ready to make some plans to go out.

Lauren suddenly remembers that she forgot to call Roxi yesterday from the apartment. Knowing Roxi will already be at work, she texts her. In the text, she apologizes and promises to meet up with Roxi this weekend. Lauren explains she feels as if she is coming down with something and wants to spend the next couple of days getting better.

Lauren's urge to go back to bed is now overwhelming. She finds herself submitting and shuffling back to the bedroom. Too much sunlight is streaming in, so she goes over to the windows to close the curtains.

A soft whispery voice floats through her mind, "Leave them open or at least keep the light on! We are connected now and they may want you too!"

Remembering the dream of the shadow people, Lauren agrees by answering out loud, "You are right. No sense in taking chances. Thank you."

Lauren figures until she starts having real interaction with people, having random voices in her head is still nothing more than her mind trying to be creative.

She crawls into bed and thinks about the dream from last night. Admit it, the dreams you are having are becoming addictive! Although unnerving and unsettling, you are beginning to crave them! No different than an addict!

Lauren sighs and has to admit there is some truth to what she is thinking. The dreams have been sucking her in; she has been enjoying the drama, the adrenaline and the fear. The rational part of her mind cuts in, but what if these dreams really happened to real people?

Lauren thinks about the poor girl Jordan in the dream she had last night. Lauren begins to wonder if people's worst nightmares could actually leave a print on reality.

Stands to reason that this poor girl Jordan would have such a nightmare. With what she experienced growing up and then her first time since the incident to turn the light off, would Jordan not be setting herself up for a nightmare? She is surprised at that idea and continues with her thought. It is no different than the concept of someone's tragic death leaving a print or trace of energy that some might call a ghost. Moreover, if that is the case then Lauren tapping into these dreams is nothing more than tuning into a scary movie on TV.

It is much easier for Lauren's mind to accept the idea that these dreams she is having are nothing more than an imprint from other people's nightmares. Who is to say that perhaps someone, out in the world, has not had a dream that had been one of her nightmares?

The more she thinks about it, the more it makes sense. Any one of these dreams could simply be the result of someone's worst fears. Or, even the person's subconscious creating a nightmare from hearing about a set of circumstances in the news or from a neighbor.

Lauren looks over at her sound machine, still on from the night before. Somehow, she feels the white noise has something to do with it. She teases herself, if that is the case she sure is getting her money's worth!

Lauren stares up at the ceiling and thinks about all of the people that live above her. Is the sound machine tapping into that energy and somehow Lauren is sensitive enough to make a connection with it?

Satisfied with her conclusion, Lauren settles in bed and looks forward to whatever dream she may have next.

Lullaby

Lullaby

Chapter One

After a long day at work Megan is happy to come home to her apartment. Sadly she realizes she no longer has the energy she used to.

Stripping down to underwear and bra, Megan endures another hot flash. For once in her life, she is happy that she is divorced and with no children. This way, no one has to see her go through the difficult stage of menopause. Megan can bitch and moan all she wants and not have to be accountable to anyone.

One of the most difficult stages of menopause for Megan has been the strange hallucinations she has been having. In all of the books she has read on menopause, nowhere does it mention the onset of hallucinations. The restless nights, hot flashes, and mood swings were all there, but no mention of hallucinations.

Megan had only told her girlfriend Teena, who in turn told her to tell her doctor. However, Megan was a little embarrassed about it so she decided to wait and see how it would progress. Certainly it had to be a "thing" connected with menopause, what else could it be? Megan is proud to say that she is not on any medication, even vitamins. She had shied away from them all her life. Something about taking drugs, any drugs, made her uncomfortable.

Even as a teenager, her parents never had to worry about her being involved in drugs. In a way, it was almost a weird aversion. It went as far as Megan hearing a sort of lullaby float through her mind whenever she thought about taking drugs. The lullaby was not only a warning but a comfort in knowing she did not have to take the drugs.

With the knowledge of not being on any medication, Megan had quickly checked that off her list of possibilities. The next was stress; however, things were going great at work. Her social life was comfortable. Even her divorce had been uneventful and happened several years ago.

For the most part, Megan was the envy of her friends for being in such a perfect time of her life. And yet, they did not know about the hallucinations.

Megan had one right before she got home this evening. As she rode the elevator, full of people, up to her floor she found herself looking around at an empty street.

A familiar man is standing over a different body. Suddenly, as if he knows she is watching, he looks over at her and smiles.

Megan can feel the people bumping into her on the elevator but her mind is making her feel as if she is on an empty street with this murderous criminal.

Megan breaks out into a major hot flash. Fearing she is about to faint, she closes her eyes very hard and wills herself to be back in the elevator.

When she finally opens her eyes she is fortunate to be in the elevator, just in time to get off at her floor. Trembling, she can't wait until she can get in her apartment and peel off all of these binding clothes!

Even though the hallucinations are tough to deal with in the moment, Megan has become used to them. They started the same time she started having hot flashes.

Each hallucination is a different scenario but with always the same man. The first time it happened, Megan had never seen the man before in her life. Now that it has happened so many times, she is familiar with the man. And no matter what horrible situation she hallucinates him in; he always smiles at her as if he is truly happy to see her.

After leaving her clothes in the middle of the floor Megan goes to the kitchen for a drink. She carefully mixes her vodka and cranberry in a tall glass, takes a sip and is satisfied with the results. Sighing, she goes to her couch, opens her laptop and casually begins to check her Facebook. Megan enjoys reading the silly stories and memes from her friends.

As she checks her notifications, she sees that she has a message. Megan looks at the sender and doesn't recognize the name. With all the scams and viruses out there she is reluctant to open the message. Megan goes to the sender's Facebook page and can see that it is in fact a real page. An older woman named Bonnie Jackson, who is a retired nurse.

Megan can't imagine why this woman would be contacting her. She looks at Bonnie's profile to see what things they may have in common. The only thing that may tie them is Bonnie lives in the same town Megan was born in. Megan takes a drink as she thinks about it, which is a stretch because other than being born in that town Megan had no other connections to that town.

Megan's parents had been traveling when her mother went into labor. They had to make an emergency stop for Megan to be born.

Intrigued, Megan decides to open up the message and see what Bonnie has to say. It is a simple message, "Megan, I think it is time we met in person. I know you will have doubts about whether you should meet with me; however, I think if you listen to your instincts you will know I mean you no harm. I need to discuss a very serious theory with you."

A slight chill comes over Megan. She is not sure how she should respond. How does this woman even know she has the right Megan?

Megan begins to type her reply, "Bonnie, I am curious about how you know you have the right Megan?"

Within seconds Bonnie replies, "Thank you for replying. To be honest, I had someone track you down for me. I would prefer not to explain here, but meet with you in person. I know you live in the city. Is there a place you would feel comfortable meeting me in public?"

Megan takes a drink, contemplating on what she should do. Meeting this person in a public place of her choice should be safe enough, shouldn't it? Megan replies, "There is a café on Fifth Street called the Retreat. They know me pretty well. I guess I would be ok meeting you there."

Bonnie is relieved, "Very good. Is there any way we can meet tomorrow after work? I feel it is that important."

Megan takes a deep breath and holds it as she quickly answers, "Is 6:00 ok?"

Before she can change her mind Bonnie replies, "Perfect!"

Megan sighs and writes, "I know the owner, I'll call now and make reservations. When you get there ask for Megan's table."

Bonnie answers, "Thank you Megan. I look forward to our meeting."

Megan finishes her drink and gets up to make another. Who could blame her after a conversation like that? This time Megan makes it a little bit stronger than the last one.

What in the world did this Bonnie chick have to talk to her about? Megan goes back to Facebook and tries to do some investigating of her own. Bonnie's page is one not used often. There are pictures of what Megan assumes her children and grandchildren. She goes back to Bonnie's profile and realizes the woman just turned 70. Megan is impressed. Here she is only 42 and feels like she is going down quick.

Megan sighs, if only she looked half as good as Bonnie when she is 70 she will be happy! Ok, so why does a 70 year old woman feel the need to meet with her? Megan is not stupid and realizes it must have something to do with the hospital she was born in. Obviously, it could be something along the lines of being switched at birth.

Megan closes her laptop and thinks about it. What if she had been switched at birth? Does it really matter now? Megan had wonderful parents growing up. Even though they had been older parents, it seemed as if they enjoyed every moment with Megan.

A pang briefly crosses over her heart. She missed her parents, especially at times like this. Megan desperately wishes she could pick up the phone and talk to her mother, but sadly that was no longer an option. Her parents had been in their 40's when they had Megan. Her father died a couple years back and her mother just last year.

Megan knows she could easily call Teena and get her take on all of this but she was not in the mood to spend all evening talking to Teena. Teena is a sweet woman and means well, but sometimes Megan can only take her in small doses. Plus she knew Teena all too well, Teena would insist on going with her tomorrow for support. Megan really did not want that. Once she finds out the whole story, of course she will talk to Teena about it.

Which brings Megan back to why would it make it any difference now for this nurse to come out and tell her she had been switched at birth? Both her parents were gone and Megan now is too old to really care. Unless the nurse wants her to meet with the baby she was switched with, or worse, meet her real parents!

Megan takes a big drink and tries to calm herself down. Slow down girl! This is all wild speculation on your part. She realizes that, but she also likes to always be prepared. So, if in a worst case scenario this Bonnie does tell her she was switched at birth, how is she going to handle it?

Megan tries to think from Bonnie's viewpoint. Perhaps Bonnie is looking for some sort of redemption, maybe even forgiveness. She wonders if she can give Bonnie that forgiveness. She reminds herself again of what a wonderful childhood she had and realizes, yes, she could forgive Bonnie. If that is indeed the case. It would not matter if she has real parents out there who might want to meet with her, in Megan's mind the parents who raised her will always be her true parents.

Ok, so Bonnie is forgiven. Is she now willing to meet with her true parents? If, of course, any of this is true.

Finally the hot flash has subsided and now Megan finds herself chilled. She gets up and goes to her bedroom to retrieve her robe. Feeling better, she goes back into the living room and picks up the clothes she had frantically gotten out of when she first arrived home. Taking them back into her bedroom she places them in the hamper. Megan can't help but giggle a little; she is having a hard time walking a straight line.

Going to the kitchen she prepares herself some dinner. She should have never had that second drink on an empty stomach. With a simple sandwich and soup, Megan carries her food into living room to watch TV. Look at that, CSI, her favorite detective show is on.

Megan thinks about the hot flashes and the weird hallucinations. Maybe it wouldn't be so bad if she did have other parents out there. Maybe she would be able to ask her biological mother if she had gone through the change at such an early age. More importantly, did she have the same symptoms Megan was having?

Megan begins to be comfortable with the idea of meeting with Bonnie tomorrow. She feels confident that whatever Bonnie has to throw at her, she will be prepared.

Chapter Two

Megan rushes from work to get home in time to change for her meeting with Bonnie. It had been a crazy day at work.

Megan prepares herself for another hot flash in the elevator on the way up but is relieved when the door opens to her floor.

Maybe by admitting to herself she is having hallucinations she is beginning to get a handle on them. It would not be the first time Megan solved her own problem!

Megan changes out of her business suit and into a comfortable pant suit. She looks in the mirror quickly and is happy with the result.

Feeling more relaxed and confident, Megan leaves the apartment for the restaurant. Butterflies begin to float around in her stomach but she quickly shoos them away. Megan chides herself, for Pete's sake! A woman in her 40's should be able to handle anything that is thrown at her! For that matter, not everything is a bad thing. This may turn out to be a good thing!

Determined, Megan enters the restaurant with a smile. Sonny, the owner, sees her from the corner and rushes over. He kisses her in greeting, "My lovely! So good to see you tonight."

Blushing, Megan hugs Sonny, "As well as it is to see you my dear!"

Sonny escorts her personally to a table in the back corner, "I reserved this table special for you! It seemed you may need your privacy tonight."

Megan shakes her head, "Sonny dear, you are such a mind reader! How in the world could you have gotten that from my call last night? All I did was ask for a table at 6:00."

Sonny smiles as he pulls out her chair, "My sweet, you never reserve a table in the middle of the week. Simple deduction is all it is."

She takes a seat and looks at him appreciatively, "Thank you Sonny. Do you think I could get my usual before they come? I have to admit I am a little nervous and it may take the edge off."

Sonny looks concerned, "Of course, is everything ok?"

Megan answers honestly, “I don’t know, we shall see.”

Sonny nods, “I will have your server bring your drink and please know that I will be keeping an eye on you tonight!”

She takes a deep breath, “That is exactly why I chose here for the meeting. Thank you Sonny.”

Within minutes the server brings Megan her favorite glass of wine. Megan is able to get in a couple of sips before she sees an older woman come through the door. The woman holds the door for a middle age woman holding a baby carrier. Megan sighs, oh please don’t let that be them!

Megan was under the impression Bonnie would be coming alone. Unfortunately, that doesn’t look like the case. She watches as the women approach Sonny. Sure enough, he starts bringing them her way. Megan plasters a smile on her face even though she is not happy with the situation.

Megan stands up to greet her guests. Bonnie comes directly to her, “I always knew you would be a beauty! Hi, my name is Bonnie.”

Megan puts her hand out, “It is nice to meet you.”

While Bonnie grasps her hand a warmness comes over her along with a distant feeling. Shaking her head a little, Megan lets go of her hand and tries to concentrate on what Bonnie is saying.

“This is my daughter Shawna and my great granddaughter Denise.”

Megan smiles, “Nice to meet you.”

Sonny had left them to retrieve a hi-chair for the baby. Quickly he returns and helps Shawna buckle the carrier onto the seat. Megan is relieved to see the baby is fast asleep. They all take their seats.

Sonny asks, “May I start you ladies off with a drink?”

Bonnie looks at the wine Megan has in front of her. “Two of those will be nice, thank you.”

As Sonny leaves Bonnie quickly begins to apologize, “I am so sorry for having to bring the baby with us!” Before Megan can answer Bonnie continues, “My daughter here watches the baby during the day while her mother works. Unfortunately, the mother had to do a double today and we could not find a sitter on such a short notice.”

Shawna speaks up, "My mother would have come on her own, but lately her sight hasn't been too well. With her not knowing for sure where she was going and being in the city, I was afraid for her to come alone."

Megan understands, "Not a problem, I'm sure it will all be fine."

Sonny comes back personally with the drinks and decides to take care of the ladies himself. "When you ladies decide, let me know and I will be happy to help."

Bonnie and Shawna look lost as they look at the menus. Megan comes to their rescue, "Ladies, do either one of you have any allergies?"

Both of them shake their head no. Megan looks at Sonny, "Sonny, why don't you choose for us tonight?"

Megan looks back over at the women, "Many times I have no clue to what to order and yet Sonny here has never steered me wrong."

Sonny blushes, "What do you say ladies, may I treat you?"

Bonnie looks relieved, "Have at it, we are game, aren't we Shawna?"

Shawna smiles, "We sure are!"

Sonny takes their menus and slightly bows, "Then I shall do my best."

Megan, Bonnie and Shawna have small talk throughout the course of the dinner. Surprisingly, the baby sleeps through the whole ordeal. Sonny outdoes himself with appetizers, salads, dinners and dessert.

After dessert, Sonny brings over coffee. All of the women complimented him on the fine dinner he prepared for them. Realizing Megan must have important things to discuss with the women, he makes it a point to stay away after the coffee, giving them plenty of time to talk.

Bonnie starts off, "I must say this was the perfect place to meet with you. I can tell you and the manager go way back."

Megan nods, "Believe it or not, I used to work here way back in the day. It is a family business. I worked for Sonny's father. They sort of adopted me when I moved to the city."

Bonnie clears her throat, "I suppose that is the best lead in I am going to get for such a delicate matter."

Megan feels bad for Bonnie, not knowing how to tell her what she needs to, "Let me guess, I was switched at birth?"

Bonnie is shocked, "Why? Is that something you always felt?"

Megan shakes her head, "No, I had a wonderful childhood growing up. I simply checked out your profile on Facebook. I realized you were a nurse in the town I was born in and figured it would be the only reason you would want to meet with me."

Bonnie is impressed, "A very smart woman. Unfortunately, there is far more to the story."

Megan's butterflies come back in full force, "Go on."

Bonnie looks over at Shawna for strength. Shawna reaches out and pats her hand. Bonnie continues, "Your parents showed up very distraught. Your mother had gone into early labor."

Bonnie thinks back to that dreadful night, "It was a very unfortunate night. The local football team's bus had been in a tragic accident. Our little hospital was swamped with injured football players all over the place and..." Bonnie hesitates... "another woman went into labor at the same time."

Bonnie doesn't have fond memories of the other woman, "She was a drug user who dragged her three year old boy with her to the hospital." She shakes her head in disgust. "The woman had taken drugs that night which induced her labor."

Megan sits there mortified, "You are trying to tell me I am the daughter of the drug user?"

Bonnie nods, "I am afraid so."

Megan is confused, "Did my parents, I mean the people who raised me, know?"

Bonnie shakes her head, "No, they were such good people. So excited for the delivery. The doctor was scrambling from room to room and did not really know who was who." Bonnie's eyes begin to glisten, "But I knew. The mother that raised you had complications. They separated her and her husband so in case something happened he would be out of the way."

A single tear escapes from Bonnie's eyes, "The baby was stillborn. The doctor didn't even realize it, he was in too much of a hurry to deliver the drug user's baby. He just handed me the baby and said clean her up."

Bonnie self-consciously brushes the tear away and takes in a deep breath, "The mother had passed out from pure exhaustion, not even realizing there had been no cries from the baby."

She looks over at her great granddaughter sleeping peacefully. "I took the baby into the other room just as a different nurse brought in the drug user's baby girl."

Bonnie sighs, "The nurse was distraught because one of her own boys had been in the bus that night and was in critical condition. Frustrated, she handed me the baby and said she had to be with her own son. She had no patience to try and save a drug filled baby."

Bonnie looks at Megan sadly, "I made a decision. I decided to give loving parents what they so badly wanted. I also gave you a chance for a better life."

Megan is overwhelmed with emotions but finds herself reaching over to pat Bonnie's hand with tears in her eyes. "Thank you! Not only for me, but for my parents. They would have been devastated!"

All three women find themselves nervously wiping their tears and laughing. Bonnie is relieved the first part is out; however, the next part will be the hardest.

First, Bonnie lets Megan ask her questions, "Did the nurse's son survive?"

Bonnie shakes her head, "Unfortunately no, this caused the nurse to take a leave of absence."

Megan sympathizes, "How many of the kids did you lose that night?"

Bonnie remembers it as if it was yesterday, "Three, the doctor unfortunately had to take a leave as well. He was not able to save his nephew."

Megan realizes what that meant, "So you were able to pull off the switch without anyone there to question you."

Bonnie nods, "There was the problem of getting you weaned off the drugs your mother had you addicted to. I was able to convince the parents that raised you that you were jaundiced and needed to stay in the hospital for a couple of days."

Megan has to know, "What did my real mother do when you told her?"

Bonnie is a little hesitant to be so harsh but knows no other way, "She was happy. One less problem she had to deal with is what she said."

Even though Megan had prepared herself, this statement still hurt. No child, no matter how old you are, ever wants to know her own mother did not want her.

Suddenly Bonnie's granddaughter begins to wake up and become fussy. Shawna takes her out of the carrier and tries to comfort her. The baby only becomes more agitated. Bonnie whispers, "Give her to me child."

Shawna gives her to Bonnie. She nestles her to her bosom and begins to hum a lullaby. Megan is shocked, "I know that tune!"

Bonnie is surprised, "My goodness, how could you? You were only a couple days old!"

Megan explains, "I don't know, but I do and it's the strangest thing! Any time I have to take any drugs or was tempted to take drugs that melody would come over me! Not only as a warning, but as a comfort as well."

Bonnie looks at Shawna with wide eyes, "See, I told you those drugs did weird things to those kids!"

Chapter Three

Shawna takes the baby to the rest room to change her diaper, leaving Bonnie and Megan to discuss what Bonnie meant about the drugs doing something to those kids.

Bonnie sighs, “About a year later, the same drugged up woman comes in pregnant again with her four year old boy in tow.”

Megan is shocked, “Why was child services not brought in for that boy when I was born?”

Bonnie shakes her head, “First thing I did was contact them and try to save that little boy, but things fall through the cracks. I guess no one ever followed through.”

Bonnie looks disgusted, “More often than not, people enable these losers by giving them handouts in hopes of them changing. They never change, they only learn how to use their kids to get more.”

Megan realizes that Bonnie must have lived a hard life to see so many innocent lives ruined. “I am sure you did your best Bonnie, you are a good woman.”

Bonnie’s eyes glisten again, “Never seemed like it was enough.” She takes a deep breath and continues, “This time your sister was born and I had no cover to give her. The chance I gave you was not an option.”

It finally hits Megan that she has a brother and a sister! Somehow, this is not comforting news.

Bonnie has a hard look come over her, “I cleaned that baby up while your brother lay in another room almost dead from an overdose.”

Megan is shocked, “Overdose? You said he was only four! How can that be?”

Bonnie looks her dead in the eye, “Your mother used to feed him the drugs she was taking to shut him up or make him less active.”

Megan is mortified, “How could she?”

Bonnie shakes her head, “Oh, it gets worse I am sorry to say.”

Megan can’t even begin to imagine, “What do you mean?”

Bonnie tries to explain, “Your mother and her boyfriend, who I assume may have been your father as well, made up a special concoction of drugs.” She lowers her voice, “When a child is born with a drug addiction we have to wean them off by using the drug the mother used.”

Bonnie looks down, “The problem was, the mother was not about to let us know her secret ingredient.”

Megan is confused, “Then how did you get me off it?”

Bonnie begins to fidget, “I could not force the mother to tell me what she was on. When they did an autopsy on the dead baby, they found no drugs in its system so they let her go.”

Megan realizes the dead baby Bonnie is talking about is the baby Megan replaced.

Megan wonders, “What about the son?”

Bonnie shakes her head, “He happened to be clean that time.”

She continues, “With you, I tried several different methods which honestly was very dangerous but I was losing you. You were a fighter though, I will give you that. Most babies would not have survived what you did.”

Bonnie thinks fondly back, “I would rock you constantly and hum my mama’s lullaby. It almost seemed as if the music was what finally saved you.”

Bonnie is curious, “Did your mother, the one that raised you, say anything about how you were when you were a baby?”

Megan smiles, “Oh yea, she used to say I was the worst baby she had ever seen. Cried all of the time. She said one day I just stopped crying. My demons had left and I was an angel ever since.”

Bonnie is impressed, “I have to give her credit, she had no idea what I was handing her the day I gave you to her.”

She continued, “With your mother delivering a baby addicted to drugs and her son near death she was put in jail, along with the father.”

Megan is concerned, “Are they still alive?”

Bonnie shakes her head, “No, they both died in jail.”

Megan is relieved, “Ok, so what about my brother and sister?”

Bonnie looks down, “Your sister died when she was a teen. Your brother is still alive, at least we think so.”

Bonnie stops Megan before she can ask another question, “We’re jumping ahead of ourselves. Let me explain what I know of their childhood.”

Shawna comes back with a happy smiling baby, “I think this one is all set to have her dinner!”

Megan can’t help but smile at the baby. It is the only time she seems to like babies, when they are clean, happy and quiet.

Sonny sees the break in the serious conversation Megan is having with the woman and comes over, “How are you ladies doing? More coffee?”

Megan thinks about it and decides, “How about a brandy for me Sonny?”

Bonnie looks up at him, “More coffee for Shawna and me if you don’t mind?”

Sonny nods, “Of course. Is there anything you need for the baby?”

Shawna thinks about it, “Is it possible for you to warm up the bottle?”

Sonny takes the bottle proudly, “Not a problem. I too have a grandbaby around the same age.”

After Sonny returns with the bottle and all of their drinks they go on with their conversation.

Bonnie tries to remember where they left off, “I tried to wean your sister, Abigail, like I did you.” Her eyes tear up. “She was not as tough as you.” She quickly dabs her eyes and goes on, “As for her brother, Roy, he was a completely different story. His little body had been force fed drugs all his life. The drugs seemed as if they became a part of him.”

Bonnie takes a drink of her coffee, “Once they were both released from the hospital, they were taken in by a local foster family. She thinks back to the Johnson’s, “Good people, really tried with the kids. Not like these horror stories you hear about other foster families.”

She shakes her head, "Those kids though were constantly at the hospital. Troublemakers, both of them. Even though the Johnson's did the best they could, by the time they became teenagers they were out of control."

Bonnie looks at Megan, "That is how Abigail, your sister, died. In a car accident after a party."

Megan wonders, "Drunk or high?"

Bonnie gets a puzzled look on her face, "Drunk, though the kids at the party said she desperately wanted to get high but something wouldn't let her."

Bonnie remembers seeing Abigail after the car accident, "When they brought her in, she was bleeding from both ears. They tried but they were unable to save her."

Even though Megan never knew her sister, she feels a heavy loss. Not sure she wants to know, she asks, "And my brother?"

Surprisingly Shawna answers this time, "He vanished right after your sister died. We figured he ran away. He was in his 20's so no one really gave it any thought."

Shawna sees Megan's confusion and explains, "My husband is a detective. Unfortunately, he has quite a file on your brother."

Megan understands, "Is it misdemeanors or more?"

Shawna is very serious, "Quite a bit more, though his visits in out of jail were only for misdemeanors. Roy bounced from town to town."

Bonnie adds, "And then he came home."

Shawna cautions her, "Or, so we think. Our poor town started having murders happen. Murders that all were identical in the killing."

Megan gasps, "Are you implying my brother is a serial killer?"

Shawna shrugs her shoulders, "My husband believes it is a strong possibility. The people that have been murdered are one way or another attached to your parents."

Before Megan can blurt out any questions, Shawna explains, "Whether they were drug dealers, neighbors, or landlords. People that had dealings with your parents, knew your parents and in some way did your parents wrong, or at least people your parents thought did them wrong."

Bonnie adds, “It seems Roy visited both your parents while in jail. He was devastated by their deaths.”

Shawna lowers her voice, “Once he was finished with revenging his parents, he began to go after people associated with Abigail. Her friends, teachers and unfortunately the Johnsons.”

Megan is mortified, “Why has he not been caught?”

Shawna is just as frustrated, “He’s good, or so he was. Now that his main targets are gone he has been killing randomly. These killings are messier, almost as if in a fit of rage. Unfortunately, they are becoming more frequent.”

Megan is afraid to ask but needs to know, “How is he killing them?”

Shawna lowers her voice even more, “The public doesn’t know this but my husband says he comes up behind the victim, grabs them around the neck and then plunges an ice pick of some sort in one ear and then the other.”

Megan gets a flash back of the hallucination she had in the elevator yesterday. She is shocked to remember seeing the bodies on the ground had blood coming from both of their ears.

Megan begins to get nervous and starts sweating. Had her hallucinations somehow allowed her to see her brother standing over his victims?

Chapter Four

Bonnie can see Megan is visibly upset. Who wouldn't be? To hear such horrible things and yet, she senses there is more. She reaches over and pats Megan on the arm, "Are you ok, my dear?"

Megan's eyes are big, "What did you mean those drugs did something to those kids?"

Her heart begins to race, the theory she had told Shawna and her husband may be true! Bonnie hesitantly answers, "The Johnsons always insisted that Abigail and Roy had a way to communicate. That it was more than a strong brother and sister bond."

Megan can't hold it inside any longer and blurts out, "Ever since I started going through menopause I started having hallucinations! Hallucinations of a man standing over someone he has killed!"

Even though it is exactly what Bonnie had feared she is still shocked, "Menopause, of course! That would kick your body into releasing hormones which in turn may have an effect on the drugs you were addicted to when you were born!"

Megan doesn't look happy, "Oh sure, it all makes sense, but what the hell am I supposed to do?"

Shawna is beyond excited, "The next time you have one, get your bearings. Look for landmarks. If there is a victim, study them, get as many details as you can and then call us!"

Bonnie can see the absolute fear Megan is having and offers, "To make yourself feel safe, hum my lullaby. For some reason, it seems to have an effect."

Megan's mind feels as if it is in a fog. She was not prepared for this, how could she be? Lullaby? Is this woman crazy? This man, her brother no less, may very well be a serial killer and Bonnie wants her to sing to him? Really?

Bonnie can see that they are overwhelming Megan. With a stern voice she explains why, "You yourself said you heard my lullaby when the taking of drugs was involved. The same must have been for your sister Abigail. Her friends said Abigail definitely wanted to try drugs but this stupid song would come over her. The more she tried the louder it would get. The only way she could party with her friends was to get drunk, nothing more."

Megan whispers, "What about Roy?"

Bonnie sighs, "He was older, had the drugs in him a lot longer. Although when he almost died at the age of four, I repeatedly sang that song to him."

Bonnie remembers, "A while later I saw him in the hospital passing through the pediatrician floor. I was holding a sick baby and humming the same lullaby. Roy heard the song and went into a blind fury, screaming to me to shut up, it hurt his ears. He literally attacked me and the baby."

Bonnie looks at Megan, "Fortunately, an orderly was close by and stopped him before the baby and I were hurt." Chills come over Bonnie. "I swear to you though, if he could have, he would have had no problem killing me and the baby just to make me stop humming that lullaby!"

Shawna interrupts, "One day my husband casually asked my mother if she remembered Roy. She began to tell him what she remembered. The two of them started putting a theory together. It wasn't until recently that my mother felt a need to come clean on what she had done with you."

Megan needs to know, "What is the theory?"

Bonnie chooses her words carefully, "I think the unknown drug, or concoction of drugs, your mother used stayed in you."

Bonnie takes a drink of her coffee, "It was the ultimate drug addiction. Since it never left the body, you would continue to crave it until the day you died."

Megan sarcastically replies, "Not unlike coffee?"

Bonnie nods, "True to a point. The craving is there but in time it can be controlled. The body can be trained to live without it. In the case of the drugs your mother used, not only could the body not be trained but the body turned on itself."

Shawna explains, "Your father was a small time drug dealer. Believe it or not, he was very intelligent and created his own designer drugs. Unfortunately, he used your mother as a test subject. When he finally perfected the drug, he put it out on the street."

Bonnie continues for her, "When your father was taken to jail he took his secret ingredients with him in hopes of scoring big when he got out. It seems he took his coveted recipe to the grave with him."

Bonnie thinks back to that dark period in her life, "Once your father went to jail, suddenly we had junkies coming in off the streets begging for us to help them. We could get them clean in their mind but their body rejected the idea and slowly began to turn on itself. Almost as if the body was searching for the drug hidden in crevices of organs."

Shawna sighs, "Your mother was the first to go and apparently your father had not even told her the ingredients. Then one of the girls off the street that died happened to be a sister of an inmate in with your father. Even while being beaten to death your father would not give up the ingredients."

Megan is confused, "Then how did the three of us kids live without it?"

Bonnie's only explanation is, "I think I simply walled it in with the different drugs I used to conquer it. We tried to do the same for the others, but I think because of their age it didn't work."

Shawna adds, "And the lullaby. As crazy as it seems, that lullaby kept you kids from doing drugs which may have activated the fatal drug already in your body."

Shawna looks over at Bonnie, "My husband seems to think the way Roy kills people is a way to stop his own demons. By piercing other people's ear drums, it's as if he is trying to stop hearing something himself."

Chapter Five

After a difficult goodbye and promises made, Megan finds herself back in her apartment before she even realizes it. She gets undressed, puts her nightie on, sits on her couch with a cup of hot chocolate, and starts thinking. There was so much information to absorb. Her mind tries to make sense of it.

Should she even call Teena and tell her what she learned? Where would she even begin? Megan reaches over to the business card she had laid on the coffee table and looks at it. It was Shawna's husband's business card. She was to contact him tomorrow and tell him about the hallucinations she had already had. Megan sighs and puts the card back down on the table. What is she going to be able to tell him? Megan always tried to forget about the hallucinations, dismiss them. Never had she tried to analyze them.

Suddenly Megan puts the hot chocolate down as she begins to feel herself get hot. No! She unbuttons her nightie and fluffs it up and down, a way to fan herself. She thinks to herself, I will not have a hot flash now! It is too soon! I need time to think and have a plan, damn it! No!

Before she knows it, Megan is standing in a dark, desolate street. She looks around quickly trying to see some landmarks but sees nothing. She intentionally avoids looking at the man, who must be her brother Roy, and a victim Roy has by the neck. She assumes that Roy can't see her, but she should have remembered the last couple of times he had smiled as if he did know she was there.

Roy calls out to her, "Are you going to stick around this time?"

Mortified, Megan shakes her head but has to ask, "Why are you doing this?"

Roy answers easily, "Because adrenaline is the only thing to mute the noise. Who are you anyway? Some mutt my father had when he cheated on my mother?"

Megan is not about to let Roy know the truth, "I guess."

Roy is not so sure, "You know my father swore he never was unfaithful. Used to say he was many things but unfaithful was not one of them. I believed him."

Megan can't help but snicker, "How could you believe such a despicable creature?"

Angry, Roy holds his victim even tighter and yells out, "How dare you! You didn't know him! He was a brilliant man!"

Megan doesn't back down, "If he was so brilliant, why did he not save your mother?"

Roy looks a little concerned, "He was in jail, what was he supposed to do?"

Megan offers, "Give the ingredient up to save her and all the others!"

Roy still defends him, "He would have, but they got to him before he could!"

Megan sadly shakes her head, "You do know the guy that killed him tried to get the secret out of him but he would rather die than tell."

Roy becomes angry, "Lies, you are no better than the rest of them!"

Roy raises a homemade ice pick up to the poor man he is holding and puts the tip in his ear, "I am just thankful you can be here like Abigail used to be, maybe you can feel the relief like she did."

Megan doesn't try to stop him but she calmly begins to hum the lullaby. Roy screams in agony as he lets go of his victim and tries to cover his own ears.

The victim, seeing his chance, runs away quickly. Roy can't follow but screams at him to stop. Megan, realizing her power, hums even louder and more confidently. After all, this was just a hallucination, she could not be hurt.

Roy charges at her. Megan is surprised to see blood running down both of Roy's ears. Megan feels Roy grab her and is surprised. Before she can protect herself Roy spins her around and holds her tightly like his victim. Without thinking he jams the ice pick in one ear and quickly changes hands to do the other.

Roy feels Megan go limp right at the same time he finds himself falling.

****

The next day Teena finds Megan in her living room. She was dead, with dried blood pooled around both ears. The final decision was that poor Megan had died of an aneurism, which not only explained the blood from the ears but also the hallucinations she had mentioned.

Meanwhile, Shawna's husband had finalized his investigation. Roy's last victim told of a strange event where Roy had been talking to someone who was not there.

The victim had remained quiet, looking for a chance to escape. He was not sure, but he thought he heard some sort of lullaby float around when Roy had suddenly released him. Screaming to make it stop, Roy had held his own ears as blood dripped down them.

Roy died of an aneurism that night too. Was it mere coincidence that these two died the same night with an aneurism or had something more happened?

All the others had died the same way, including Abigail.

Perhaps the strongest side effect of the drug was to cause an unexpected aneurism to happen at any given moment.

To this day Bonnie's family speculates and give their own theories, but in the end they all agree. A simple lullaby, sung with love and compassion, has a power all in itself.

White Noise Stories Continued

Upon waking, Lauren finds herself staring at her ceiling thinking about the dream she just had and what she had been thinking about earlier.

This last dream is a good example. What if the woman in the dream, Megan, had found out that she was adopted? Perhaps even had that bizarre meeting with the nurse and her daughter.

Isn't it plausible that Megan came home that night and had the dream Lauren just dreamed herself? A dream that gave off so much energy and terror from Megan's mind that it left some sort of print that Lauren was able to tap into and see for herself?

Lauren gets up and goes to the bathroom with every intention of coming back and dreaming some more. A brief thought comes over her that she should probably eat something but the desire to see what the next dream holds is too strong and she quickly dismisses the idea of food.

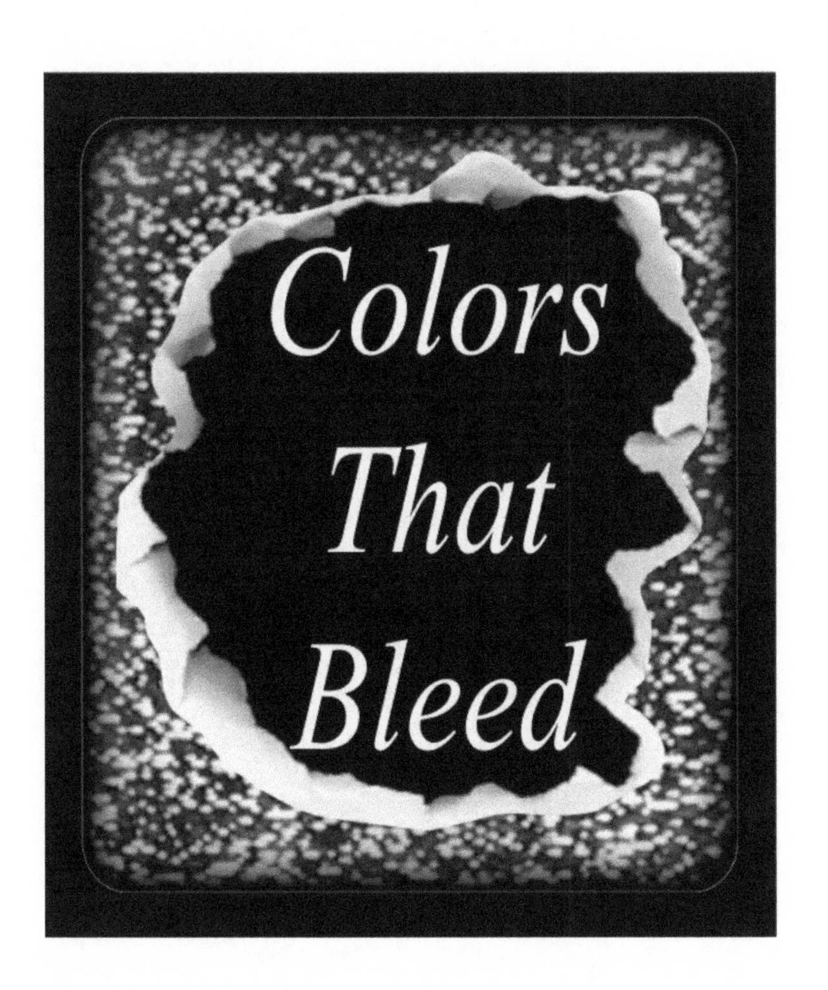
Colors
That
Bleed

Colors That Bleed

Chapter One

Bryan quickly grabs his art supplies and rushes out of his apartment. He had promised himself he would not be late for the boardwalk again, but for some reason promises to himself are always easy to break.

Bryan works at the boardwalk in the summer, painting portraits for the tourists. A buddy of his, Mark, keeps his little stand at his store. This saves the hassle of bringing the stand with him every day which also saves him an immense amount of time by allowing Bryan to simply show up. There really isn't a specific time that he has to be at the boardwalk, since he is his own boss; however, there are peak times when customers shop more than others. Lunch time is one of them. Smart enough to at least pack his lunch the night before. Bryan munches on a sandwich as he rides the train to the boardwalk.

People think he is crazy for living in the city, especially since he works at the boardwalk; however, the boardwalk is only a summer job. In the city Bryan can work all year round and he loved being near the art district. Slowly but surely, he had begun to make contacts in the business. Although his work was still considered mundane, he had hopes of fine tuning his art. What better way than to mindlessly practice his art while making money?

Bryan does have talent, he can paint a portrait of a customer within minutes. He is also smart by already having a collection of backgrounds painted for the day. When a customer picks a background, he can paint the customer onto the background they have chosen.

To mix it up a bit, Bryan also has paintings on novelty things as well, anything from little surfboards to sea shells. Many would not think he would make enough to support himself, but quite the contrary, he makes great money, he has to for him to live in the city. Although he doesn't have much of a life in the summer due to the long hours he works, come Labor Day he has enough money to coast through the winter. This allows him to work on his private collection during the winter season. If funds begin to get low, Bryan can always work the holidays on the street, giving him more than enough money for rent, food and art supplies.

It definitely is a nice set up; however, Bryan craves more. He wants to break free of the bonds of having to work for money. He is an artist! Once the art world takes notice, money will flow in without him giving it a second thought.

His stop comes up quickly. Looking at his watch he is pleased to see he will have plenty of time to set up before the peak time. Enjoying the sunny day, Bryan makes his way over to Mark's store.

Mark has the typical store for the boardwalk, souvenirs galore. In fact, it is how Bryan gets his souvenirs at a bulk rate.

Mark and Bryan went to school together. Bryan even worked right along with Mark during the summers. Mark's parents owned the store. Once Mark proved himself after high school by running the store, Mark's parents retired and gave the store to him.

Bryan walks into the store and sees Mark, "Hey bud, how's it going?"

Mark smiles, "Look at you! A little bit earlier than most days, feeling ok?"

Bryan blushes, "Believe it or not, I had every intention of being here even earlier but I tried painting after I got home last night. Before I knew it, half the night was gone."

Mark looks a little concerned, "How is it going, any break-through?"

Mark is the only one that knows about Bryan's dry spell. No different than writers, painters can have "painter's block". A time in which either the painter doesn't know what to paint or whatever he does paint lacks passion. Unfortunately Bryan is having both. Nothing seems to interest him in painting it, let alone show passion in his painting. It is becoming quite frustrating.

Bryan sighs, "Believe it or not, I went back to the basics and tried painting a bowl of fruit."

Mark can't help but laugh, "Basics? This coming from a man who has never had an art class?"

He enjoys Mark's teasing, "Hey, when it comes naturally, why force it to conform to a box?"

"So, why the bowl of fruit?" Mark has to ask.

Bryan has to admit, "Ok, something Mrs. Jones taught us in high school. If you can make fruit look real enough to eat you have done something marvelous."

Mark laughs again, "Good ol' Mrs. Jones. I remember her. Big black horn-rimmed glasses, going around pointing at your pictures saying 'Marvelous dear, simply marvelous!' She was a riot."

Now it is Bryan's turn to tease Mark, "If I remember correctly, she said that about everyone's paintings except yours!"

Mark nods, "Got that right. One day Mrs. Jones told me, "Honey, maybe you would do better in choir. I would hate to see this grade bring down your GPA."

Bryan is stunned, "Dude! I never knew she said that to you!"

Mark smiles, "I told her I didn't care. My future was already set with my parent's business. What did I care about my GPA? I wanted to see my buddy paint!"

A warmness comes over Bryan. If it had not been for Mark's encouragement and determination for Bryan to create his art, he would probably be on the same street his mother was. Or at the nearest local bar, eventually bumping into the father he never knew. No, Mark's family had sort of adopted Bryan through the years.

Bryan is always invited for the holidays and Mark's mom, Sheila, always makes sure to give him a birthday present. If not for her, he would have never had a birthday present. He was not even sure his real mom knew the date of his birth. This reminds him, "By the way, tell Sheila I got my birthday present. So very sweet of her!"

Mark helps Bryan pull out his stand from the back and set it up on the boardwalk, "Don't let her fool you, she does it for herself too. That woman gets the biggest kick out of her quests for the perfect presents for everyone."

Bryan smiles, "You are lucky to have such great parents!"

Mark nods, "I know, 'we' are lucky to have such great parents. You know, by default, you are one of us!"

Bryan looks out to the ocean feeling grateful, “Stop man, you keep giving me these warm fuzzy feelings. How will I ever be the cutthroat businessman today if you do that?”

Mark looks back at his store full of pride, “Remember, it has always been the motto of ‘honey attracts more’, especially when it comes to these tourists.”

Bryan looks around and starts to see the boardwalk beginning to fill up, “Yea, we love to hate them, don’t we?”

Mark smiles, “That we do. Hey, what did Mom get you anyway? Should I be jealous?”

Bryan opens up his box of paints and pulls out a handcrafted paintbrush and hands it to Mark. “Sheila said she found this on the islands when her and your dad went on vacation.”

Mark looks at the brush, intrigued, “This is gorgeous, and the markings on this thing are unbelievable! What are the bristles, horse hair?”

Bryan shrugs his shoulders, “I am not sure, it could even be boar since it was on the islands.”

Mark hands it back to Bryan, “Do you think you will ever use it?”

Bryan nods, “Yea, she said the villagers told her to have me use it every day. It is practically invincible.”

“Did you use it to paint your fruit?” Mark wonders.

Bryan shakes his head, “No, I had it packed it away with my work paints so I could show you. I will try it out today to see how it works and go from there.”

Mark looks at his watch, “Ok bro, you are on your own. I am expecting it to be a busy one today according to the books.”

Bryan laughs, “You talk about me not having art classes behind me but look at you! You definitely did not need any college classes, you are quite the natural in your own right!”

“I have to say, you are right! Did you know I have increased sales by twenty percent since last year?”

Bryan is impressed, especially with the competition on the boardwalk and the economy in the tank. “Good for you!”

Mark and Bryan say their goodbyes. Bryan sets up his little stand and opens his large umbrella. Once he is all settled, he prepares for the wait.

As he is waiting for the tourists to become interested in him Bryan studies the paintbrush Sheila had given to him. It was quite remarkable. He hopes she did not pay too much money for it.

In fact, the brush is so nice, Bryan is not sure he should even use it! Maybe, he should use it as a display. And yet, when he holds the brush it has a nice feel to it. It has just the right amount of weight to it, the brush practically balances itself. He looks at it more closely. Even though the brush is a dark red muddy color, Bryan is beginning to wonder if the brush may not be made out of bone. The bristles are another interesting thing. It is almost as if the hair is growing out of the bone. On closer inspection, Bryan for the life of him can't figure out how they attached the bristles!

His first customer startles him by clearing his throat, "Hey, I like your work! Would it be possible for me to get a portrait on that one there? The surf on that background looks wicked!"

Bryan can't help but laugh, "It does, doesn't it? And you, my friend, will look awesome in front of it!"

Bryan points to the chair beside him, "Have a seat, this will only take a few moments."

As the customer has a seat, Bryan pulls out the supplies he needs and begins, not even realizing he is using the brush Sheila had given him.

Chapter Two

Bryan and the customer talk easily while Bryan begins to lightly sketch the customer onto the canvas. The customer's buddy comes up with some food. The customer looks concerned, "Dude, am I allowed to eat while I sit here?"

Bryan smiles, "Not a problem."

The customer is relieved, "Awesome! I am starving!"

Bryan continues to work on the portrait while the customer happily chomps on his sandwich. Out of nowhere a seagull dives for the customer's sandwich.

Bryan is used to the pesky birds but never had he seen one go in for such an attack. Startled, the customer stands up and bats at the bird; however, the seagull is relentless. It would be funny if the customer was not so terrified and the bird not so determined.

Surprisingly the customer lets out a big scream, "He bit me!"

Bryan is shocked as he sees the customer start flinging his finger around which is bleeding at a pretty good pace. He immediately jumps up and helps the customer.

Once all the panic is done and the customer has a towel around his finger, Bryan sits back down to a canvas splattered with blood. The customer bleakly peers over the canvas and sees the damage. "Dude, I am so sorry! Do you have to start over? Will I have to pay for that one too?"

Bryan shakes his head, "No worries, just sit there and relax. I think I can fix this."

The blood is still fresh enough that Bryan can wipe the majority of it off. There are parts where it has stained the canvas but he thinks he can just mix the colors and fix it up.

Bryan goes to work at mixing the colors up and blending them into the scene. He is amazed how easy the cleanup is going. In fact, it almost seems as if the accident is going to make the portrait even better.

Bryan is amazed how nicely the new brush is working. It takes very little effort to clean up and use different colors, and for some reason the brush seems to swirl the colors into a perfect blend.

Within minutes the portrait is completed, “Ok, all done.”

The customer is shocked, “Really? Let me see.”

The customer looks at it with a big smile on his face, “Dude! It is perfect! I can’t believe what a great job you did and nowhere can you see the blood!”

Bryan looks at the painting with a smile, it really was good! In fact, it has to be the best portrait he has ever done! The portrait seems to have a life of its own, the colors bright and vibrant. Bryan almost wishes he could keep it for himself.

Both the customer and him are admiring the painting so much that neither one of them notice Mark approaching the stand. Mark clears his throat to get their attention. “I heard you guys had quite a dust up with one of the locals. Everyone ok?”

Bryan looks up and nods, “Yea, we live to die another day.”

Mark hands the customer a band aid, “I thought you may need this just in case, wasn’t sure if Bryan had any out here.”

The customer takes the band aid gratefully, “Thanks! Did you see how awesome my painting turned out?”

Mark takes a peak and is surprised, “Wow! That is good Bryan!”

Bryan agrees, “It is, isn’t it?”

The customer happily pays Bryan for the painting adding an additional twenty dollars for a tip, “You, my man, are going to be busy the rest of the afternoon because I’m going to be showing this to everyone I see!”

Bryan accepts the money and blushes, “My pleasure. I will be here until we close tonight.”

Mark waits until the customer leaves, “Bud, what the hell? That painting is amazing!”

Bryan smiles, “I know, I almost did not want to sell it to him!”

Mark nods, “I can see why! What made it so different?”

Bryan thinks about it, “I guess the new brush your mother gave me?”

Mark is proud, “Good for you, maybe you found a new talisman to get you back on track.”

Looking at the paintbrush, “I think you may be right!”

Mark leaves to go back to his shop as a new customer approaches Bryan’s stand inquiring about a painting she saw a man carrying.

Bryan happily shows her the different items he has to put her portrait on. Just as she takes a seat another person comes up. Before long Bryan has a line of people waiting to have their portrait done.

Bryan works non-stop the rest of the day. Mark is surprised to see Bryan still working after Mark has already closed his store. Mark walks over to see how much longer he will be.

Bryan looks up from his painting to see Mark walking over, “I am just finishing up.”

Mark comes up behind Bryan to watch him as he paints, although the painting is nowhere near as good as the first customer’s painting, it still is better than Bryan’s previous work.

“Looking great, bud!”

Bryan can see what Mark sees but doesn’t mention it in front of the customer, “It is, isn’t it?”

Finishing up Bryan hands it to the customer and the customer is all flustered. They continue to stare at it as they complement Bryan over and over. Finally the happy customer pays and leaves.

Bryan begins to put his art supplies away so Mark can put the stand in the store. Mark and Bryan work in silence until the customer is far enough away. Mark starts off, “A very busy day for you, you did not even break for a dinner. For that matter, a bathroom break! I don’t know how you do it!”

Bryan groans, “Don’t remind me, I don’t know which is worse, my hunger pains or my bladder pains!”

Mark and Bryan carry the stand to the store. Mark quickly unlocks the store, “Bryan, go on and go, I will get this.”

“Thanks man!” Bryan practically runs to the bathroom. He has to go so bad it takes a moment for him to relax enough to start. But once he starts, it goes on and on. Finally finished, he walks back to the front of the store where Mark is waiting for him.

Mark and Bryan do a quick check and lock up the store. As they walk on the boardwalk Mark asks, “How about I treat you to some dinner before you go home?”

Bryan shakes his head, “I appreciate it but I really want to get home and do some painting. The fever has hit me and you know what that means.”

Mark smiles, “Yup, there will be no living with you!”

Mark hesitates, “Can I ask you something?”

Bryan already knows what he is going to ask, “Why were the other portraits not as good as the first portrait?”

Mark sighs, “They were good, don’t get me wrong. In fact, it seemed as if you jumped a level just from last week!”

Bryan nods, “I don’t know why, but for some reason today I was in the zone. Though I admit that first painting was amazing, but no matter how hard I tried throughout the day, I could never get the same results.”

Mark thinks back to the first portrait, “I am far from being an art critic; however, there was just something about that first painting that popped! Like in your face, this is art!”

Bryan can’t help but laugh, “I know and I want to find that again!”

Mark is curious, “Was there anything else different that happened while you were painting that one?”

Bryan thinks back, “Not really, other than the bird incident.”

Mark chuckles, “Oh, that’s right, he was the bird man! My workers called him that for the rest of the day!”

Bryan gets serious, “It must have looked funny from afar but dude, that bird was vicious! I have never seen anything like it before! The damn thing actually bit him! He flung blood all over!”

Suddenly it hits Bryan, “That’s it! There was blood on the canvas! In fact, I had to mix the colors with the blood to be able to still use what I had started.”

Mark cringes, “Blood? That’s gross!”

Bryan is not deterred, “What if the blood is what made the painting pop?”

Mark sighs, “I suppose it could be the reason.”

Bryan thinks more about it, "Yea, when I was painting it I was surprised at how easily the colors merged."

Mark shakes his head, "What does this mean, are you going to go all vampire on me now?"

Bryan laughs, "No! Of course not! I just need to do some research on using blood in paint. Maybe it is a thing?"

Mark still doesn't like the feel of it, "I don't know man, seems a little dark art for me."

Bryan ignores him, "I can't wait to start researching. In fact, I should be able to research on the train trip home!"

Mark is a little concerned, "And what about those hunger pains of yours?"

Bryan's mind is racing a mile a minute, "Uh? Oh yea, I don't know maybe I will get something on the way to the station."

Mark knows Bryan has no intention of stopping so he stops at a restaurant at the boardwalk, "I am getting myself something to eat and you still have time until the next train. Come and eat with me, my treat."

Bryan is reluctant but his stomach pains win out, "Ok, if you insist."

Mark teases him, "That's more like it. Never known you to be one to turn down free food!"

Bryan feels a little guilty, "After the day I had, I should be buying the dinners!"

Mark smiles, "That's ok, it was a good day for me too! Believe it or not, the people waiting in line for you kept sending their friends in to my store to kill time which, in turn, led to more sales. So it's all good."

Bryan is happy to hear it, "That's awesome, after all you and your family have done for me, I am more than happy to share the wealth!"

Mark and Bryan have a nice little dinner and then Bryan is off on his way to take the train home. Although his brain was itching to begin the research, it was nice to just hang out with Mark.

However, now that Bryan is waiting for the train his mind quickly thinks of questions he wants answered from the internet. The most important is how does blood affect your painting?

Chapter Three

Bryan gets settled in on the train and immediately does a search on painting with blood. Interestingly enough a Wikipedia page comes up on a Vincent Catiglia. Vincent is known for his figurative paintings delving into the most unusual subject matters. They often examine life, death and the human condition.

What Bryan finds fascinating is that Vincent paints exclusively in human blood on paper. Vincent's paintings were exhibited at the H.R. Giger Museum Gallery in 2008 and closed in 2009. Many view Vincent's work as an examination of the human experience, the cycle of destined decay. Although a dark theme, Vincent also has an undercurrent of survival and victory throughout the paintings.

Vincent's ability to attract and repel is apparent due to his ability to transmit blood into something other than fear, giving way to a pathway of truth and realization. In Vincent's work you can see a comparison of birth and growth to decomposition and decay. Vincent seems to confront these issues by exposing their reality.

Bryan is impressed to see that Vincent Catiglia has even been compared to Michelangelo, among other famous artists, who delved in contemporary expressionist and mythologism.

Vincent has done several album art, even movie posters. Bryan finds all of this very fascinating, but he is more interested in how Vincent does it.

It says that Vincent uses only blood and water. However, the technique in which it is applied is what gives it a tonal and textural range. Vincent was influenced by another painter, Elito Circa, who is known for his hair and blood folk paintings.

The article continues to explain that the first colors used by man were red and black. The red color has a source of iron oxide pigments. Its name, hematite, is derived from the Greek word hema which means blood. Early man coveted this color due to the spiritual and symbolic significance.

It looks like Vincent uses a bloodletting process for his art. A modern day practice to combine his own life force into his art. Combining artist and art in every sense of the word.

Bryan is surprised to see that blood is technically tissue. Essentially, Vincent is using actual tissue to not only give an optical view but a literal transference of blood and flesh to his paintings.

Bryan looks up from his phone and out at the racing scenery passing him by. He is not sure if it was the late dinner he and Mark had, the subject he is researching, or plain motion sickness, but he suddenly feels sick to his stomach. Trying to focus on the seat in front of him and ignore the racing scenery, he begins to feel a little better. Perhaps doing research on the train was not such a good idea.

Bryan thinks about his research. The article included pictures of Vincent's work. Although very intricate and extremely talented, Vincent's work was not what he wanted to do. Although pictures never do an artist's work justice; Vincent's work seemed to be done mostly in red. No other vibrant colors were used. While the portrait that Bryan had painted so well earlier had red in it, all of the colors seemed to bleed together creating an amazing, life-like image.

He rubs his eyes. Maybe he is crazy thinking the blood had anything to do with the painting turning out so great. It could all be coincidental. Bryan thinks about it and the one thing that doesn't seem coincidental is the brush Mark's mom gave to him. It really seemed to make a difference!

Bryan has every intention of trying the new brush on the art he is working on at home. He has never been a superstitious person but for once in his life he understands why sometimes athletes attach significance to a specific item when they have a brilliant breakthrough. If this new paintbrush is going to be Bryan's new lucky charm, then so be it!

Finally his stop has come up. Even though he should be exhausted, Bryan can't wait to get back to the apartment and paint.

Rushing to his apartment, Bryan wastes no time in getting started; however, when he sits down in front of the painting he had started last night he is disheartened. The painting is so blah, no depth whatsoever. Disgusted, he throws the painting in the trash. Setting up a new canvas he scolds himself, "This is not high school anymore for God's sake! Get over yourself and grow up!"

Bryan easily traces his outline with the new brush. Again he is amazed at how easy the brush makes painting. Feeling encouraged, he begins to mix the paints.

For some reason he can't get the red on the fake apple in the bowl in front of him right. Bryan takes a moment and tries to relax. He glances at the painting in the trash. He can clearly see the red he used for the apple in that painting was not right either.

Bryan gets up and carefully picks up the fake apple out of the bowl of fruit and looks at it. He brings it over to where his paints are and closely studies the color of the apple. Not getting a good handle on it, he takes a knife and cuts a piece of the apple off. Flakes from the fake apple fall down onto the paints he already has on his palette for the painting.

Frustrated, Bryan uses his brush to try and remove the flakes. As he does, the colors become mixed. Too tired to care now, he randomly throws the colors up on the painting. He is shocked to see that the colors are becoming the exact colors he needs for each piece of fruit. Bryan works feverishly to finish the painting.

When the painting is done, Bryan shakes his head. It is almost as if he had come out of a trance. Funny, but that is exactly how he felt this morning after painting the first customer's portrait. Blinking his eyes several times, his vision begins to become clear. He is shocked to see in front of him yet another outstanding painting!

Bryan's excitement is overwhelming! Now this is a piece of art he can proudly take to the gallery this weekend! Even though it is a typical painting of a bowl of fruit, in so many ways it is not! The colors are the most vibrant he has ever seen! Somehow, it is as if the colors are swirling together to create an illusion of the bowl of fruit, and yet, the colors are an entity of their own. It is the only way Bryan can explain it.

He grabs his phone and takes several pictures, even video. The video and pictures don't give the painting the true respect it deserves, but it does show some of its attributes. Excited, Bryan forwards the pictures and video to Mark. Even though it is very late, he can't wait.

Within minutes he gets a call from Mark. Bryan answers the phone, "Hello?"

Sleepily Mark answers, "Dude! What the hell did you do? I have never seen such a bowl of fruit! Who knew?"

Bryan giggles nervously, "I know right? It is the most amazing thing! I am definitely taking this one to the gallery this weekend!"

Mark agrees, "Definitely, you have outdone yourself! I am telling you this is amazing shit! I am so proud of you!"

Bryan smiles, "I am sorry I woke you. I just had to show someone!"

Mark shakes his head, "No, that is quite alright. I am so glad to be part of this. I am not bullshitting, this is amazing! I can only imagine what it must be like in person!"

Bryan is looking at the painting as he is talking, "To be honest, I was surprised the pictures and video caught what it did, but yea, in person it just seems to be alive!"

Mark tries to get a handle on all of this, "This is all because of the paintbrush my mom got for you?"

"I think so! I don't know if it is just the power of suggestion, you know, like now I have this invincible brush I can paint. Or, the brush is really that good."

Mark sighs, "Well, whatever it is, it is yours now!"

Bryan hesitates, "I am thinking about staying home tomorrow. Maybe get a couple more paintings done for the gallery this weekend."

"I think it is a good idea," Mark says. "You made more than enough money today and my motto is strike when the iron is hot!"

Bryan is happy, "Thanks Bud, now go back to sleep. I promise I will not bother you the rest of the night."

Mark yawns, "I think I will take you up on that, but you do know I am always here for you man."

Bryan gets a little sentimental, "I know, and I appreciate it more than you will ever know. Night Bud."

Mark says his goodnights and snuggles back down in his bed. He takes his phone out to look at Bryan's pictures one more time. A little surprised, the pictures are not as good as when he first saw them. A little disappointed, he tries to convince himself he is too tired to be so critical. This painting of the bowl of fruit is the best painting Bryan has ever done, hands down.

Mark puts the phone on the bedside table and tries to go back to sleep. Unfortunately, it is not as easy as he thought it would be. Something is bothering him. He lays there looking up at the ceiling. Could it be jealousy? Mark throws that thought out immediately. He has never been jealous of Bryan. Bryan was like a brother to him and he truly wants to see him succeed.

So, what is it that is bothering him? Mark can't put his finger on it but something feels wrong. Like a premonition of doom that he can't seem to shake.

Maybe tomorrow he should call his mother and find out more about that paintbrush. Mark fears there may be a price for Bryan's impending success. Thinking about calling his mother makes him uneasy. Doesn't knowing about a fear increase the fear?

Chapter Four

Bryan sleeps in longer than he had planned. Groggily he goes to the kitchen to make himself some coffee. While the coffee is brewing, Bryan looks at the painting from last night. A little disappointed, he notices the colors are not as vibrant as he remembered them being. Sighing, he picks up the painting and takes it to the window to see it in better light.

The colors pop as soon as the sunlight shines down on the painting. Shocked, Bryan is pleased to see the painting almost come to life again. Satisfied that it is only the lighting in his apartment, he takes the painting into his bedroom. There he places it on an extra easel and covers it with a piece of white linen to protect it.

Not used to being in the apartment during the summer, the apartment feels stuffy. Bryan decides to open the windows to let some fresh air in. Although the noise from outside can be a distraction, he had learned at an early age how to tune unpleasant noises out. Whether it had been the short time his father lived with them and the yelling never seemed to stop, or when his mother decided to bring a different man home for the night and work her magic on him. Either way, Bryan would much rather hear city noises or the noises inside his apartment than what he heard while growing up.

Bryan goes back in the kitchen to see if the coffee is done and fortunately it is. He gets his cup of coffee and sits at his painting area as he contemplates what he should paint next. Sometimes it can be very frustrating choosing the next project.

As Bryan allows his mind to wander, a large thump comes from his bedroom. He quickly gets up to see what it could have been. Once inside his bedroom he realizes a pigeon has flown in. While flying in the pigeon had bumped into the lamp on his night stand. Bryan closes the door behind him, leaving the pigeon no escape except back out through the window.

Bryan tries to keep the annoyance out of his voice as he speaks to the pigeon, “Sorry Buddy, but I am not interested in having any roommates.”

The bird looks at him like he is the stupid one and then, as if to make its point, leaves a nice pile of goo on his floor.

Bryan yells, “You son of a bitch!”

Frightened, the bird takes flight, flying randomly around the bedroom. Suddenly it veers towards the window at full speed; however, it’s the top of the window that is closed. The bird hits the window hard and falls to the floor.

Sighing, Bryan grabs a nearby towel and approaches the bird on the floor. At first glance, he can tell the bird is dead. An animal lover at heart, he feels sad for the bird. Tragedy had come and he could not help but feel responsible.

Before picking up the bird, he decides he better close the window so no other birds could fly in. As Bryan closes the window he notices at the top right corner there is a little crack. Great, his landlord is going to love that! Well, hopefully it will be too small to notice if he ever decides to move out of this place.

Bryan carefully picks up the bird and takes it back to his painting area, placing it on the table next to the bowl of fruit. He notices there is a little blood on the towel he used to carry the bird.

Looking at the bird, Bryan begins to get an idea. He takes the bowl of fruit away and quickly goes back in his bedroom, looking for something. After finding it, he comes happily back into the room. Picking up the dead bird once again, he puts it on his chair and places a sky blue beach towel onto the table.

Not wanting to, Bryan picks the bird up with his hands. He finds the area where the blood had come from. Already the blood had started congealing at the wound. Trying not to think about what he is doing, he grabs a little paint cup and squeezes the bird’s blood into the cup. After getting as much as he can, he carefully cleans up the bird and places it face down onto the beach towel. Bryan spreads the poor bird’s wings out as far as he can. With a lot of imagination, it almost looks as if the bird is flying away in a pretty blue sky. With that image in mind, he quickly begins to sketch his idea out on a new canvas. Once the image is sketched out, he carefully begins to mix the bird's blood with the colors he plans on using.

Bryan begins to paint, using the brush Mark's mother had given him. As he paints, it is as if he is flying right along with the bird.

****

Meanwhile, Mark is taking his lunch break and decides to call his mother. Fortunately, he has a great staff that can usually handle everything on their own.

Letting his staff know that he will be sitting right outside the store if they need him, Mark finds a bench and calls his mom. Sheila, his mom, is surprised to see it is Mark who is calling her, "Mark, is everything ok?"

Mark smiles, "Well hello to you too Mom!"

Sheila shakes her head, "Stop teasing me! Why else would you be calling me at this time unless there is something wrong?"

Mark realizes she is right, "I just have one question, were you born a mom? You know, with the mom instincts, or were they learned over time?"

She laughs, "It is a natural ability. Obviously, nothing major is wrong so how have you been?"

Mark enjoys the warm sunlight cascading down on him, "Fine, and you and Dad?"

Sheila gets comfortable in her chair. She can always tell when Mark has something on his mind and it looks like it may take him a while to explain it. "Oh, your father is on this kick of making bird houses, be warned he's going to try and get you to sell them at the store."

Mark shakes his head, "Thanks for the heads up. Are they any good?"

Sheila lowers her voice, "Not bad, but the painting is horrendous. I think he should leave that for Bryan."

Mark is happy that she brought Bryan up. "Speaking of which, he is one of the reasons I called."

Now Sheila is beginning to get concerned again, "Is Bryan ok?"

Mark reassures her, “Oh yea, he’s fine. In fact, better than fine. His painting seems to have taken a turn for the better.”

Sheila is relieved, “Good! That poor kid deserves some sort of happiness. How he ever survived his childhood is beyond me!”

Mark has to give her credit, “Well, if it had not been for you and Dad, I am sure he would have turned out quite differently.”

Sheila is a little confused. If Bryan is doing so well, why did she hear concern in Mark’s voice? “So, tell me what’s going on.”

Mark sighs, “Not sure how to even explain it. First of all let me say that birthday present you got him was unbelievable!”

Sheila blushes, “It was, wasn’t it? He called me the day he got it and told me how much he loved it. Did he actually use it?”

Suddenly the sun seems too bright and Mark shades his eyes. “Yes, actually, he used it yesterday for the first time.”

Sheila is proud of herself, “Really? I honestly thought he would just use it as a display brush. Never dreamed he would actually use it for painting.”

Mark agrees, “I know, it was so intricately carved and unusual I was a little surprised he did too. By the way, is there a story behind it?”

Sheila thinks back to her trip, “Why yes, there is. When your father and I were on our trip we sort of separated from the group.”

Mark knows what that means, “You two wanted to do some exploring on your own.”

Sheila confesses, “You know us too well, we like to get off the beaten path. Anyway, we stumbled on this shack of a place that had strange items. At first, we weren’t even sure if any of the items were for sale; however, this old man sitting cross legged on the floor told us to look around and if we saw something he would consider letting us purchase it.”

A slight chill comes over Sheila as she remembers, “Most of the things were made out of bones and hair. Usually your father is the one that loves to study everything but in this case he was ready to leave.”

Sheila chuckles, “So, your father gave me the clue he wanted to leave. We thanked the man and just as we were about to leave this item fell onto the floor in front of me. It was the paintbrush I got for Bryan. I picked it up and looked it over. At first, I was not sure what it even was, then when I realized what it was I instantly thought of Bryan."

Sheila hesitates, "It was the strangest thing. It was as if the man knew what I was thinking. He spoke up and said it would make a fine birthday present for someone back home. I realized Bryan's birthday was coming up so I bought it."

Mark is curious, "Did the man say anything about the paint-brush?"

Sheila tries to remember, "Oh, you know me, I started gushing on about how fine of a painter Bryan was but recently he seemed to be having some sort of painter's block. As the man wrapped the paintbrush up he told me that this was a special paintbrush made out of bone and hair of a wild boar."

Sheila goes on, "He explained that his people would make tools out of the bones of animals they had killed. Their belief was that the bones they used had the animal's spirit captured inside, thus giving their tools even greater power."

Sheila, a little embarrassed, laughs nervously, "You know at the time, both your father and I fell for the whole tourist trap thing. Looking back now, I see how silly this all is."

Mark is not so sure. Not wanting to concern his mother, Mark answers, "Nonsense, it's a story you can tell your grand-children!"

Sheila becomes hopeful, "Why? Are there any prospects on the line?"

Mark sighs, "No Mom, but I assure you, you will be the first to know!"

Disappointed, Sheila understands, "When you least expect it is when you will find your connection."

Mark doesn't want to get into this long and detailed argu-ment again, "Mom, I better get back to the store."

Sheila wishes she had not said anything. When will she learn to keep her mouth shut? Changing the subject, Sheila asks, "Is Bryan going to be ok?"

Mark stands up, "I think so. I guess I am worried because now that he has had a couple of good paintings he is going to want more."

Not understanding Sheila answers, "Of course he's going to want more. That's no different than when you want the store to succeed."

Mark nods, "I know Mom and I am being very supportive, I just feel like something is going to happen."

Sheila tries to comfort him, "It just may be that you see Bryan going a different direction than you and that bothers you. However, I can guarantee you honey, he will always be a part of your life."

Mark sighs, "Maybe you are right. Thanks Mom, I knew you would make me feel better."

Mark says his goodbyes and goes back to the store. Although he does feel a little bit better, he still has that gut feeling. Mark tries to shake it and thinks about what a kick Bryan will get out of the story behind his new paintbrush.

Who knows, maybe that paintbrush has some sort of voodoo power in it that is making Bryan's paintings turn out so well. Even though Mark had thought of that as a joke, deep down inside of him wonders and for some reason, while the sun is baking down on him, Mark has goose bumps coursing all up and down him.

Chapter Five

Mark is not surprised that it has been a couple of days since he has talked to Bryan. Whenever Bryan gets going on his art he becomes totally immersed. However, Mark is a little worried and decides to try calling him after work. This time it is Bryan that answers the phone groggily, “Hello?”

Mark instantly knows Bryan had been sleeping, “Sorry, I was hoping you would still be awake. Nothing important, go back to sleep.”

Bryan clears his voice, “Nah, that’s ok. How’s everything?”

Mark sighs, “Good, the store is pulling in great numbers, though I have to admit it’s not the same without you here.”

Bryan chuckles, “When I am there we rarely see each other. Only at opening and closing do we get a chance to catch up.”

Mark nods, “I know, but I like those times.”

Bryan teases him, “Aw, I love you too man. Don’t worry, I have not forgotten about our bro-mance.”

Mark laughs, “Actually, you may be taking second place from now on. That girl Lori from the candy store is becoming a thing.”

Bryan is shocked, “Get out of here! See, I told you she had a thing for you but you would not listen!”

Mark sighs, “I know. I guess I finally grew to see it for what it is. I have to admit, it is nicer to date someone other than a tourist.”

Bryan understands, “Those tourists can be tempting but they are also temporary. Lori is a great girl; I can definitely see you ending up with her!”

Mark blushes, “Thanks, we have gone out a couple of times. In fact, I am on my way now to take her out for a late dinner.”

Bryan is happy for his friend, “It is awesome that she works the same as you. Her parents own that shop, right?”

Mark answers, “Yea, but fortunately her sister is next in line to take over. Lori is quite pleased about that, it is not something she wants to do the rest of her life.”

Bryan is curious, "What does she want to do?"

Mark thinks about it, "Write, I believe. Right now she is writing short stories but eventually she wants to write a novel."

Bryan is impressed, "Look at you, hanging out with the intellectuals!"

Mark shakes his head, "Believe it or not she is a lot like you. No writing classes or college. It seems to come naturally to her. Speaking of which, how is the painting going?"

Bryan looks over at the two covered pictures on easels in his bedroom, "I can't complain. I now have two paintings done and am working on my third."

Mark is a little disappointed, "You didn't send me any pictures of the second one."

Bryan is surprised, "Really? I thought I had; here let me send it to you now."

Bryan quickly finds the pictures he took of the pigeon and sends them to Mark. Mark gets them instantly and is looking at them as he is talking to Bryan, "Woa! That is wild! What made you think of that?"

Bryan sighs, "It is a long story. This dumb bird flew in my window and then tried flying back out but hit the top of the window and died. While cleaning it up I had this idea to use that blue beach towel I have as a background. Before I knew it, the painting was done."

Mark is curious, "These two paintings are a lot like that first portrait. Have you figured out the secret?"

Bryan hesitates, "I think I have, but you are going to think I am crazy!"

Mark is a little nervous, "Try me."

Bryan explains, "It is like I have to have something of what I am painting added to the paint."

Mark is confused, "What do you mean?"

Bryan thinks about it, "The portrait had the customer's blood on it. For the bowl of fruit, I could not get the color of the apple right so I cut a piece of it to examine it more closely. Flakes of it fell into my paint."

Mark doesn't understand, "Flakes?"

Bryan nods, "Yea, the apple was fake. When I cut it, the color flaked off."

Bryan goes on, "Then when the bird had hit the window he had bled a little. I used its blood in the paint and you can see how awesome it turned out."

Mark wonders if he should tell Bryan about what his mom said about the paintbrush. Just as he is about to, Lori comes walking up to him. Completely forgetting about what he was going to say, Mark clears his throat, "I'm sorry Bryan, Lori is here. I should get going."

Bryan smiles, "I know, ho's before bro's."

Mark is afraid Lori was able to hear Bryan and whispers, "Dude!"

Bryan laughs, "I am just teasing! Tell Lori hi for me and after this weekend we can all get together."

Mark appreciates it, "I will, in fact, since you are busy this weekend, Lori and I are going to make plans."

Bryan is shocked, "On a weekend? Good for you!"

Mark blushes, "I know, but Tim is very trustworthy and we will be staying close to the boardwalk just in case."

Bryan is proud of him, "Go for it, you both deserve it. We will talk later."

Mark says good bye and then focuses on Lori, "Look at you, all dressed up! Very nice!"

Lori blushes and curtsies slightly, "Thank you sir, all for you."

Mark puts his phone away and steps closer. Still a little awkward, he leans in for a kiss; however, the awkwardness quickly fades and the kiss suddenly becomes quite passionate.

Stepping back Mark catches his breath, "Now I could get used to that!"

Lori grabs his hand and starts walking, "So, how is Bryan doing?"

Bryan is the furthest thing from Mark's mind right now. Trying to focus, Mark answers, "He's doing fine. His painting seems to be in full swing right now."

Mark had already told Lori about the paintbrush, what his mom had said, and even the uneasiness he felt about the whole thing.

Lori asks, "Did you tell him the origin of the paintbrush?"

Mark shakes his head, "No, I was going to but you showed up."

Lori looks a little concerned, "I think you should have, may give him a reason to be a little cautious with it."

Mark is a little surprised, "Why? Do you believe in weird things like that?"

Lori nods, "I do. I also believe in respecting something I know nothing about. Take Ouija boards, I would never mess around with such things."

Mark has to agree, "Yea, those things always bothered me too. Why tempt fate?"

Lori blurts out, "Exactly!"

Mark thinks about it, "However, doesn't voodoo only have power if you believe in it? I mean, if that stupid paintbrush is voodoo related, maybe it is best that Bryan knows nothing about its dark side."

Lori shrugs her shoulders, "Maybe. And yet, we are not even sure it is voodoo related. It could be something else we know nothing about. Has anything bad happened to Bryan since he started using the paintbrush?"

Mark thinks about it, "Not that I know of. It's just this feeling I can't shake. Even now as we are talking about it, I get this anxiousness. It is hard to explain."

Lori squeezes his hand, "You are a good friend. Hopefully it is something as simple as not wanting change."

Mark is surprised, "That is exactly what my mom said! I tell you, you two are going to get along great!"

Lori smiles, "Does that mean you are willing to take me home to meet the family already?"

Mark laughs, "You know, I think I am! I know it has only been a couple of days but I feel so comfortable around you. Another thing my mom always said was that I would know instantly if it is right."

Lori stops and looks up at him, "I feel the same way! Why in the world did it take us so long to connect? We're only three stores away from each other!"

Mark sighs, "I guess I was too interested in the tourists, trying to live through their lives. I quickly found out it was not for me."

Lori agrees, "And I was too busy with my nose in a book to try and find something real."

Mark wonders, "What prompted you to come to my store?"

Lori blushes, "I happened to see you go out and check on Bryan and his customer after the bird incident. I saw you give the guy a band aid and for some reason it really touched me."

Mark thinks back to that day and realizes maybe something bad did happen to Bryan while using the paintbrush. If the seagull had not attacked the man, there would have been no blood. In fact, if the pigeon in Bryan's apartment had not flown in, there would be no painting of it. Mark thinks about the bowl of fruit and realizes there really is nothing there to tie it to the other incidents.

Mark decides to keep his theory to himself; instead he leans down and kisses Lori again. For a fleeting moment he wonders about what sort of painting Bryan is working on now, but with Lori passionately kissing him back, he suddenly forgets everything but her.

Chapter Six

Once Bryan was done with the pigeon painting he began to wonder what he should paint next. As he sat in his painting area he thought about the paintings he had already done. Suddenly an idea comes to him. He quickly sets up a mirror on the table in front of him. He had never attempted a portrait of himself. How cool would it be to paint a painting of him painting himself?

Pleased with himself, Bryan begins to get the project underway; however, before he starts he realizes maybe he should mix his blood with the paint like he did for the others.

Not wanting to hurt his hands which in turn may hurt his painting, Bryan decides to cut one of his legs. A small nick, just enough to give him blood for the paints. Whoever thinks cutting yourself intentionally is easy must have never done it! He takes a deep breath, closes his eyes, and then runs the knife quickly over his leg.

Tears instantly well up in his eyes. Looking down at the wound, Bryan is pleased to see a lot of blood gushing out. He takes a paint cup and starts collecting it. Once he has enough, he cleans the wound and bandages it.

Before painting, he gives himself some time to catch his breath and clear his eyes. Now ready to paint, Bryan begins. As usual, the sketching is the easiest. Bryan happens to look over at the clock and realizes hours have gone by. Surprised, he decides to take a break. Stretching, he walks around the apartment and notices a foul smell. He realizes he still had not disposed of the pigeon.

Disgusted, he peers into the trash bin and is shocked to see maggots already infesting the body. How can that be? The bird just died a couple of days ago! Shaking his head, Bryan seals up the trash bag and takes it out. Fortunately, no one is around to see him throw it in the bin.

Walking back to the apartment, he is still amazed at how quickly the bird had decayed. Bryan wonders if maybe the bird had already been sick when it entered the apartment. The idea that the death of the pigeon may not have been all his fault makes him feel better. Perhaps he had only speeded up the poor bird's death.

Once Bryan is back in the apartment, he is again visited with a strong foul smell. Bryan had always prided himself on not being the typical bachelor. Usually, his apartment is fairly clean. Sure, his paint area looks a little messy; however, the rest of the apartment is always clean and he never leaves dishes in the sink.

Bryan folds up the blanket on the couch. He had worked so late last night that instead of going to bed he had crashed on the couch. Wrinkling his nose, Bryan can't stand it anymore and goes in search of a can of air freshener in one of the cabinets in the kitchen. Fortunately, he finds one and practically empties it. Not great, but a little better, so Bryan goes back to painting.

For some reason, this painting is taking up an immense amount of time. When Bryan stops concentrating on the painting and looks at the clock, again he is surprised at how many hours have gone by. Literally forcing himself to stop, Bryan takes a break. In fact, Bryan decides to leave the apartment all together and go out and get something to eat.

Completely exhausted, Bryan clumsily walks out of the elevator towards the front door. Surprised, a doorman holds the door for him. Bryan smiles, "Wow, did not know we had a doorman. Must have not gotten the notice of my rent going up?"

The doorman smiles, "Hopefully, Mr. Walkens, that will not be the case."

Impressed, Bryan stops before going through the door. "And you know my name too, impressive. What is your name?"

The doorman answers, "You can call Mr. Akeru."

Bryan puts his hand out to shake, "Mr. Akeru, it is a pleasure to meet you."

A little surprised, Mr. Akeru returns the handshake, "As it is you, Mr. Walkens. Have a good night."

Bryan walks out into the cool crisp night. He can tell summer will be over soon. A little sad, he thinks about Mark. Maybe, he should give him a call. Then he realizes this is the weekend Mark will be going out with Lori. Bryan doesn't want to be the needy third wheel.

A little frustrated at how much time has flown by, Bryan realizes there is no way for him to get his portrait done in time for the art gallery this weekend. He takes a deep breath and tries to calm himself, remember all good things come to those who wait. Besides, it will be more impressive to have several good paintings to show instead of just one or two.

Bryan goes to a nearby café and orders a light dinner. While he is waiting for his dinner he finds himself self-consciously picking at the skin on his arm.

The waiter brings his dinner and is about to place it on the table, "Dude! That's gross!"

Confused, Bryan looks at the waiter and then looks to what the waiter is looking at. Shocked, he sees a pile of dead skin on the table. Bryan quickly wipes it off, "Oh my God! I am so sorry, I had no idea!"

The waiter places his food gently on the table, avoiding all contact with him, "Probably should get that checked out!"

Bryan shakes his head, "It is not that big of deal, really. I am a painter and it is just paint dust."

Completely relieved the waiter feels better, "Oh, that makes sense. Probably should have washed your hands before now."

Bryan nods, "You are right, my head is spinning from all I did today. Where is the restroom?"

The waiter points to the back and leaves.

Bryan washes his hands in the bathroom. After drying them he examines them more closely. They look normal. He raises his shirt sleeves to look at his arms and as he does small little hairs fall to the floor. Terrified someone may come in, Bryan quickly kicks them to the side so no one will see them. Knowing this is not the time or place to be examining himself, he goes back to his table.

Bryan picks at his food, his appetite completely gone due the circumstances. The waiter comes back to check up on him, "Would you like a box to take that home?"

Bryan smiles, "I think that might be best, maybe at home I will not be so distracted about work."

The waiter already has a box and places it by his food, showing Bryan he doesn't want to wrap it up. Bryan takes the box and dumps his food into it.

The waiter, not wanting to lose out on a tip, suggests, "You know stress can be an evil thing. Loss of appetite, sleep, you name it."

Bryan pays the waiter in cash with a nice tip, "I suppose you are right. I just need to take a deep breath and let things happen in the time they want to happen."

The waiter notices the nice tip and thanks Bryan. However, as the waiter goes back to the kitchen he has every intention of making himself too busy to clean up that table! The waiter shivers at the thought. God only knows what sort of disease that guy has with that much loss of skin. Paint dust my ass! For all he knows that guy could have that flesh eating disease!

Leaving the café, Bryan walks back to his apartment thinking about what the waiter had said. Stress could be a big part of what was happening to him. In fact, it makes perfect sense! He had never been under so much stress; his body is not used to it. He reassures himself that stress is all there is to it. Seriously, what else could it be?

Chapter Seven

Bryan works feverishly through the night and the painting is finally finished by early morning. Bryan leans back and admires his masterpiece. It truly is a masterpiece, his best painting ever!

As Bryan admires his painting he subconsciously scratches at his skin. Before he looks down to the spot on his arm that is itching maddeningly, he notices a dull spot in the painting. Irritated, Bryan dips the paintbrush into the mixture of his own blood and touches up the area. Suddenly the itch on his arm is gone. He looks at his arm and realizes it is in the same spot that he just touched up in the painting.

Before Bryan can begin to try to figure out what it all means, he is overwhelmed by a horrific stench that seems to be coming from his bedroom. He goes to his bedroom to investigate. He had not been in the room since he started painting his self-portrait.

Upon opening the door, he quickly covers his mouth as his eyes begin to water up. The stench is unbelievable! What could be causing such a smell?

Bryan walks timidly into the room, his eyes are drawn to his paintings on the easel. He notices paint dripping from both canvases. He screams, "No! Not my paintings! What the hell?"

Bryan carefully steps around the puddles on the floor. Before he takes off the white linen covers on the paintings, he notices something odd about the bowl of fruit he used as a reference when painting the first painting. The fruit had turned rancid! It was all bruised, discolored and had maggots wiggling in and out of it. Disgusted, Bryan runs to the kitchen, grabs a trash bag, and carefully picks up the bowl and drops it all into the bag. Trying to shake off the heebie jeebies, he quickly ties the bag tightly so none of the bugs can get out. In fact, he decides to take it immediately to the trash bin.

Once it is in the trash, Bryan thinks about it as he heads back to the apartment. How is any of this possible? The damn fruit in the bowl was not even real, it was all fake!

Bryan grabs more trash bags and cleaning supplies as he goes back into his bedroom. Not wanting to, but knowing he has to, he takes the white linen off of the first painting. Shocked, he can't comprehend what he is seeing. In front of him the painting seems to be oozing off the canvas onto the floor. The colors bleeding into one another. As bad as all of that is, the painting itself makes no sense. It is as if Bryan painted the bowl of fruit exactly the way it looked when he took it to the trash!

No longer is it a beautiful, intensely colorful painting. Instead, it is a morbid painting of decomposed fruit with worms and bugs wriggling around. In fact, as Bryan is looking at the painting, a fly that was portrayed as flying around the bowl of fruit in the painting literally comes out of the painting and starts flying around him! How is that possible?

Bryan quickly takes his phone out and snaps a picture of the painting. Then he places the canvas into a trash bag, tying it up tight so none of the bugs can get out. He then sops up the mess on the floor, collecting maggots and flies that had dripped off the painting. Bryan tries not to think about what he is doing but simply tries to hurry up and get it all cleaned up.

Where the first painting had been is now all cleaned up. Bryan is reluctant to begin on the next painting but knows he has to do it. He gently pulls away the white linen protecting the painting. Bryan immediately begins to start to gag as he looks at the painting. The once beautiful painting of the pigeon flying in the perfect blue sky is nothing more than a poor beast trying to escape its own mortality. The painting is not as decayed as the first painting; however, he reasons that is because it has not been given enough time to decay.

Bryan takes a photo of this picture as well, amazed at how the portrait has transformed itself from its original state. Bryan sends the photos to Mark so he can see what the paintings are becoming.

Bryan watches as the bird seems to be flying in pain. Yes, the painting is in motion. The bird still has its back to Bryan, but he can see that one wing is broken. He can even hear the bird scream in agony. Different spots on the bird are red with blood and the blood is what is dripping down onto the floor. He desperately wants to put the bird out of its misery but is not quite sure how to.

Bryan gets an idea and goes into the living room to retrieve the paintbrush. He dips it into the paint he was using and quickly goes back to the bedroom. He begins to paint over the bird, very difficult to do while the bird is still in motion. However, every brush stroke of paint Bryan puts on the painting doesn't become part of the painting; it simply stays as individual brushes of paint.

Not able to handle the bird's screams of agony, Bryan takes the painting and puts it in his bathtub and lights it on fire. Tears roll down his face as he watches the bird wither in agony as it is consumed in the flames. Finally all becomes quiet.

Exhausted, Bryan can't get himself to clean up the mess. His only recourse is to call Mark and try to explain to him what just happened.

Bryan anxiously waits as the phone rings several times. He knows Mark is with Lori, but hopefully he will answer. Mark, unfortunately, is at the movies and has turned his phone off. Bryan decides to leave a message. "Mark, some crazy shit is happening! I sent you pictures of the paintings I painted. They are changing, dying!"

Bryan realizes how crazy it sounds but he has to make Mark understand, "I tried to fix the one with the bird but I couldn't."

Bryan suddenly realizes why he couldn't, "The paint I tried to fix it with was with my blood, not the bird's!"

Bryan sighs, "Ok, I know what I have to do, but it's going to be hard to keep it up. Please, when you get this message come straight over, I will leave the door unlocked. I need your help!"

Bryan takes one last look at the bathtub and grimaces. He then goes to the front door and unlocks it. After that Bryan goes back to his painting area.

Sighing, Bryan takes off his pants and picks a new place to cut for the blood he will need. Bryan knows it is going to be a very long night.

Chapter Eight

Mark wakes up beside Lori refreshed and happy. He thinks about the wonderful night they had last night. Dinner, a movie and then home for dessert!

Mark is a little surprised that he did not hear from Tim last night after the closing of the store. He quietly reaches for his phone, not wanting to disturb Lori. Suddenly he remembers that he turned his phone off during the movie and never turned it back on. Damn! Hopefully no one tried to get a hold of him last night!

Mark, feeling anxious, checks the phone. There was only one missed call and it was from Bryan. Whew! That means Tim handled everything with the store fine last night and that is a relief! However, he is surprised to see that Bryan had not only left a message but a couple of texts earlier in the night. He opens up the texts and looks at the pictures that Bryan sent.

They were two pictures of Bryan's paintings that Mark had already seen, the one with the bowl of fruit and the one with the bird. Maybe Bryan had forgotten Mark had already seen these?

Lori begins to wake up, "Is there a problem?"

Mark shakes his head, "No, I think Bryan is losing it. He sent me pictures of paintings he had already sent."

Lori rubs her head a little, "That's a bit more about pictures than I needed to hear this morning!"

Mark smiles, "Looks like someone may not be able to handle the wine they had last night?"

Lori nods carefully, "Among other things."

Mark kisses her on the forehead, "Poor baby, let me get you some aspirin. As for the other things, I'm not sure what to do about those."

Lori watches him get out of bed and blushes, "The other things I am afraid may become just as addicting as drinking wine!"

Mark comes back in with a glass of water and the pills, "I don't know, it seems to me you are a lightweight when it comes to drinking. Who is to say you won't be the same for the other things?"

Lori takes the pills and then looks up seductively at him, "I have a feeling my endurance for the other things will only improve. Are you up to the challenge?"

Mark plops back in bed, "Wouldn't that be enabling the addict?"

Lori laughs, "I am willing to take that chance!"

As Mark is about to start the challenge he remembers he did not listen to Bryan's message. "I'm sorry, before we start do you mind if I listen to Bryan's message? He normally doesn't leave one and I have been a little worried about him."

Lori agrees, "Of course, gives me a chance to freshen up."

Mark watches her as she hops out of bed and heads for the bathroom. Already he is beginning to get excited at the possibilities that lay ahead of them. He sighs and listens to Bryan's message. Suddenly his excitement is gone and his whole body kicks into panic mode. He quickly starts to get dressed as he yells out to Lori to do the same.

Lori and Mark arrive at Bryan's apartment in record time. Mark had tried calling Bryan several times but to no avail. Wishing with everything in his soul that they are not too late, Mark opens Bryan's door.

An overwhelming smell of smoke and decay come over both Mark and Lori. Mark stops Lori from going in, "Call the police and stay out here."

Lori nods, secretly relieved to not have to go in. Mark timidly walks into the apartment calling out, "Bryan, dude where are you? You ok? Answer me, please! I am so sorry I did not get your message sooner!"

Mark is answered by an eerie silence. Then he sees Bryan slumped over in a chair in what he called his painting area. Tears roll down Mark's face as he runs over to his best friend. Before he gets to Bryan, he sees the large pool of blood around him and realizes it is too late. To make sure, Mark carefully reaches over to Bryan and forces his body to sit upright.

Mark is horrified to see the paintbrush his mother gave to Bryan sticking out of the jugular vein in Bryan's neck. Mark can't possibly begin to understand what has happened. Obviously Bryan committed suicide with that damn paintbrush, but why? Things were going great for him, Bryan finally had the break he so desperately wanted for his painting.

Mark looks at the painting in front of Bryan and is shocked at how good it is. The colors seem to swirl into a delightful picture of Bryan looking at a mirror as he paints a self-portrait of himself. Never had Mark seen such brilliant colors!

Mark forces himself to look back at Bryan. This time he notices that the blood from Bryan's neck is not what covers his legs. He forces himself to look closer without touching anything. Yes! There, all up and down his legs, it looks like Bryan had been cutting himself. Confused, he looks at Bryan's arms and there too are several slices in the skin. Mark looks around on the floor and there lays the knife Bryan had been using to slice himself.

What the hell? Then Mark sees pots of blood spilled into the colors that Bryan was using to paint his self-portrait. Bryan must have thought using blood was what made his paintings so good; therefore, Bryan used his own blood to make his self-portrait. But why did he need so much? Obviously the painting was finished.

Mark steps carefully around and looks at the painting from the side. He is shocked to see layers upon layers of paint were applied. In fact, looking from this angle Bryan's image of himself is literally 3-D.

Lori breaks Mark's thoughts, "Is he going to be ok?"

Mark softly answers, "No, I'm afraid he is already gone."

Time seems to have no relevance in the next few hours. Police came and asked questions. Bryan's body was then finally removed. The police were curious about why the apartment smelled so bad and why the painting in the bathtub was burned. Their only conclusion was the bird Bryan had painted had still been in the apartment and decayed. There were some messes on the floor in Bryan's bedroom which suggested that, also forensics found feathers in the bathtub.

No one is certain why Bryan felt a need to burn the bird and the painting instead of disposing of it. If anything, it gave the police an idea of where Bryan's mind was at the time. The police wrapped it up as simply an artist that went crazy and committed suicide.

Mark on the other hand had his suspicions. It was not until the next summer that he realized Bryan had been a victim himself. A customer came in one day asking, "Do you know how I can get in contact with the guy who used to paint in front of this store?"

Mark sadly shook his head, "I am sorry, Bryan is no longer with us."

The guy nodded solemnly, "I am sorry to hear that, he was an awesome painter!"

The guy introduces himself, "My name is Joe. Bryan painted this awesome picture of my buddy Ron here on the boardwalk."

Mark smiles, "Yea, he painted a lot of portraits."

Joe shakes his head, "No, this was different. For some reason the colors on this painting just popped out at you!"

Mark's smile suddenly fades. He had told the police about the first painting Bryan had done that had blood on it. The police tried to track down the subject in the painting to tie up any loose ends. Unfortunately, it had been a cash transaction and Bryan had not kept any records. It had been a dead end. However, now stands in front of him a person who knows the person in the painting Bryan did. Mark is curious, "Is your buddy with you?"

Joe shakes his head, "No, I am afraid he is no longer with us either."

Shocked, Mark has to ask, "What happened?"

Joe is a little reluctant to say, "Believe it or not, a strange flesh eating disease."

Chills come over Mark as he lowers his voice, "How did he catch that?"

Joe shrugs his shoulders, "No one knows. It was a very painful death; in the end his mind was totally destroyed. He kept saying that the painting was disintegrating and he needed to fix it so he would get better."

Mark's heart sinks, "What of the painting?"

Joe shakes his head, "Beautiful as the day it was painted. In fact, a gallery has it now and wanted me to try and track down the artist. It's a real shame Bryan's no longer with us; from the sounds of it he would have become quite famous!"

Mark agrees, but can't help but think about how many more that damn paintbrush would have killed if Bryan had not thought of doing a self-portrait first.

White Noise Stories Continued

Lauren wakes up not knowing where she is. As her eyes adjust to the light, she realizes she is in bed in her apartment. A longing to be in her old bedroom back at her parents' home comes over her.

As before, her dream comes back to her in vivid color. Lauren shivers a little as she thinks about her choice of words. Color. The dream had been about colors that bled.

Lauren not only feels a sense of sadness from the dream but also a sense of fear. Could something like the dream really have happened? Is she so naïve that just because it has not happened to her, it could not be true?

While in the bathroom Lauren can't get the dream out of her mind. As she finishes up, Lauren can't help but glance at the bathtub. She is shocked at what she sees. The image of the live painting of the bird, squirming under the flames of fire, plays out for her. Mesmerized, she watches as the flames dance around the poor bird trying to escape from its torture. A horrible stench of burnt feathers and flesh come over Lauren, shaking her back to reality. She quickly runs from the bathroom back to her bed.

Although Lauren had liked entertaining the idea that her dreams were nothing more than an imprint of another's person nightmare, she doesn't care for that idea to appear outside her dream state. Hearing voices and seeing images or hallucinations is going too far. Is this what it feels like to be slowly going mad? Lauren shakes her head. There has to be a logical explanation.

Perhaps there is something in the water, but if that were the case the whole building would be filled with crazy people. What about something just inside her apartment? Had she not heard somewhere that paint can have an adverse effect on you? Paint that has lead in it? Lauren shivers again at the thought of paint; flashes of the paint on the portraits dripping down onto the carpet overcome her.

Another thought from the dream comes to Lauren's mind and she can't help but get out of bed to check. Unfortunately, there it is. A crack in the top window where the bird in the dream had hit the window. The crack Bryan had noticed and hoped the landlord would never notice. Apparently, they had not. Lauren takes a deep breath and wonders what she should do. There had been someone who had died in her apartment!

Exhausted, Lauren crawls back into bed. What is she going to do? Is this Bryan and his live paintings going to haunt her? Lauren tries to be reasonable. Nothing strange has happened to her in the apartment other than the dreams, occasional voices that were not even Bryan's, and a real time flashback.

Lauren's mind is going into overdrive. What if, since Bryan did die in her apartment, it opened up a portal? The portal in turn is intensified by the white noise sound machine.

Which brings up her first thought, can the dead dream? Is that what Lauren has tapped into, the dead dreaming? Suddenly, the idea of sharing dreams with the dead is not as entertaining as sharing someone's memory of a dream.

Feeling very alone and vulnerable, Lauren snuggles back under the covers. Listening to the white noise, Lauren finally gets enough courage to reach over and quickly bat at the sound machine to turn it off.

Lauren feels a sense of relief as she hears the outside noises flooding down on her. Suddenly the noise of the barking dog and baby don't seem so bad.

Lauren's eyes begin to feel heavy. She realizes her poor body must be exhausted and allows herself to fall asleep once again. If anything, with the noise machine off, if Lauren sleeps normally without any dreams this will be her test.

The
Fallen

The Fallen

Chapter One

Angie sits in the living room in front of a roaring fire, enjoying a movie on Netflix with her husband. It was a cold gray day that happened to fall on a weekend, giving them the perfect excuse to do absolutely nothing.

The phone rings. Noticing it is her son Kyle, she quickly pauses the movie to answer it. "Hey Kyle, what's up?"

Kyle's voice seems strained, "We are on our way to the emergency room. Don't worry, I am fine, however my leg not so much."

Angie sits up, "What hospital are they taking you to?" She quickly grabs a pen and writes down the hospital, "Ok, we will be there as soon as we can!"

Kyle shakes his head, "No Mom, don't worry, that will not be necessary! Rose is right here and taking great care of me."

Angie relaxes a bit but rolls her eyes at the mention of Rose. Rose and Kyle's relationship is a fairly new one. Kyle desperately wants his mom to like her, so he constantly tries to put Rose in a good light.

Honestly, Angie had not quite made up her mind about Rose; she had only met the girl twice. Unfortunately, both times had not made Angie fall in love with her like Kyle had.

For months Kyle has been telling Angie what a great girl this Rose is and how much fun they are having in the relationship. Angie truly thought this one might be the one.

Kyle had mentioned in passing that Rose came from a wealthy family; however, he would constantly emphasize how much of an independent woman she is, having a job and her own apartment. Compared to his previous relationships, this was refreshing to know. In addition, when Kyle talked about her you could tell he admired her. There was no drama like so many girls have these days.

To be honest the first meeting with Rose was a nice one. She was an attractive girl, same age as Kyle, and seemed to have a good head on her shoulders. When Kyle called the next day anxious to know what Angie thought, she agreed that Rose seemed to be everything that Kyle had told her.

However, Kyle instantly knew there was a "but" that Angie was going to say. Frustrated, he raised his voice, "What is it about this one you don't like Mom?"

Hesitant, Angie did not even want to mention it, "I like her and we had a nice time!"

Not letting it go, Kyle persisted, "Mom, you said you would tell me if there were any red flags! So just spit it out now instead of playing games."

A little hurt, Angie did not feel like she was playing games, she honestly did not know if it was a big deal or not, "I guess it is that you can see that she comes from a wealthy family."

Confused, Kyle blurts out, "And what do you mean by that?"

Angie stumbles around for the right words, "I just noticed that not once during the night did she say thank you."

Kyle sighs loudly, "Geez Mom! Is that the only thing you could find? For Pete's sake, she was nervous about meeting you and Dad for the first time! I assure you she was very thankful, afterwards all she could talk about was how nice you two were!"

Feeling a little guilty, Angie apologized, "I am sorry, I should never have brought it up. You are right; she is a very sweet girl."

A couple more months go by before they meet Rose again. Kyle and Rose's relationship was getting deeper. In fact, so deep they were thinking about moving in with each other in the spring when Rose's lease was up on her apartment.

Angie was genuinely excited for Kyle. He seemed happy in the relationship and it did seem the logical step to be taking. However, the second visit with Rose was no better than the first. In fact, it was worse. Not that they all did not get along and have a good time; it was just that Rose would not say thank you if her life depended on it. This infuriated Angie. They had paid for Kyle and Rose all through the day and not one single thank you.

Kyle was aware of it too and tried to overcompensate for Rose by saying how much "they" enjoyed the day and how "they" were thankful.

The next day Kyle revealed to Angie that it was beginning to bother him as well, many times he would do things for Rose and she would not acknowledge any gratitude.

Knowing how much Kyle wanted the relationship to work, Angie tried to dismiss it as something Rose must have grown up around. Perhaps she did not even know she was doing it.

A couple more months passed and her relationship with her son was changing. Kyle was becoming more distant and more involved with Rose. Angie knew that, truthfully, when you are in a relationship that is how it is supposed to be. Although Angie missed her son, she was happy that he was finally in a relationship he wanted to be in.

Focusing back on the conversation at hand, Angie asks, "How did you hurt yourself?"

Kyle laughs a little, "I wiped out on the mountain and ski conditions were not quite perfect today. Since it is so late in the season there is more ice than snow. Unfortunately, I hit ice and lost control."

Angie knows Kyle too well and can tell he is trying to make light of the situation, "How bad is it Kyle?"

Kyle knows he can never get anything past his mom, "It is pretty bad. I have a gash that goes all the way to the bone so I am sure I will need a lot of stitches and the knee, well..." Kyle closes his eyes willing the pain to stop, "it is messed up."

Angie sighs, "Are you sure you don't want us to come? We could be there in a couple of hours."

Kyle smiles, "No Mom, I will be fine. I have Rose right here and anyway, was it not you that said you were so happy I finally had someone else to take care of me?"

Angie laughs a little, "You are right. Tell Rose to call me as soon as you find anything out, ok?"

Kyle agrees and after a quick love you, hangs up. Angie hates not being able to play mom to Kyle in person. However, at least he did call her to let her know what happened.

Feeling a little guilty, Angie turns the movie back on; after all, kids do grow up and learn to deal with things on their own. It is what you strive as a parent to accomplish, but being a mom, you never seem to grow out of that responsibility nor do you want to.

Chapter Two

Two months passed while Kyle waited for surgery on his knee. It had been agonizing waiting in his apartment alone for days on end. Rose was only able to visit one day which was on the weekends.

They had continued to pursue the idea of moving in, in fact, Kyle was able to secure a beautiful two bedroom apartment on the top floor with a river view. He timed it perfectly with Rose's lease ending on her apartment and after his surgery.

Of course his mom could not understand why Rose did not stay a couple more nights during the week, especially since Rose was going to be moving into the area eventually. Her drive to work would be no different than what it would be when she would be living with Kyle.

Kyle hated to admit it, but deep down he agreed with his mom; however, Kyle had always been self-sufficient and hated asking for help from anyone. So, stubbornly, he tried to make things work. It was tough though, not being able to drive was harder than he thought. Sometimes, not being able to move around, he would go for days without having any real food in the house.

The trash stacks up and the laundry is out of control. It embarrasses him that the apartment is such a mess, but there is literally nothing he can do. It is hard enough just getting to the bathroom, let alone try and carry anything while he is on crutches.

The day of his surgery he had to ask his mom to take him since Rose could not get off work. His mom happily agreed, although taking his car, which is a manual, into downtown New York is a bit overwhelming for her.

Angie maneuvers Kyle's car through the dense traffic. Trying to keep her calm, Kyle says, "You are doing a great job Mom, we are almost there."

Angie doesn't feel so confident, "I hate to say it, but even though I have not driven a stick for a while, it does seem easier to move your car around in traffic than it would have been with my SUV."

Kyle nods, "I knew you could do it. I was just worried that the SUV would have been too big for the parking garage. It would have been a tight fit."

Relieved, Angie finally pulls into the parking garage and helps Kyle walk a block to the hospital. "I can't believe they don't have their own garage Kyle!"

Frustrated with the pain of walking so far Kyle agrees, "I know Mom, but what can we do?"

Realizing the poor kid has enough on his mind with the surgery, Angie tries to change the subject. "Just think, in a few short hours this will all be over! The next couple of months you will actually be healing instead of just waiting for the surgery!"

Kyle sighs, "You are right, I can't wait to be normal again!"

Angie helps him get checked in and goes into the back with him to see him off to surgery. Patiently, she waits for him in the waiting room. Eventually the doctor comes out and goes over Kyle's procedure with her.

Angie had no idea how extensive the damage to Kyle's knee was. If she had known, she would have been a lot more worried about the surgery!

The doctor proceeds to show her pictures of the surgery he performed. "Right here is where I placed the cadaver tendons."

Angie has to stop him, "Wait a minute. Did you say cadaver?"

The doctor answers, "Yes, ma'am."

A little shocked, Angie asks, "Cadaver, like in dead parts?"

The doctor smiles a little, "Yes, ma'am."

Angie has a slight chill go through her, "Did Kyle know about this?"

The doctor nods, "Yes, he knew it could be a possibility. I could not be sure until I had the knee opened up and saw how extensive the damage was. Don't worry, this is a common practice."

Eventually Angie is allowed to go back and see Kyle. Expecting a happy son coming out from under the drugs, she is surprised at Kyle's reaction. Kyle looks angrily at her, "It is about time you got here!"

Confused, Angie replies, "They just now let me come in, how are you feeling?"

Frustrated, Kyle answers, "How do you think I feel? It freaking hurts!"

Angie looks over at the nurse, "Wow, when you come out from under are you not usually a bit loopy? You know, silly like? In fact, I had planned on getting my phone out and tape him, hoping to get something funny to put on YouTube."

The nurse laughs and shrugs her shoulders, "Different people react differently. It mostly plays on your emotions. With Kyle here, it seems to be playing on his anger."

Apologetically Angie answers, "I am sorry, I have never seen him act like this before. Usually he is very polite and easy going."

The nurse shakes her head, "No problem, we know it is out of his control. We don't take it personally."

The nurse hands Kyle's clothes to her, "If you don't mind, you can start getting him dressed and then we can get you out of here."

Kyle struggles to sit up, "I am sorry for being so short with you, Mom. I don't know what is wrong me. I just feel so angry for some reason. Did you talk to the doctor?"

As Angie helps him get dressed she answers him, "Yes, I did. The doctor was very nice."

Kyle proudly agrees, "He is, isn't he? They say he is the best. He does surgeries on famous dancers and even Olympic athletes."

Angie is impressed, "Well, he certainly seemed quite confident in what he did for you."

She hesitates, "Unfortunately though, he was not able to do what he told you this morning. When he opened up the knee there was more damage than he thought so he ended up having to use the cadaver parts."

Kyle suddenly stops what he is doing and starts crying uncontrollably. Not sure of the reason for the outburst Angie automatically thinks he hurt himself as they were getting him dressed, "Oh my God, did I hurt you?"

Kyle wipes his eyes angrily, "No Mom! I am sorry; I just was not expecting that. I mean, I know the doctor had mentioned there being a possibility of using them, but still…" Kyle is not even sure how to finish the sentence.

Angie understands, "Honey, he said it was a common procedure. I am sure it is not a big deal."

Kyle finishes putting on his shirt, "I know! It was the weirdest thing. The moment I heard 'cadaver' an immense sadness came over me."

Angie sighs, "I am sure it is still the medicine coursing through you, give it a little more time. The thing to focus on is that the surgery was a success and the doctor is quite pleased with the results."

Kyle forces a smile, "Ok Mom. Let's get the hell out of here!"

Butterflies suddenly invade Angie's stomach. She is definitely not looking forward to the drive back out of the city. "As long as you can get me to the Lincoln Tunnel, it will all be good!"

But of course nothing is ever easy. Angie had to retrieve the car herself from the garage, pick Kyle up in front of the hospital, with three lanes of crowded traffic. The poor kid had to hobble around the car which put him right in the traffic and try to carefully seat himself into the car. Once in, Angie quickly merges into traffic.

As they are driving through the middle of Times Square, Kyle begins to scream in agony, "Oh my God, this hurts so bad! Where are my pills?"

Trying to concentrate on the traffic and help Kyle, Angie answers, "Right here in my purse. I also have a bottle of water in there you can use."

Still stuck in traffic, Kyle begins to calm down a little as the medicine begins to take hold. Angie tries to tease with him, "Honey, you have to stay with me until I get to the Lincoln Tunnel because I have no idea where I am."

Frustrated, Kyle raises his voice, "Just follow the damn signs Mom!"

Angie takes a deep breath, desperately wanting to throw her hands up and say I can't do this, she tries to focus on driving. A bus nearly hits them as it squeezes in, a taxi suddenly stops to pick someone up with no warning, and a man just casually crosses in front of them.

Kyle is so angry he reaches to the back to get his crutch. Mortified, Angie yells out, "What the hell are you doing?"

Determined, Kyle answers, "I am going to get out and beat the shit out of that guy with my crutch!"

Angie quickly locks the door, "No, you are not! Look, he is gone now and there is the exit for the tunnel. We are almost out of this crap!"

Seething, Kyle just sits there until he realizes a cop is motioning them to go straight, instead of allowing them to turn towards the tunnel. Kyle suddenly rolls down the window and yells out at the cop, "What the hell man? We have to go that way to get to the tunnel!"

The cop looks bored and calmly answers, "Just go around dude, nothing I can do about it."

Angie quickly rolls up Kyle's window and inches forward past the cop. Kyle screams over at her, "I was not finished talking to that cop!"

Angie has had enough, "Kyle, just chill out! It is hard enough to deal with all this traffic, let alone not knowing what you are going to do next! Look, the next street will take us around the block and then the tunnel should be right there."

Sure enough, that is exactly what it did. Once in the tunnel Angie begins to relax. Now, heading down the highway at a pretty good clip, she looks over at Kyle and is surprised to see him fast asleep. The pill must have finally kicked in.

What a nightmare this whole day had been! Never in her life had she seen her son so consumed with anger. As her line of thinking continues, she realizes Kyle had never acted like this before the surgery.

She reaches down to turn the AC lower as a chill comes over her. It was as if a different personality had emerged from Kyle.

Angie's imagination gets the best of her and she can't help but wonder, can cadaver parts carry personality traits with them?

Chapter Three

Two weeks later and Angie is finding herself taking Kyle back into the city for his two week appointment, "I thought Rose was going to be taking you to this appointment?"

Kyle answers her sharply, "Mom, I told you she could not get off work!"

Angie sighs as she tries to maneuver her way around the city yet again. Desperately, she is trying to bite her tongue on this whole Rose thing. It was bad enough the girl was not there for Kyle's operation, even worse that Rose did not come and stay with him the night of the operation. It frustrated Angie no end that Rose did not think about it being dangerous for Kyle to spend the first night alone. Fortunately, Angie made sure he was taken care of and then checked on him the next day.

Rose works at a freaking bakery for Pete's sake! You would think her boyfriend's well-being would be a little more important!

Kyle can sense his mom wanting to say more about Rose so he tries to cut her off, "Rose came by on Sunday and we started boxing things up for the new apartment."

Angie knows how excited Kyle is about the new apartment, "When do you move in?"

Kyle excitedly replies, "In two weeks, I can't wait!"

Angie pulls into the parking garage, relieved to be finally out of the traffic. "That should be right around the time you start physical therapy. How is the knee doing?"

Kyle is relieved to have his mom on a different subject, "It is doing better. I have to admit though, these pills do a number on me."

Angie is curious, "How so?"

Kyle shrugs his shoulders, "I don't know how to explain it, I just get so angry."

Angie is surprised, "Are you frustrated that you can't walk around?"

Kyle thinks about it, "I guess, but I feel like it is more. I don't know why because everything is going great for me right now. I have Rose, the new apartment, and work has been great about the accident. I really have nothing to complain about. Plus, I know the knee is just a temporary thing and I will be back to myself in no time."

As they walk to the office Angie is surprised at how well Kyle is doing, "You were right Kyle, you seem to be moving around a lot easier."

Kyle smiles, "Just wait until I get that brace off today, there will be no stopping me then!"

Angie has to ask, "Has Rose noticed a change in your temper?"

Kyle sighs, "Thankfully no. I have not seen her that much so I have been able to keep everything upbeat."

Angie wants to say more but the waiting room is small and it doesn't seem the right place to get into an argument about Rose.

After a long wait, the doctor finally sees Kyle. When Kyle comes out he hands Angie the brace happily, "I will not need this anymore."

Both in a good mood, they retrieve the car from the garage. Once in traffic though, their moods change drastically. Kyle yells at Angie so much she is close to tears. Trying to focus on the road in front of her Angie has to say, "Why are you being so mean? I am doing the best I can!"

Kyle takes a deep breath trying to calm himself down, "I hate all these cars! Not one of them is paying attention to anything around them! It is a wonder we are not all dead!"

"I agree, but we are almost to the tunnel and then it should lighten up." Angie has never seen Kyle so angry, other than after the surgery. She wonders out loud, "When was the last time you took a pill?"

Kyle sighs, "Last night Mom. I was going to wait until after the appointment to take another one."

Angie is surprised, "That is smart, seems like you are doing real well on not getting addicted to them."

In the tunnel they both begin to relax. Kyle answers her, "Yea, I have been making a point not to take too many. I did ask the doctor about my anger issues and he said not to worry. Actually, he doesn't even think it is the pills. A lot of patients experience different emotions. Apparently mine just tapped into anger for some reason."

Angie offers, "I am sure as you heal your emotions will go back to normal as well."

Kyle looks a little concerned out the window, "That is what I am hoping for."

After lunch and stopping at the store for more groceries, Angie drops Kyle off at the apartment. On the way home she can't help but think about Kyle's outbursts. Never had Kyle spoken to her the way he did. What is going on with that kid?

Exhausted, she finally reaches home only for Kyle to call her as she is going in the house. Concerned, Angie answers, "What's up?"

Kyle answers solemnly, "You will not believe me when I tell you."

Worried, Angie can tell by his voice it is serious, "Are you ok?"

Kyle answers disgustedly, "Physically I suppose ok, mentally is a whole different issue. Rose just called frantically crying. She finally was able to get out that she is not ready to move in and that she can't handle it anymore."

Shocked, Angie asks, "Wait, did you tell her how good the appointment went?"

Kyle sighs, "I did. I texted her about how great it felt with the brace off and that the doctor said everything was healing perfectly."

Angie is still in shock, "It just doesn't make sense. How did Rose act last weekend?"

Kyle shakes his head, "Great, told me she loved me and helped me pack for the new apartment. I swear, by her actions I never saw this coming!"

Although Angie had a feeling Rose was not into taking care of Kyle, Angie never expressed it to him for fear of another argument. Not that it would have done any good, because Kyle would have instantly defended Rose. However, it just was not right that Rose had not been there for him. She was this spoiled little rich girl who had never had a day of responsibility in her life. You could tell, it had to be about her or she was not interested.

Angie disgustedly puts it out there, "I guess she could not see the big picture. You are getting better and things will be back to normal eventually. In the grand scheme of things it really is such a short time for her to have to help you."

Kyle agrees miserably, "I really did not ask much of her Mom, you know me and how stubborn I am. I hate asking people to do things for me. You have no idea how many nights I did not have food in the house. Thank God for delivery!"

Angie just realizes it and blurts out, "What about the new apartment?"

Kyle sighs, "Fortunately I had not signed the papers. I have already called the landlord and told him what happened. He was so disgusted for me; he could not believe Rose did this to me!"

Angie feels sorry for him, "Kyle, I know how badly you wanted that apartment but I am glad you passed on it. I think it would have been a little hard on you to do it by yourself."

Kyle agrees, "I know Mom, but it was such a nice place!" Sadly, he mumbles, "I guess it is what it is."

After talking to his mom a little longer, he gets off the phone and wonders what to do. Although Kyle is not supposed to start physical therapy for another two weeks, he is anxious to get started.

Kyle has to do something to get his mind off this whole Rose business. Even though exhausted from the day, he has the urge to go for a walk. Before he knows it, he is outside hobbling down the sidewalk with his crutch.

The warm sunlight beats down on him but a slight breeze keeps him cool. Kyle has to admit it is a nice day for a walk. He starts thinking about his situation. Surprisingly, he is not as upset as he thought he would be. In fact, it almost feels like a relief.

Although deep down Kyle desperately wants to settle down, he also realizes he doesn't want to do it with the wrong girl, and for some reason Rose no longer seems like the right one even though before the surgery he had every intention of living the rest of his life with her.

Kyle stops for a moment and rubs the ache in his knee thinking, crazy how quickly things can change.

Chapter Four

Physical therapy had been hard and tedious but the hardest part seems to be behind Kyle. He now can walk pretty well without the use of a crutch.

Every night after work Kyle takes a nice long walk. At first he simply let his feet do the walking with no destination in mind; however, each night he would find himself walking in the same direction and going further. A little curious as to where he would end up, he continued to walk until he would get winded and then turn around for home.

Kyle was surprised to see he was now up to several miles from his home which sometimes made the walk home almost unbearable.

After reaching one particular neighborhood, which looked no different than any other neighborhood he had passed, his curiosity seemed to be quenched. This was the neighborhood Kyle would walk to, then turn around and walk home.

Before he had found the neighborhood Kyle had casually walked the route. Now that he knew where he was going, his mind took on a new task of getting there by a particular time.

Day by day Kyle began to cut chunks of time off of his walk. Once in the neighborhood, he would slowly walk around to ease his pace before returning home. As Kyle would walk around the neighborhood he began to recognize people. Some would even wave at him.

Even though the breakup with Rose had left Kyle a little bitter, he found himself noticing a girl in the neighborhood who seemed to start her run every day the same time he arrived. It was almost as if the girl was using her run to punish herself. Of course not able to keep up with her in a run, embarrassed Kyle watched from afar.

The girl never seemed to notice him; her focus is the side-walk in front of her and the music in her headphones. However, that did not seem to bother Kyle. In fact, he found himself thinking about her during the day and anxious to get home from work so he could see her.

After a week of hanging back, Kyle decided to start being in the path the girl traveled. It only took a couple of days before the girl would actually nod back at him in recognition. Encouraged, Kyle tried to figure out a way to casually meet her; however, everything he could think of seemed lame.

Fortunately, fate kicked in. As Kyle was about to pass her, he stumbles on a crack in the sidewalk. Embarrassed, he tries to compose himself but for some reason his knee completely gives out on him. Before he knows it, Kyle is on the ground in front of her.

Startled, the girl suddenly stops. "Oh my! Are you ok?" Quickly she turns her music off.

Kyle's face turns slightly red as he tries to get back up, "Yea, so stupid! Must have tripped over the sidewalk!"

The girl can see he is struggling and without asking, grabs his arm to steady him, "I am not surprised, these sidewalks are dangerous! Believe it or not, I have taken a tumble a couple of times because of them. That is why I am always so focused on what is in front of me."

Kyle is not sure if she is lying to make him feel better or not but he appreciates it, "I am surprised you don't run on the road?"

She looks out at the road as cars pass by, "I would rather take my chances on a scraped knee than be hit by one of those idiots."

Seeing that he is fine she casually drops her arm. Afraid that she might turn her music on and continue with her run, Kyle quickly extends his hand out, "I am Kyle."

Smiling she shakes his hand, "I am Rae."

Without thinking he laughs, "Aw, my 'Ray of Hope'."

Her smile suddenly fades as she quickly looks down.

Kyle chides himself for using such a dumb cliché. "I am sorry, you have probably heard that a million times. I am afraid I am not too original."

Rae quickly composes herself and looks back up at him, "Not at all, 'Ray of Sunshine' is what I normally hear."

Lowering her voice she hesitantly says, "Only one other person ever called me their 'Ray of Hope'."

Kyle can sense her discomfort but for some reason needs to know, "And who would that be?"

Uncomfortable, Rae answers, "My ex-boyfriend."

Kyle has to be honest, "Well, at least now I know there is an ex which in turn may mean you might be interested in going for a drink?"

A little surprised, Rae begins to shake her head, "Oh no, I have to finish my run. Anyway, I don't have my ID on me."

Kyle will not take no for an answer. He points over to a little café nearby, "I am sure they will serve you some water with no ID."

Rae blushes, "You are persistent, aren't you?"

Kyle starts walking towards the café, "Yup, now come on, we deserve it."

Rae and Kyle have their first date at that little café. They spend hours talking. Kyle doesn't get home until very late that night, but that is ok because he came home with her phone number.

Days turned into weeks as their relationship grew. Kyle revealed everything about himself including his fiasco with Rose and yet Rae's ex-boyfriend was one thing she never spoke of.

Kyle is now almost one hundred percent healed. He is back to driving and has ridden his motorcycle around a couple of times.

Rae doesn't seem too interested in his bike. It is not like she is afraid of it, she just doesn't seem to want any part of it.

After weeks of pressuring her, Rae finally agrees to allow him to take her on a date with the bike. Kyle shows up promptly at her door, all excited.

Just as they are about to take off, a pain shoots through Kyle from his knee. It is so intense that Kyle almost drops the bike.

Rae quickly gets off, "What is the matter?"

Kyle rubs his knee disgustedly, "This sharp pain in my knee came out of nowhere."

Rae takes her helmet off and heads to her car, "Ok, well that settles it. Park the bike and we will take my car."

Not wanting to ruin the evening, Kyle does what she said.

Before Rae gets into the car she looks at him concerned, "Are you ok to drive or would you like me too?"

Aggravated, Kyle mumbles, “No, I will be fine.”

They drive in silence until they come to a stop due to traffic. Kyle angrily looks down at the dash clock, “Great, just what we need! I hope we still make the movie in time!”

A little surprised at his anger Rae simply agrees, “This is crazy, wonder what happened?”

Kyle strains to see, “Looks like a multiple pile up!”

Rae looks at him wide eyed, “You do realize that if we had left when we did on your bike we may have been in that accident as well?”

Kyle nods, “Yea, the thought had crossed my mind.”

As Kyle drives slowly by the wreck Rae looks sadly at all of the twisted cars, “You know my ex-boyfriend died in a car crash.”

Kyle had no idea, “I am sorry.”

Rae shrugs her shoulders, “It is ok. I had been trying to break up with him for quite a while.”

Kyle’s knee begins to ache.

Rae thinks back, “I loved him dearly but he had such anger issues. Sometimes I was afraid of him.”

Rae explains, “He lived in the city, in fact, he had just moved into a new apartment. He had also just bought this new bike which he stored at my place. Had a phenomenal paint job on it, quite rare.”

Rae shakes her head, “When he got the new bike it was as if he began to get worse with his anger, especially with road rage. It was out of control.”

Rae closes her eyes, “The night of the accident we had a fight. He stormed out on his bike and later I received the call.”

Kyle’s knee is now throbbing, subconsciously he rubs at it.

Rae opens her eyes and looks back at the wreck, “Even though I did not cause the fight, I still blame myself.”

Kyle is not sure what to say. Before he can think of something she continues, “You know, even though he had a hard time controlling his anger he loved people. In fact, his mother told me he donated his body to science. I like to think his one life gave life to many more.”

Kyle’s knee aches so much now that Kyle is on the brink of tears. Lost in her own thoughts, Rae doesn’t notice Kyle’s pain;

however, she casually lays her hand on his knee and softly caresses it.

Instantly the ache in his knee subsides. As it does, a calm comes over Kyle. Kyle realizes no matter what it takes, he will keep his anger in check for Rae.

A thought, not of his own, rises up. He was given a second chance and this time he was going to appreciate her. In Kyle's mind, he reasons this thought simply meant a second chance at another relationship.

Destiny had brought them together; therefore, it was his duty to do his part in keeping them together.

From the cadaver parts inside him, the thought is that destiny had nothing to do with it. It was about the will from the love of an ex-boyfriend. A second chance to be with his 'Ray of Hope'.

White Noise Stories Continued

Lauren wakes up to conflicting thoughts about her last dream. To her, on the surface it was a sad horrific love story. And yet, if it is not a story but a true event, what is it then?

Lauren tries to put herself in the same situation. If something overtook you to find their lost love and during the process you fell in love with that person; would that not be a good thing for all concerned? She is not so sure. How would you ever know for sure that the feelings you had for that person were yours and not someone else's? Who is to say the rage from what overtook you would not become stronger and bitterer? It would always be a love triangle.

Lauren can't help but smile, as if dating is not hard enough without having to consider this on top of it! Suddenly though, her smile quickly fades. As she props herself up in bed she realizes her sound machine is on! How is that possible? Lauren distinctly remembers turning the sound machine off before she went to sleep!

Obviously, she must have reached over and turned it on without realizing it. The damn thing had become such a part of her life; it must have become a subconscious habit for her to have it on. So much for her test. Lauren timidly reaches over and turns the sound machine off again.

Forcing herself out of bed, Lauren feels dehydrated and weak. She wanders into the kitchen to find something to eat. Not really hungry, but she knows she needs to drink and eat to get her strength back up.

Lauren makes some toast and coffee. She has no idea what time it is until she sees the time on the microwave. Shocked, she is surprised to see she has slept the day away! She should feel rested, but if anything, she feels even more tired.

Lauren picks at her food as she thinks about the most recent dream. If a soul dies, is it tied to the last place it lived? And yet, this Rae's ex-boyfriend seemed to have found a way to escape, to have his soul live in body parts he had donated.

If that were the case, Lauren argues with herself, why would his soul still be attached here, if he indeed lived at this apartment complex? How can she receive his dream if he is off living, if you want to call it that, somewhere else?

Tired of trying to make sense of all of this, Lauren's mind still races to come up with a solution. Perhaps the desire to live in this apartment complex one day, with the love of his life, kept him emotionally attached to this place. She had often heard that things unresolved in your lifetime could be something that keeps your soul here. Not at rest.

Are dreams not nothing more than the subconscious trying to resolve issues in your life? Would this explain why some of these dreams continue on after the death of the main character? The continuation of the dream could be the soul's way trying to figure out a better outcome or possibly the outcome in general.

Not really hungry, Lauren pushes her food to the side. What about her? How does she feel about this idea of living in an apartment where someone died? She knows all too well what her mother and Roxi would think!

Lauren looks around the cheerful little apartment, but this was her home. She really has no desire, or energy, to move somewhere else. Although, Lauren has to admit to herself, now would be the time to make the decision since she still has time before her new job starts. Does she risk the opportunity to move?

A fog comes over her mind as she hears the distant hiss of the white noise coming from the sound machine. Lauren feels a strong desire to go back to bed. It is as if she is being called back to dream.

Lauren's actions are no longer hers; quietly she gets into bed without thinking about turning the sound machine off. In fact, Lauren realizes it is even hard for her to think. It is easier to simply go to sleep.

DNA
&
Me

DNA and Me

Chapter 1

Ashley finishes up her work and heads to the break room. Bored, she gets her lunch out of the fridge and sits at a nearby table.

Erica comes in like a gust of fresh wind and places her salad on the table next to Ashley's lunch, "Lunch time could not come fast enough for me today!"

Ashley smiles, "Still trying to stay on the diet, good for you!"

Erica blushes, "Yea, well it is only Monday. Come Wednesday I am making no guarantees!"

Ashley nods, "How was your weekend?"

Erica plops down in a chair next to her, "Not bad, did this long questionnaire thing. It was interesting."

Ashley is curious, "What kind of questionnaire?"

Erica explains, "You know how I went on that kick about my ancestry history?"

Ashley laughs, "How could I not? I thought for sure when you found out one of your ancestors was a knight we would all have to start calling you Princess!"

Erica sighs, "Ok, I admit I did get a little over excited about that which in turn made me want to delve even deeper. I decided to try out that DNA and Me setup."

Ashley teases her, ""What are you hoping to do now, prove you are an offspring of the Queen?"

Erica giggles, "Stop teasing me! This is serious stuff."

Ashley laughs, "If you say so."

Erica explains, "It is pretty cool. You send in a sample of your DNA for analysis."

Ashley, being the cynic she is, replies sarcastically, "Great, now the government has you on file."

Erica shrugs her shoulders, "Like they don't already?"

Ashley smiles, "Got me there."

Erica continues, "Then they ask you a butt load of questions."

Ashley can't help herself, "Sounds like the morning after a bad date. First they get your DNA and then ask you a butt load of questions."

Erica is exasperated, "Would you stop? Look, believe it or not, I got you a set up too. I thought it would be fun to do it together, you know… compare notes."

Erica rummages through her purse and pulls out a small box and pushes it towards Ashley. "I know you did not like the whole ancestry thing because of your family and all but everyone is curious about their own DNA."

Ashley feels bad as she looks at the box in front of her, "Erica that set up costs a lot of money. We have not been friends long enough to warrant such a purchase!"

Erica smiles, "No worries, I had a coupon. Anyway, it doesn't matter how long we have known each other. I think it will be fun to compare the end results."

Ashley picks up the box, "Are you sure it is not your way to gloat that you are some sort of princess and I will be your chambermaid?"

Erica shakes her head, "This breaks down your DNA, not what your ancestors did for a living."

Ashley has to admit it does sound interesting, "What do you have to do?"

Erica is happy that Ashley is beginning to show interest, "You spit in this vial and mail it away in the box they give you."

Before Ashley can come back with a sarcastic reply Erica continues, "Once you mail it, you go online and register. Then the questions begin."

Ashley is curious, "What kind of questions?"

Erica thinks back, "Normal ones like what are you allergic to, do you have any diseases, and so on."

Ashley looks a little concerned, "Family history?"

Erica hesitates, "Some, but remember if you can't answer the questions it is not a big deal. They already have your DNA and will be giving you your results from it."

Ashley wonders, "What kind of results?"

Erica smiles, "All kinds. The region you originated from, any health related concerns if you are thinking about having children. It is all online when you register."

Ashley has to admit she was jealous when Erica was all into finding out about her ancestry, especially since Ashley had no real way of finding about hers. She realizes Erica must have picked up on that and is genuinely touched that she found a way for her to be able to look into her own past.

Ashley looks at her watch and realizes it is time for her to get back to work. Awkwardly she gives Erica a quick hug, "It was very sweet of you to do this for me, thank you!"

Erica, pleased with herself, returns the hug warmly, "You are very welcome. I look forward to our discussions on what we find out!"

Ashley walks back to her desk thinking, although she doesn't like the idea of someone having her DNA on file, the idea of knowing more about her own history is tempting.

For far too long she had heard other people brag that their family was from Ireland or Italy or wherever, meanwhile, when asked Ashley would joke and say she was nothing more than a mutt.

For once it would be nice to throw out where her family was from. Who knows, maybe it will explain why she is the way she is.

Chapter Two

That evening in her apartment, Ashley gets to work on registering with DNA and Me. She had to admit the research they were doing was very impressive.

Although there were a ton of questions, they were easy. In fact, it was kind of fun answering the questions. Even the ones Ashley could not answer did not bother her because, like Erica said, the site would eventually know by analyzing her DNA.

The next couple of weeks Erica and Ashley have quite a few lunch conversations about what some of the reasons the DNA and Me site questions were for.

With Erica having sent her DNA a couple days earlier than Ashley, it stands to reason she will get her results faster. Sure enough, one day Erica comes in and announces she finally got her results. Curious as hell, Ashley pleads with her to tell her what they were; however, Erica holds her ground and tells her not until Ashley gets hers in. Then, and only then, they will discuss their results together. Surprised at her resolve, Ashley has no choice but to agree.

The same day Erica receives her results, Ashley receives an email from the site. It is an entire new packet of questions they need her to answer before they can finalize her results. A little disappointed, Ashley hurries through the questions with far less enjoyment than the first batch.

The next day at lunch Erica notices Ashley seems a little down, "Hey kiddo, what is up with you today?"

Ashley moans, "Tired from last night."

Erica is curious, "And what kept you up so late on a work night?"

Ashley, annoyed, answers roughly, "You did!"

Erica is surprised, "I did? What did I do?"

Ashley answers, "You got me involved in this dumb DNA shit. They sent me another packet of questions to answer before they will send me my results."

Erica tries to brush it off, "I would not worry. They said right on the site that sometimes they need more information from certain people to make sure the results are accurate."

Ashley nods, "I know, but these questions are out there!"

Erica is curious, "Like how?"

Ashley answers, "Questions like, are your ear lobes attached? Do you have extra rows of teeth? One of the really strange ones was, do you have inner eyelids?"

Ashley looks at Erica, "Seriously? What the hell! How many people in the world actually have those things to warrant them to even ask those questions?"

Erica is shocked, "Are you kidding?"

Ashley shakes her head miserably, "No, I wish I was!"

Before Erica can even think of a response, Ashley continues with her rant, "By the time you answer all their questions you can't help but wonder if there is any need for them to even test your DNA! They already know everything there is to know by your answers to these stupid questions!"

Erica is now beginning to wonder if this was a good idea. Seeing Ashley this angry over something so little is beginning to unnerve her. Erica apologizes, "I am sorry. I thought this would be fun for the both of us. I really enjoyed our conversations the last couple of weeks."

The condescending tone in Erica's voice only adds to Ashley's simmering fury; however, she realizes she is at work, in public, and now is not the time to lose her temper. She takes in a deep breath and forces a smile, "No, I am sorry. It is not your fault. I admit I am just a little nervous about finding out the results."

Ashley decides to cut her lunch short and gets up, "Please understand, I have never done anything like this before."

Erica tries to reassure her, "It is nothing to get worked up about. I should have let you look at my results. It is nothing more than knowing the color of your hair and your eyes."

Erica sees Ashley's doubt, "Really, I will bring my results in tomorrow and you can see for yourself. The one thing I think you will appreciate most is; it does tell you where you originated from."

Ashley nods, "Thanks, I need to get back to work. Lots to do today but we will meet up tomorrow. Maybe it will help if I see your results."

Although Ashley leaves the break room on good terms with Erica, she goes back to her desk still seething. Sure, easy enough for that bitch! She already knows her results! She takes in another deep breath, this is not that big of a deal – let it go! Ashley sits down and counts to ten. She begins to feel her temper subsiding.

Trying to tease herself, Ashley thinks maybe soon I can say that is just the Irish in me! However, her little joke falls flat even on herself.

No, for some reason her gut instinct is telling her that something is not right. And as usual, it is best she follow her instinct. Perhaps it is time for her to move on again.

Chapter Three

Back in her apartment, Ashley contemplates on what her next move should be. She looks over at boxes she had not even unpacked from her last move. Frustrated, Ashley sits down in front of her computer to start scanning for her options. Noticing she has an email, Ashley is surprised to see her results have come in from DNA and Me.

A bit nervously, Ashley opens up the email. Complicated reports fill her screen. Taking a deep breath, she tries to understand what the reports mean. From the looks of it, the diseases they tested her DNA for had no variants for any of them. Ashley supposes that is a good thing, though honestly probably ninety percent of them she had never heard of.

Here was something interesting, looks like her DNA links her to European heritage, a whopping ninety-five percent. She can't help but smile as she thinks that now she can say she is an English mutt.

Flipping through the reports she finds one that catches her eye. Yes, her ring finger is longer than her index finger. Yes, her big toe is the longest. So far, she had fallen in line with the percentages of her reports being what she expected, except a couple of things did seem off. Supposedly, she only had a thirteen percent chance of green eyes. And yet, her eyes are solid green. Her ear lobes had a seventy-five percent chance of being detached and yet hers are attached. And lastly, only a nineteen percent chance of being a dark blonde. Again, Ashley's hair is the very description of dirty blonde.

She sighs as she thinks, so much for technology! After going through the whole report, there is one thing that has her going back to try and understand. Apparently she had 286 Neanderthal variants which put her at sixty-four percent more than most of their clients. Pretty cool to think that her DNA could be traced back to Neanderthal times and yet a little strange that she is in such a high percentage.

Ashley decides to do some research on Neanderthals. By the end of the night she has some impressive information to share. She prints it all off and puts it by the door to take to work tomorrow. Lunch tomorrow should be quite interesting when she compares her results to Erica's.

The next day Erica is surprised to see Ashley sitting in the break room smiling. For no reason, Erica has a chill come over her. Erica shakes the feeling off and smiles, "Looks like someone must have gotten their results!"

Ashley nods, "I did, and did you bring yours in?"

Erica waves a printout in the air, "I promised you I would."

Erica sits down beside Ashley and they both spread out their results. Erica proudly speaks first, "My results showed a seventy-eight percent chance of being European which falls right in line with all of the ancestry history I had found out."

Ashley tries to ignore the bragging tinge in Erica's voice. Pleasantly Ashley replies, "I guess we were neighbors. Mine showed a ninety-five percent chance of being European."

Now it is Erica's turn to be a little jealous, "Really? Good for you!"

Erica hesitates, "I know how much that meant to you since you had no way of looking up your ancestry, being adopted and all."

Erica's words cut deep. Ashley wished to God she had never told Erica she was adopted. The only reason she had was to keep Erica from nagging at her about her family history. The real truth was that Ashley had never been adopted. She had bounced around from one foster home to another. The truth of the matter is that Ashley is the only one who knows her birthday.

On her birth certificate there was no father listed and the mother's name had been redacted to keep her identity a secret. Anger boils up in Ashley as she thinks about her mother's identity being kept safe. At least her mother had an identity, more than she had been given! She stops and reminds herself that was until now. Mommy dearest may have not wanted to give her an identity but at least technology had.

Ashley is curious, "What were your variants for Homo Sapiens?"

Erica flips through the report, "I am not sure. Oh wait, here it is. They said I fall in the average range."

Ashley's heart begins to beat faster as she is excited to present her finding, "It says on mine that I fall in the top sixty-four percent of being Neanderthal."

Erica, without thinking, bursts out laughing, "Oh you poor thing! Your DNA is mostly caveman?"

Ashley had never dreamed she would be made fun of. She quickly starts to defend herself, "No, they were nothing like that; I did a lot of research on them last night."

Ashley thumbs through her notes, "To date, bones of 400 Neanderthals have been found. They died out in Europe between 200,000 – 250,000 years ago." Ashley can't help but add sarcastically, "That puts your finding of your Knight, in Cheshire England, in 1633 to shame!"

Erica instantly regrets her outburst, "You are right! I am so sorry, how very interesting! Tell me more of what you found!"

Ashley is not convinced that Erica is sincere but wants to share her information nonetheless, "They may have had red or blonde hair."

Erica replies, "There you go! That is where your blonde hair comes into play."

Encouraged, Ashley continues, "Their eyesight was better due to larger sockets and larger areas of the brain devoted to vision."

Erica sighs, "How many times have I told you how lucky you are that you have never had to wear glasses!"

Ashley looks down at her notes, "This was interesting, their craniums were larger. Scientists did this 3D scan test where they projected the brain from infancy to adult. Then they compared it to modern humans and the brain was much larger in adulthood. This could explain their advanced tools, their ability to have fire on demand, there is even evidence they used canoes."

Ashley doesn't give Erica a chance to reply before going on, "They lived in complex social groups. They were much stronger than modern humans, having strong arms and hands. They were predators and made dwellings out of animal bones. They also practiced burial behavior, intentionally burying their dead."

Erica cringes a little at the thought of living in houses made of bones. Curious, Erica has to ask, "How did they die out?"

Ashley had not missed Erica's cringing; obviously she is only going to focus on the bad. With less enthusiasm Ashley answers, "There are three possible reasons; one being climate change or volcanic catastrophe, another is they bred with Homo Sapiens and disappeared through absorption, or their interaction with Homo Sapiens could have caused their demise."

Realizing that Erica probably thinks of her now as nothing more than a monster, Ashley decides to give her the darker side of her family history, "They were outnumbered by Homo Sapiens nine to one. This lower population could have caused mutations due to inbreeding."

Erica gasps, "Oh my!"

Instead of being offended Ashley takes pride in her finding and continues, "Bones found showed signs of defleshing, suggesting victims of cannibalism. With there being food shortages they would have been victims of survival cannibalism."

Erica is shocked, but tries to remain civil and clears her throat, "How very interesting, though a bit much for lunch time conversation! Interesting nonetheless."

Ashley smiles but tries to shrug it off, "I know, a bit too much information but you asked."

Although the girls finished their lunch amicably, both knew for some reason things had changed between them. Erica knew that she was the reason, but then again, she could not help thinking Ashley was being over sensitive.

Ashley on the other hand, remembered why she never let people get close to her. It was no different than all the other places she had lived and she knows all too well, more than likely, it will be no different if she moved away.

However, moving away is always best. It gives her a fresh start and allows her not to have to deal with her present situation. Most find moving a chore, Ashley on the other hand, had become accustomed to it being a necessity.

Chapter Four

Once Ashley is home from her day at work, she hops on the computer and starts making plans to move. Strange, but it is almost as if her primal instinct is kicked into overdrive.

Finding a job is never a problem for Ashley and even though she had only been in this city for a short time, her savings was pretty decent. Even with breaking the lease on her apartment and paying for a deposit on a new place, she is confident she has enough to coast her through until she gets settled. Realizing she has many things to do, she had even asked her boss for tomorrow off. With a plan in mind, she begins to do a check list.

Late in the night Ashley finally goes to bed exhausted but excited. There are many things she needs to accomplish tomorrow, getting a good night's sleep will only help.

Ashley wakes up early, fresh and ready. She quickly gets dressed so she can get her first task done as soon as possible. By lunch time she is back in her apartment and ready to prepare her lunch. Suddenly her buzzer sounds off. Annoyed, Ashley answers, "Yes?"

"Miss Simmons?"

Ashley replies, "Speaking."

"You have two gentlemen here from DNA and Me who wish to meet with you."

Ashley looks around the apartment to see how messy it is, realizing it is fine she sighs, "Ok, you can send them up."

Ashley wonders, what could the people from DNA and Me possibly want from her? She cleans up the kitchen, putting all the ingredients for her lunch into the fridge. Lunch will have to wait until after they are gone.

Within minutes there is a knock at her door. Straightening her hair, Ashley opens the door, "Yes?"

Two men in dark blue suits smile at her. The taller one speaks, "Miss Simmons?"

Ashley nods, "Yes?"

The taller man offers his hand, "My name is Nick and this Sean. We are from DNA and Me."

Without moving Ashley asks, "What is this about?"

Nick clears his throat, "It is about your results. We found them quite amazing and wanted to go over them with you in more detail."

Ashley is still cautious, "I thought all interaction was done online, why was I not notified of your visit?"

Nick looks a little confused, "Sean, didn't you tell her we would be in the area today?"

Sean, a little flustered, answers, "I am sure I did!"

Ashley sighs and opens the door wider, "Come on in, it is ok. Actually, you caught me at a good time. Normally I would be at work but today I took off."

Once the men are inside, Ashley leads them into the living room, "Please, have a seat."

Both men sit on the couch while Ashley sits on the love seat across from them. She watches intently as they open files and lay them on the coffee table in front of them.

Nick starts off, "As I said, we were most impressed with your test results and would like to go over some of the data."

Ashley feels special and blushes, "Of course."

Nick points at a spreadsheet, "You are listed quite high on the Neanderthal side."

Ashley nods, "Yes, I know. I was quite surprised about that."

Sean is curious, "Do you know anything about Neanderthals?"

Ashley smiles, "A little, I tried to research them when I received my results."

Nick shakes his head, "Of course, it must have been so exciting to see your DNA could be traced back so far!"

Ashley agrees, "Especially since I know nothing about my family history."

Nick looks at his notes, "Ah yes, it does say here that you were adopted."

Ashley feels no need to keep secrets, "I never really was adopted. I sort of bounced from one foster home to another."

Sean's voice softens, "That must have been very hard for you."

Ashley shrugs it off, "It was but I also think it made me stronger."

Nick notices the boxes, "I see you recently moved here?"

Ashley laughs subconsciously, "Some things I never unpack in case I get the desire to move again."

Sean is surprised, "Do you move a lot?"

Ashley's extinct is beginning to sound warning bells, a little cautiously she answers, "I do, I have yet to find the right fit."

Sean senses her withdrawal and sympathizes, "I don't know how you do it. I hate to move! The packing, the changing of addresses, meeting new people. I am afraid I am too much a creature of habit!"

Nick offers, "I don't know, it sounds kind of adventurous. Must be nice to be able to pick and go when you want a change."

Feeling more comfortable, Ashley admits, "You are right, in fact, I am thinking about a new change already."

Nick smiles at her, "Good for you!"

Ashley looks down at the reports in front of them, "So, what is this all about anyway?"

Nick answers, "As you know on our site we clearly state we use your DNA for research."

Sean adds, "You can only imagine how much scientists would like to know more about a descendant of a Neanderthal!"

Ashley has never felt so important, "Really?"

Nick agrees, "Oh, most definitely! So, it is our job to screen you to see how you would feel about answering more questions and even come in and do more extensive testing."

Sean can't help but jump in, "They are even willing to pay you!"

Nick nods, "He is right. A select set of scientists have offered to pay you for your time."

Ashley can't believe her luck! What a windfall! This could be perfect for her until she finds another job. "Where would the testing take place?"

Nick answers, "Our facility is in Texas."

Ashley is surprised, "Texas? I have never been to Texas. How long would the testing take?"

Nick shrugs his shoulder, "We don't know for sure, it would all depend on the scientists."

Ashley has to ask, "Would it warrant me moving to Texas?"

Nick nods, "It could and I am sure the scientists would even pay for your move."

Ashley could not be happier, "Then I see no reason not to get started! What do we need to do first?"

Nick pulls out a large envelope filled with papers, "In here you will find new questionnaires and more information on the scientists you will be working with."

Sean reaches into his briefcase, "Before we leave, could we get a sample of your urine, if you don't mind?"

A little surprised, Ashley takes the cup from Sean, "Not at all, is there anything else?"

Nick gathers his papers up, "No, as soon as Sean and I leave I will contact the main office and tell them you are on board. I will also let them know you are interested in moving to Texas. They will take care of all the details and then get back with you."

The two men sit there looking at her. Suddenly she realizes what they must be waiting for, "Oh, of course, the sample. Let me take care of that right now and I will be right back. Would either one of you like a drink or something?"

Both of them decline. Nick answers, "Actually, Sean and I are due for lunch. Perhaps you would like to join us?"

Excited, Ashley nods, "That would be lovely. Let me take care of this, freshen up and then we can go."

Sean nods, "Take your time, we are in no hurry."

Ashley excuses herself and goes to the bathroom. Once inside she notices that Erica is beginning to come around. Oh no, now is not the time! She quickly grabs the chloroform from under the cabinet and opens the shower curtain. She whispers quietly, "Now Erica, I can't have you waking up right now!"

Erica's eyes suddenly fly open but Ashley already has the chloroform over her mouth and nose. Within seconds, Erica is unconscious again. She checks Erica's gag and finds it secure.

Noticing the bandage on Erica's leg has begun to bleed again, she quickly cleans it up.

As Ashley takes her urine sample she looks at Erica in the tub. It was a shame that she was going out to lunch, she had really been looking forward to her lunch at home. Oh well, there will be dinner tonight. Ashley cleans up and is finally ready to leave. She opens the bathroom door and announces, "Ok, I think I am ready."

Surprised, she sees Nick standing in her kitchen with the refrigerator open. The plate he is holding has a nicely carved piece of Erica's thigh.

Without thinking, Ashley lets her instincts take over and she dives for the nearby desk. Before she can open the drawer Sean yells out, "Don't do it Ashley, I will shoot!"

Ashley's primeval instincts to survive take over and she reaches for her own gun in the drawer. Sean has no option but to shoot her.

Nick screams out, "Don't kill her! We want to take her alive for research!"

Sean had every intention of keeping her alive. His first shot was to the shoulder; however, he had no choice but to shoot again as Ashley continued to reach for her gun. This time his shot hit her in the leg but there seemed to be no stopping her. Determined, Ashley now has her gun and is aiming at Sean. Before she can shoot Sean's own instincts kick in and he shoots her in the head.

Nick drops the plate and runs over to Ashley but he can tell she is already dead, "Such a shame, she would have been great to research."

Sean agrees, "I know, but hopefully we saved the victim!"

Nick peers into the bathroom and yells out, "She is unconscious but will be ok."

Nick comes back out and looks at Sean, "Good call on seeing the pattern in her results!"

Sean sighs, "Thanks! I am just happy we finally have a set up where maybe we can start catching these killers."

Sean looks over at Ashley's limp body, "They were such vicious killers. Even though they had been absorbed to look like normal humans their primeval instinct is always there. Predators and cannibalistic, two very strong traits that are not a good combination!"

Nick nods, "Who knows how many this one has killed? Unfortunately, another trait they were good at was burying their dead!"

White Noise Stories Continued

Before even considering the ramifications of her last dream, Lauren's phone rings loudly. She gets out of bed and stumbles around to find it before it stops ringing. Lauren finally finds it and is surprised when she sees the battery is almost dead, "Hello?"

Lauren's friend Roxi answers cheerfully, "Hey girlfriend! It is Friday night, are we ready to party?"

Her heart races, Roxi must be playing with her! If it is Friday that means Lauren has lost some days! Trying not to sound scared she sighs, "This week sure is flying!"

Roxi, too caught up in her own good mood to notice Lauren's reserve, disagrees, "Not for me, this has been one long ass week, especially since I did not get to see you last weekend!"

Lauren explains, "You know how tough a move is, you lose track of time."

Roxi realizes what that meant, "Oh no you didn't! Don't tell me you did not know it is Friday night. Girl, you better be ready when I come to pick your ass up!"

Lauren frantically runs into the bedroom and pulls clothes out for the evening, "What time do you think you will be here?"

Roxi smiles, knowing full well Lauren is rushing to get ready, "You have about fifteen minutes to make yourself gorgeous!"

Lauren needs more time, "Tell you what, I will meet you at the bar. Get us a table, order a drink, and I will be there before you know it."

Roxi is a little disappointed, "Girl, you know I hate making my entrance alone. Alright, but don't leave me there alone for too long!"

Lauren promises, "I won't, see you in a few."

Lauren takes a shower and gets dressed in record time; however, looking gorgeous is another matter. She is shocked to see how skinny and sickly she looks. Not liking what she sees in the mirror she glances down. Lauren notices a glass from the kitchen she did not remember using. At least during her loss of time her subconscious had the sense to keep her hydrated.

Upon closer inspection she notices crumbs as well. Lauren is happy that she must have eaten something during that time but she is not happy that she doesn't remember it.

Lauren forces herself to look back at the mirror. Fortunately the bar will be dark, she has good concealer, and she can wear something to hide her weight loss. She has to admit the gray in her hair probably doesn't help but there is not enough time to color it.

She finds Roxi easily at the bar. Roxi's drink is already half empty which could either be a good thing or a bad thing. Lauren puts on her best smile and hopes for the best, "There's my girl!"

Fortunately, the drink had calmed Roxi down and she is genuinely happy to see her friend, "Lauren sweetie, have a seat!" Lauren sits down and orders her drink. All the while Roxi is watching her intently, "Are you ok?"

Lauren blushes, "Of course, just a little rattled after rushing. I am sorry I let the time get away from me."

Roxi brushes it off, "No problem, I remember how I was when I moved into my apartment. Although I did not have the luxury of having a whole month off like you!"

Lauren sighs, "I know, but if it counts for anything, I had the apartment all finished in the first week."

Roxi nods in approval, "Nice, so what have you been doing with yourself since?"

Lauren thinks about it, a little confused, "I checked out how much time I would need in the mornings. I did some exploring but for the most part just relaxing."

Roxi doesn't want to be mean but she can't hold back a comment on Lauren's hair, "I never realized you had so much gray in your hair."

Lauren subconsciously pushes her hair away from her face, "Me either. Believe it or not I colored it on Monday but it must not have taken."

Roxi offers, "Perhaps it was a bad batch. Are you giving it time to grow out a little before you color it again?"

Lauren realizes that is a good excuse, "I think so, maybe right before I go to work will be long enough to risk coloring it again."

Roxi looks critically at Lauren, "Have you lost weight as well?"

Lauren becomes defensive, "What is it, pick on Lauren night? Do I look that bad?"

Roxi quickly apologizes, "No, not at all. I just worry about you."

Lauren lightens her tone, "I may need to see a doctor. I looked up the gray hair and it could be stress or even thyroid issues."

Roxi is a little relieved, "Thyroid could be the reason for the weight loss too. You definitely need to have it checked out!"

Lauren looks around the room to see if she sees anyone she knows. Her attention is immediately drawn to a young couple sitting at the bar. Who are they? Lauren strains to see them better, but for the life of her she can't figure out how she knows them. A deep fear sets in as Lauren feels she should know them.

Roxi looks around the room quickly, "What is it, an old boyfriend? Oh God, please don't let it be one of mine!"

Lauren laughs, "No, not anyone I think you would know. Not even sure if I know them."

Roxi is confused, "Ok, but for a moment there, the way you looked at them it was as if you saw a ghost."

Lauren tries to brush it off casually, "Really? I guess I am a little frustrated with myself that I don't know how I would know them."

Roxi shrugs her shoulders and changes the subject. Lauren and Roxi get caught up on gossip. However, while they talk she finds herself repeatedly looking back over at the couple.

It must have become obvious because the guy notices her watching them. Lauren tries to focus back on Roxi as she goes on a long dragged out conversation about all the gossip at work.

Roxi suddenly gets up, startling Lauren, "I am going to the bathroom."

Lauren looks at her, confused, "What?"

Roxi rolls her eyes, "I get the feeling you are not all here tonight. When I get back, let us get some food in you and talk about where your head has been tonight!"

As Roxi leaves, Lauren notices out of the corner of her eye the couple is getting up to leave. She holds her breath as they walk by, the guy allowing the girl to walk further ahead of him. Once she is far enough ahead, he pauses by Lauren and lowers his voice, "Some of them do escape, yet somehow some of us stay tied to that place. You might want to start thinking about your escape."

Lauren looks up at him startled, "Excuse me?"

The guy shakes his head as if to clear his thoughts and apologizes, "Oh, I am sorry. Do we know each other?"

Lauren is not sure she heard him correctly the first time and merely shakes her head, "At first I thought I knew you both, but now I realize I was mistaken."

The guy gives her a friendly smile, "No problem, it is a small world sometimes." Lauren watches as the guy walks away with a slight limp.

Roxi suddenly appears and is ready to eat. You would think Lauren would be starving, but if anything, the alcohol she had after not eating in several days was not the wisest choice. Roxi sees her friend is distraught, "Are you ok? Honestly hon, you don't look so good!"

Lauren is almost in tears with gratitude, "No, I am sorry, I am not ok. I really think I should go home. Do you mind?"

Roxi grabs her coat and comes over to help Lauren get up, "Not at all, but you are not going home alone!"

Lauren nods, "You are such a good friend, thank you."

Lauren is surprised to see Mr. Akeru standing out front ready to open the door for her. She stops Roxi right before they get to the apartment complex. "Thanks for walking me home Roxi; however, if you don't mind can I go up to the apartment alone?"

Roxi is concerned, "Are you sure?"

Lauren nods gratefully, "I am. I left the apartment a mess before going out. I want the first time you see it to be perfect!"

Roxi sighs, "Ok, I understand."

Lauren looks around, "Do you want me to call you a taxi?"

Roxi shakes her head, "No, I have been enjoying the walk. It is pretty over here. I have to say I am already jealous. I can only imagine how nice your apartment is!"

Lauren smiles, "It is, isn't it? I just love the area, everything I could possibly need is right here. The apartment is a little small. It's nothing spectacular, I can assure you, but for now it will be fine."

Lauren and Roxi say their goodbyes. Lauren walks up to Mr. Akeru, "My goodness, it is a bit strange seeing you work so late!"

Mr. Akeru opens the door and follows Lauren inside, "Someone called out, and I filled in. In fact, my shift is ending now."

Mr. Akeru looks at Lauren concerned, "I have not seen you in a couple of days. Everything going ok?"

Now that Lauren is inside the building all of the memories of the dreams she has been having flood down on her. Chills come over Lauren. Is she beginning to lose her sanity like the voices in the elevator told her she would? Has she been in total denial the entire time? Lauren has to know.

"Mr. Akeru, I have some questions for you."

Mr. Akeru is all ears, "Of course Ms. Lauren, what would you like to know?"

Lauren's mind spins frantically, where does she begin? More importantly, how much can she reveal without having Mr. Akeru think she is crazy? She blurts out, "Where the explosion happened, did the girl just move in? Was there a couple that disappeared from their bedroom? Did a woman die in her apartment from an aneurism? What about a young man who died in a motorcycle accident? And oh my God, did a cannibal used to live here?"

Mr. Akeru tries to absorb all the questions Lauren just threw at him, "That is a lot of questions Ms. Lauren!"

Lauren looks apologetically at him, "I know and I am sorry. It would be easy enough for me to look all this up on the internet, I just thought I could ask you first."

Mr. Akeru nods, "Of course, I will be all too happy to try and answer your questions."

Lauren asks impatiently, "Well?"

Mr. Akeru smiles, “There were people who lived in this building that had the incidents you are talking about happen to them.”

Lauren is not sure that is the answer she wanted to hear, “Really?”

Mr. Akeru lowers his voice, “Now, Ms. Lauren, my question to you is, what is going on?”

Lauren appreciates his concern, “I honestly don’t know. I have been having these vivid dreams of the incidents we are talking about.”

Lauren lowers her voice, “Is this apartment complex haunted?”

Mr. Akeru chuckles, “Oh goodness no! As I said, I have been here a long time and I would know more than anyone!”

Lauren is not convinced, “I heard voices in the elevator.”

Mr. Akeru wonders, “Did you hear them spoken aloud or were they inside your mind?”

Lauren admits, “At the time I believed my mind was being creative.”

Mr. Akeru is impressed, “You are a very smart girl in trying to be so reasonable. Let me ask you, are you afraid of your apartment or anywhere else in the complex?”

Lauren looks around and shakes her head, “No, now that you mention it, I can’t say that I am. However, the dreams can be very terrifying!”

Mr. Akeru sympathizes, “I am sure and then when you think about the dreams they spook you even more?”

Lauren looks down a little ashamed, “Yes, I suppose they do.”

Mr. Akeru sighs, “You are not the first person to have mentioned this to me.”

Lauren becomes hopeful, “You mean others have had similar dreams?”

Mr. Akeru nods, “They have, and it has been going on for years.”

Lauren is confused, “Then the complex is haunted!”

Mr. Akeru disagrees, “Not exactly.”

Lauren has to know, “What do you mean?”

Mr. Akeru thinks about it, "I think it is nothing more than stories being handed down from the tenants."

Mr. Akeru realizes he needs to explain more, "It's like when people gather around a water cooler and talk about gossip, but in this case the gossip is traveling through dreams."

Lauren becomes excited, "I had thought the same thing! I convinced myself that I was merely dreaming other people's nightmares. Nightmares that had been so powerful they left some sort of trace that someone else could tap into."

Mr. Akeru is surprised, "That is an interesting way of looking at it."

Lauren ties her theory in with Mr. Akeru's, "It is basically no different than me being able to hear people several floors above me through the heating duct!"

Mr. Akeru adds, "Incidents that happened in the building travel from one person to the next. It would not be unreasonable to think that if a person hears about an incident they would dream it."

Lauren understands but is a little skeptical, "The dreams seem so real and are in first person. If the story is being told through dreams, wouldn't some of the facts change?"

Mr. Akeru shrugs his shoulders, "Perhaps, even adding a different ending?"

Lauren becomes excited, "That would explain why some of the dreams continue after the main person has died!" She is relieved, "This is much better than the alternative idea."

Mr. Akeru is curious, "Alternative? What would that be?"

Lauren feels foolish saying it out loud, "The dead being able to dream."

Mr. Akeru can't help but laugh out loud, "My poor child, you have been giving yourself quite a scare!"

Lauren has to admit, "If you were having these dreams, you would be questioning your sanity too!"

Mr. Akeru smiles, "You are not going crazy, although I admit not too many are going to believe our theories."

Lauren nods, "I have not told anyone but you. To be honest, when I leave this place I forget all about the dreams!"

Mr. Akeru is not surprised, “It is as if the complex is an amplifier. When you leave the dreams become like any normal dream, ones you can barely remember.”

Lauren needs to know, “How did the others cope?”

Mr. Akeru thinks about it, “There are only a handful of stories to be told about this building. Once they dreamed all of them the dreams stopped. The ones that told me this in private, every one of them were new tenants and after a few weeks they forgot about the dreams.”

Lauren laughs a little nervously, “And here I thought the noise was going to be the biggest thing I would have to learn to live with!”

Mr. Akeru shakes his head, “Give it time and everything will fall into place.”

Lauren agrees, “Thank you for listening, I feel so much better! Now you get home, it has been a long day for you!”

Mr. Akeru sighs, “That it has. Good night Ms. Lauren.”

“Good night Mr. Akeru.”

Lauren walks over to the elevator and waits for the doors to open. Riding up she thinks about her conversation with Mr. Akeru. It was nice to know she has not been the only one; however, what a strange phenomenon!

As she thinks about their conversation something nags at her. What is it? She has the same annoying feeling that she had back at the bar. That’s it! The bar! The guy she saw was definitely from her dream! In fact, so was his girlfriend! The dream about the cadaver parts from the ex-boyfriend! The more Lauren thinks about it the more it makes sense. She had even noticed the guy at the bar had a limp when he walked away. That would have been due to the surgery on his knee!

What was it she thought he said? Something like, “Some of them do escape, yet somehow some of us stay tied to that place. You might want to start thinking about your escape.” If the guy at the bar said what she thought he said, how does that fit in with her and Mr. Akeru’s explanation? It doesn’t! If these were mere nightmares, why would this guy say what he did?

The more Lauren thinks about the interaction with the guy at the bar, the more it makes sense! The poor guy had shaken his head after saying what he did and then acted as if he hadn't said anything at all. Almost like someone else had spoken up for him. Like a possessed part of him was reaching out to her! Suddenly, the doors of the elevator open up frightening her.

Timidly she walks to her apartment thinking about the dreams she has had. Lauren had assumed most of them had happened distantly in the past. Had not Mr. Akeru said the explosion happened back in the eighties? And yet, the couple she saw tonight is present day!

For that matter, if there was a story about a guy dying on his motorcycle here at the apartment complex, even if someone did know the guy was a donor, how would they have known about the guy who had surgery on his knee? How would Lauren have known what the couple looked like unless the dream came directly from the guy that died on the motorcycle!

So, now she is back to believing the dead can dream! Is it not unreasonable to believe in one strange phenomenon and not entertain that there could be an even stranger phenomenon? Lauren reasons with herself, it may. However, she is the one living alone. For her to be able to go back in that apartment and sleep normally she has to convince herself it is nothing more than what she and Mr. Akeru had concluded.

Once inside the apartment, Lauren looks around and forces herself to take a hard look. Does she feel afraid in the apartment? Looking at the nice cozy home she has made for herself she realizes, no, it is beginning to feel like home.

She goes into the bedroom and forces herself to do the same in there. Not only does she not feel afraid, she is ready to go to bed! Lauren walks over confidently and turns on the sound machine.

As she undresses the sound machine seems to take all her worries away. Crawling into bed and snuggling under the blankets, Lauren is looking forward to a good night's sleep.

One last sane reason comes to mind to comfort Lauren. If she is terrified she would not be able to go to sleep so easily, would she?

Bling

Bling

Chapter One

Emma is surprised when Howard asks her to go with him to see the motorcycle show at the convention center. She had almost given up on their relationship, if you could call it that, due to their complete lack of having anything in common. It makes it next to impossible to even communicate.

Howard is a lawyer, a lawyer who has never had an interesting story in his life. He means well, but the man is as boring as boring can get.

Emma is a bailiff and works in the same building as Howard. She had thought herself to be quite lucky to have a lawyer show interest in someone like her. A lawyer and a bailiff never seem to interact. Now she knows why, and yet being lonely in the city it is nice to have a relationship, even if it is with a lawyer.

Emma is the complete opposite of Howard. Although they are the same age, she enjoys life. One of her many passions is her motorcycle. Most people opt for public transportation in the city; however, not Emma. She loves the challenge. Easily moving her motorcycle in and out of traffic gives her mind a puzzle that needs to be solved quickly.

Not only does she love the power and control, but to be honest, she loves the attention. Emma intentionally lets her long hair flow around her helmet to make sure everyone knows there is a woman riding this complicated machine.

Knowing that Emma rides, Howard knew the motorcycle show would be something she would like. He wasn't sure why she fascinated him so much. Deep down Howard knows that Emma is nothing more than a bright flame and once he gets too close he will be burned. And yet, just like a moth he can't help himself.

Howard meets Emma in front of the convention center. He is surprised to see her roll up on her bike. Emma flips her helmet up and yells out to Howard, "I have a friend that will let me park this in back. Stay here, I will be right back."

Howard simply nods and smiles. He watches in amazement as she whips the bike around to the back. Within minutes Emma returns.

To see her walking up, you would have never known she just got off a bike. Her long hair untangled, freely flows softly in the wind. Her outfit for the day is a modest one, jeans and a sweater. Her leather jacket must be with her bike.

Emma comes up to Howard and is surprised to see him in jeans. She smiles, "Look at you! One of the common folk today?"

Howard blushes. Emma had teased him before about being over dressed. The jeans he has on are the only ones he has, and he has them only because of a quick stop at the store the night before. He leans over and gives her a quick kiss, "I could never look as good as you do in yours!"

Emma is shocked. Maybe there is hope for this guy after all! Emma begins to relax and grabs his hand casually, "First jeans, next on the list for you is a motorcycle!"

Howard squeezes her hand and laughs, "I think you missed a couple steps, like boots and a leather coat. Then we will see!"

Emma and Howard walk around the convention like a normal couple. Emma is surprised that Howard seems to be genuinely enjoying himself.

Howard is thinking to himself how lucky he is. The girl beside him is not only beautiful but confident. Unlike some of the woman here, she also seems soft, not harsh.

Although Emma can be tough when her job calls for it, Emma can also fit in anywhere. Howard would never be embarrassed to take her to a fancy gala event; therefore, he needs to make sure she will not be embarrassed with him in a situation like they are in today.

Howard may be boring but he is smart enough to know he is beginning to lose Emma. They had only dated for six months but he can tell she is becoming uninterested, when in truth, Howard is becoming deeply attached to her. If having to change a little meant keeping her, he is willing to do it.

After walking around for a while Howard offers, "Would you like for me to get us some drinks?"

Emma nods, "That would be nice. I will meet you over at the Harley stand."

Emma is curious about what Harley has to offer this year. Looking around she finds herself drawn to a bike. Of course a salesman is quick to notice her interest. "It is a beauty, isn't it? The latest CVO Breakout."

Emma admires the color, "I have never seen a color like this. What would you call it? Black chrome?"

The salesman nods, "Yup, they only made 700 in this color. It definitely is unique!"

Even though Emma is quite happy with the bike she owns now, this bike is a whole other story! Not only is the color unique but it is dripping in chrome.

The salesman looks around a little curious, "I am sure the Mister would enjoy this, where might he be?"

Emma is instantly offended, "I ride my own bike, and this would be for me, not him."

The salesman is a little taken back, "This is a pretty big bike. I have a Sportster I can show you that may be more your speed."

Emma is barely able to contain her anger as she easily strides the bike and balances it between her legs, "For your information, I ride a Dyna Wide Glide right now!"

The salesman quickly realizes his mistake and begins to apologize but Emma is not having it, "Who is in charge of this booth?"

Hearing raised voices another salesman quickly appears, "That would be me. Is there a problem here?"

Emma careful tilts the bike back down on its stand and gets off, "This man thought my "Mister" would be the only one to ride this bike!"

The guy in charge shakes his head, "Gary, why don't you go help someone else. I will be more than happy to help this customer."

Gary mumbles as he walks away. The guy in charge sighs and apologizes, "I am so sorry, he had no right. You looked great on the bike; it is obvious you are a rider! I am Joe, how can I help you today?"

Emma looks back at the bike lovingly, "Have you sold this floor model yet?"

Joe shakes his head, "No, we are not allowed to take offers until tomorrow, the last day of the show."

Emma looks him square in the eye, "I will give you $5,000 over the list if you sell it to me. It can stay here until the show is over."

Joe is shocked, "You do know the list price is $32,000?"

Just then Howard walks up with their drinks. He hands one to Emma. "What's going on?"

Emma looks back at the bike, "I am trying to buy that bike right there."

Howard is surprised, "Really? Good God! It is gorgeous!"

Emma proudly nods, "I know."

She looks back at Joe questioningly, "What's the verdict Joe?"

Joe smiles at her, "The verdict is, you have yourself a new motorcycle! I can tell it will be going to a good home!"

Chapter Two

During the next couple of days, Emma gets everything in order for her new ride. The sale of her current bike is a breeze and that enables her to put a big chunk down on the new bike. Between insurance and the monthly bike payment she is happy to see her new purchase only adds $50 to her monthly expenses.

Relieved to know she can actually afford her new big purchase, Emma begins to get excited.

Surprisingly, Howard is supportive. Emma had figured Howard would lecture her all the way home the day she made the deal for the bike. Instead, he treated to her a nice dinner to celebrate. After dinner they went back to her apartment for dessert. Emma is surprised again with Howard's passion. She definitely likes the changes he is making.

A couple of days pass and Emma finds herself smiling as she walks from the subway. Life is good. This will be the last day she will have to use public transportation; her new baby was ready to come home!

Walking into the motorcycle shop she quickly finds the salesperson who helped her at the show, "Joe! I hear she is all ready for me?"

Joe smiles, "That she is. We put the new pipes on that you wanted, and I must say the inner primary definitely makes a difference!"

Emma agrees, "It was the only two things I needed to add."

Joe explains, "Because it is a CVO, they pretty much load them up. Special editions."

Joe looks around and lowers his voice, "I have to say, I really caught hell for selling it to you early. These things are in such high demand the owner had planned on auctioning this one off; however, since I had already sold it he couldn't."

Emma feels bad, "I am sorry. I thought the $5,000 over list would more than compensate for any problems."

Joe sighs, "So did I, unfortunately he may have gotten more, but that of course is always a gamble. He simply auctioned off the slots for first orders received. Don't worry, it all worked out."

Emma is relieved, "They are in that much of a demand?"

Joe's eyes get big, "You have no idea! Most dealerships are already on back order and don't even have one to display! That's another reason they wanted to hold on to this one a little longer. The person who would have won the auction would have still waited two months before they were going to release this one."

Joe smiles, "Enough of what could have been, let's concentrate on what is! I felt $5,000 over list was too much to accept, so to make it a little better for you, I threw in a matching helmet and, believe it or not, the suit that they had on the mannequin at the show. It is all the same color as the bike!"

Emma is shocked, "That is awesome! Thank you so much!"

Joe takes her into his office and they finalize the papers. At the end, he hands her a small container of paint, "This is for any touch ups you may need. I can't stress too much how important this is, the color on your bike is like no other. It is very difficult to get your hands on this color."

Emma puts it in her backpack along with the papers. She looks up at Joe a little concerned, "Since I am driving the bike home now, I will need to condense all of this as much as possible. I will wear the suit and helmet; may I leave all the packaging with you?"

Joe nods, "Of course, and you should be able to strap the helmet you brought with you on the back seat."

Emma begins to get nervous at the thought of riding the new bike, "I guess we are ready to go see Bling."

Joe looks confused, "Bling?"

Emma laughs, "Yea Bling, I have already named her. She is dripping in bling, don't you agree?"

Joe shakes his head chuckling, "Nice one and quite appropriate. Let's go get you your Bling."

Even though Emma had taken several pictures of Bling at the convention center, none of them did Bling justice. In fact, most of them were a blur. Although Emma tried remembering how pretty the bike was, seeing it today left her breathless.

Emma walks up timidly to the polished bike, runs her hand over the embroidered seat. Softly she whispers, "Oh Bling, you are the most beautiful thing I have ever owned!"

All the men in the shop watch enviously as Emma straddles the bike and starts it up. She had been so impressed with Bling's appearance she had not even given a thought about how she would sound. The roar of the engine is almost deafening. Smiling she can't help but rev it up a little to hear the pipes cackle. All of the men hoot and holler.

Emma takes a deep breath and turns it towards the doors to leave. Nervous that everyone is watching she puts it in gear, holds her head up in a confidence she doesn't feel, and rolls it out into the street.

Once on the street Emma is careful, making sure she is comfortable driving. At stoplights, she fixes the mirrors to see better.

Feeling more confident, Emma heads out of the city to the highway. Without having a choice, she kicks it in. The power is there in an instant! As she drives effortlessly on the highway she is amazed at how this feels like a Cadillac compared to her old bike. The seat cradles her perfectly, the engine is more powerful, and the handlebars are at the perfect angle.

She finds herself driving for hours with no place to go but the open road. Looking down at the digital clock she sighs. Time to call it a night.

Chapter Three

Howard had been happy with the direction their relationship was going until she bought that damn bike! He admits it probably is nothing more than simple jealousy. He is jealous over the time Emma spends on her bike where she could be spending it with him. However, Howard is a patient man. He reminds himself that soon Emma's new toy will lose its magic and then they can go back to concentrating on their relationship.

A nagging thought tugs at Howard. Emma had changed since the new bike. As much as he tries to minimize it, she had changed. She had become more distant and moody. At first he had feared she had met someone else, but he quickly realized there had been no time for another. The bike had consumed her time which probably accounts for her moodiness.

She had to be exhausted because as soon as Emma was finished with work she would hop on the bike and not get home until late into the evening only to start it up the very next day. As for the weekends, forget about it. She would take off Saturday morning, leaving the city behind, and Howard wouldn't hear from her until late Sunday night. Emma's sister lived in the suburbs and Emma would crash at her house on Saturday night. Occasionally she would go on rides with others, but for the most part she liked to ride alone.

Howard's phone rings. He is surprised it is Emma, "Hi stranger! How are you doing?"

Emma sounds pissed, "Not good! I got a recall letter in the mail today. They are forcing me to have my bike repainted. It says for some reason the paint job gives authorities a hard time to recognize it, including toll plazas!"

Howard had never heard of such a thing, "Really? That's crazy! Do you have to pay for the paint job?"

Emma shakes her head, "No, they say they will cover the cost, but I don't want to change the color! The color is one of the main reasons I bought the damn thing!"

Howard lets his lawyer side slip out, "Well, the law is the law."

Disgusted, Emma yells before hanging up, "I should have known that's what you would say!"

Furious, Emma leaves her apartment and hops on her bike. Weaving in and out of traffic, her fury knows no bounds.

Several times she cuts people off and surprisingly it feels good! They deserve what they get! One BMW pushes his luck with Emma; however, she is not having it. Quickly she cuts in front of the BMW and speeds through a red light. A car swerving to miss her crashes into the BMW.

Emma simply laughs as she races away. Making quick turns to confuse any cops that may have seen the accident, she rolls up to the back of the bike shop where she bought the bike.

A couple of guys come over admiring the bike. She quickly gets off and strikes up a conversation with them. One of the guys whistles as he looks at the bike, "She looks as clean as the day you picked her up!"

Emma nods proudly, "Believe it or not it's been real easy to take care of her."

One of the guys looks around before he asks, "How have those free tolls been going for you?"

Emma laughs, "Ever since you told me to paint the plate with my touch up paint not a single toll. Thank you!"

Another guy lowers his voice, "I hear that's not the only thing you can get away with. These bikes are freaky. A couple of them have been involved in accidents and yet no one is able to identify them. Not cameras or eye witnesses. It's almost as if they are invisible."

Emma feels relief flow over her as she thinks about what she just did, "Well, I guess all of that is about to change with us being forced to change the paint!"

Emma looks pleadingly at the guys, "Unless, of course, there is something you can do for me?"

They look at each other as they think about it. One finally speaks up, "You could leave it here for the time it would take to paint it so we can bill for the hours, and then we will give you the information needed to change the color on the title." The man winks at her, "We will just never paint it."

Emma looks concerned, "Won't the license branch find out?"

The other guy speaks up, "How? There are no inspections on bikes anymore, and the license branch has no way of knowing other than looking at the information we provide for them."

Emma's eyes sparkle, "If you would do that for me, I would be eternally grateful!"

The guys agree, "A bike this unique needs to be saved; just promise us if you ever want to sell her, you will sell her back to one of us!"

Emma smiles, "Deal, but don't hold your breath! I would have to be long dead and buried for that to happen!"

Chapter Four

For the next couple of days Emma frantically searches the papers for any mention of her hit and run. Nothing is to be found. Her confidence in being able to get away with road rage increases, in fact, she begins to find herself looking for a reason to have road rage. Encouraging it. Causing it.

Emma has now begun to lose count of how many accidents she has caused. Throughout the months she begins to see some of the accidents being tried in her own courthouse.

On break, Emma notices Howard alone in the hallway and approaches him, "Hi Howard, it's been a while. How have you been?"

Howard sighs, "Overloaded with work right now, these road rage cases are getting out of hand."

Emma nods, "I noticed that too, kind of odd. What are your thoughts?"

Howard hesitates, "It seems most of them complain of a burst of light, or something, that causes them to be distracted. Before they know it they are running into another car."

Emma simply replies, "That is strange."

Howard nods, "There have been incidents where when a new skyscraper is built the sun reflects on it causing distractions. I thought at first this may be a good connection; however, there seems to be no pattern. Different times of the day and night and of course different locations."

Howard changes the subject, "You need to be careful out there. How do you like your new bike? Did you get it painted?"

Emma stumbles, "It is great! The paint job turned out to be nothing more than a clear coat. Looks the same."

Howard is surprised, "Really? That's good. Maybe we could get together again?"

Emma sighs, "I am sorry, I know I have been a bit consumed with the bike. Pretty soon with the winter coming I will have to put Bling away. Give me a little bit longer and I promise to put my full attention on us. You have been so understanding, it is only fair I pay you back."

Howard is hopeful, "I understand. I have to say it is probably wise for me right now too. Until my work load lightens up I am not sure I would have the time either."

Emma smiles, "Then in a month we shall meet up, fair enough?"

Howard agrees, "Fair enough."

Howard goes back to his office smiling, yet a thought keeps nagging at him. Emma's bike Bling. He never understood why Emma's bike had to be repainted in the first place. He remembers all too well when Emma first told him about it and then hung up. It had been days before she would even take his call after the fight, and then Howard found himself apologizing for something when he was not sure exactly what he had done. But of course men have been doing that for centuries. It certainly is nothing new and not something he had given much thought to until now.

Curious, Howard starts doing research on the computer about the reason Emma's bike needed to be repainted. The recall is still in effect; however, from what he can gather, it is not just a simple clear coat. It is a full color change. Why would Emma lie to him?

Howard can't let this go. Finally he is able to get in touch with the manufacturer itself. Using his credentials he is surprised when his call is transferred to their legal department. Fortunately, the lawyer who answers is friendly, "Hi, this is Tom. How can I help you?"

Howard replies, "Tom, this is Howard Kline with Kline, Hofstead and Anders Association. I just have a couple of simple questions in regards to the recall for a paint job on a CVO Break-out."

Tom becomes more guarded, "I will try to answer them as best as I can but understand this is already being investigated. I can't reveal anything during the investigation."

Howard is surprised, "Certainly. My only real question is why was the recall done?"

Tom is a little relieved, "We explained it clearly in the letter. Due to the paint it is hard for it to be recognized."

Howard doesn't understand, "Recognized how?"

Tom will only reveal what is in the letter, "Through toll plazas, for example, the cameras are having trouble capturing a clear image."

Howard realizes what this means, "Would that mean the human eye may have trouble registering it too?"

Tom hesitates, "I suppose it could."

Howard replies, "Thank you Tom, that is I all I needed. You have a nice day."

Tom is relieved, "You too."

Howard leans back in his chair as he looks at the stack of folders on his desk. Could the bright light that distracted so many be a motorcycle? It makes sense, the different times of day and the different locations. People in their cars with their radios on, along with all the other noise the city has to offer, may not have even heard a motorcycle or thought anything about hearing a motorcycle.

Howard leans forward and grabs the folder on top and quickly looks for a phone number. If his hunch is right, this could resolve so many of his cases. Howard pauses for a moment. If he is right this also could mean Emma may be involved. He takes a deep breath, before getting ahead of himself he needs to check the facts first.

By late that day Howard finishes calling the last folder in the stack. To his surprise, every one of them remembers hearing a loud bike just before the crash.

The judge is not going to want to hear this. Without more proof it will just look like an excuse. It is so easy to blame a motorcycle, but rarely does it get you off. Bottom line, you as a driver are required to look out for motorcycles at all times, no matter if the bike is at fault.

Howard looks at all the cases and shakes his head, this is different. It is not one or two cases but several and that is just in his office alone. How many were there throughout the city and even ones not reported? He takes it a step farther, what if this is a serial attacker? Someone empowered by knowing they can't be caught. Can't be seen.

Howard knows it is time to make a call to Emma, the one call he has dreaded the most during the day. There is no answer; she must be out for another ride on her bike.

He looks at his watch and realizes the shop Emma bought the bike from is still open. Howard quickly heads to the street and flags down a taxi, talking to them in person will be better than on the phone.

Howard timidly walks into the show room and a perky girl comes up, “May I help you?”

Howard smiles, “Yes, my girlfriend just got her bike repainted here. They forgot to give her the touch up paint and sure enough, wouldn’t you know it, a bicycle parked next to it scuffed it up a bit. Is there anyone in the back that could help me out with this?”

The girl nods and points to the back door, “Sure, go on in the back there and tell them what you need. They are still there but not for much longer, we are getting ready to close.”

“I will be quick, I promise.”

Howard walks into the back room and finds several men hanging out. Howard clears his throat, “Excuse me, I am sorry to bother you. My girlfriend Emma brought her bike in to be painted some time ago.”

The youngest pipes up, “Oh yea, did she have any problems down at the DMV?”

One of the older ones glares at the kid and interrupts, “What can we do for you?”

Howard realizes Emma must have struck a deal with the guys and quickly tries to think of something, “She wanted me to stop in and see if everything cleared on your end. I have to say I can’t thank you guys enough, she is so happy!”

The older man is relieved, “Not a problem dude. A bike like that should have never been touched to begin with, everything went fine on our end. In fact, we did it for another kid. Just doing our part to stick it to the man.”

Howard now feels very uncomfortable in his suit and tie, “I hear you, sometimes this tie feels like a noose. But when we get on the bikes, there is nothing stopping us! I know you are closing, that’s all I needed. Thank you.”

Howard is able to leave without the perky girl seeing him. He quickly flags down a taxi and thinks about what he just learned. Obviously Emma never got her bike painted and somehow the guys made it look like she did. More importantly, they did it for another guy.

A few streets over, Emma revs her bike looking for the next accident she can cause. Sure enough there is a man to the right of her in a Mercedes. Men in expensive cars always seem to be the easiest to pick on. It is as if they have to prove themselves. As predicted, the Mercedes cuts off a woman in a Toyota.

Emma kicks it in and swerves around the Toyota and races beside the Mercedes, only to cut him off right as the light is changing. Instead of stopping, the guy in the Mercedes kicks it in, pissed, and tries to keep up. The next light is already red but that doesn't stop Emma as she zips by egging the Mercedes to follow her. He does.

As they are going through the intersection they both are blinded by a light. It is the last light many see that night.

Howard's taxi suddenly stops, "Oh my God! Did you see that?"

Howard had not seen anything but had heard the sickening crunch of metal on metal. He quickly looks forward and sees cars mangled together. He jumps out of the taxi and starts running to see if he can help. His heart quickens as he sees a motorcycle, it looks like the one Emma owns.

Forcing himself to lean down next to the body he gently removes the helmet. Relief floods over him as he sees it is a young man. The relief quickly becomes remorse, as he realizes the young man is dead. He looks around at the crash scene and sees others trying to help.

Across from him Howard notices another bike and a bystander pulling the helmet off its rider. He instantly recognizes Emma's long flowing hair. Like the young man in front of him, she too is dead.

Months go by and a lot of lawsuits are settled. Howard had been right; a motorcycle had been the cause of the many accidents around the city.

The irony of two bikes painted the same way meeting in a final crash was not lost on Howard. Although he would like to think only the young man had been responsible for all the road rage accidents, it was highly unlikely when some of the accidents happened at the same time in different parts of the city. Obviously, both Emma and the young man had been at fault.

To add to the irony, both the guy and Emma lived in the same apartment complex. Apparently, the guy had been keeping the bike at his girlfriend's house and had just recently moved into that apartment complex. The city is not as big as everyone thinks.

Howard can't help but wonder, had the knowledge of not being able to get caught caused a primal urge to boil up in the two of them, or had the paint or even the bikes themselves caused the desire?

Across town the police auction is over. Both CVO Breakouts are sold to different people in different states.

The new owners are amazed at what they had bought. Both bikes supposedly had been in a crash, but neither bike had been damaged. The only stipulation on the bikes is they are to be repainted. Neither owner has any intention of changing such a unique color.

White Noise Stories Continued

Lauren stretches lazily as she thinks about the latest dream. Such a small world, what were the odds that two people would live in the same apartment complex and have the same unique bike?

Lauren can't help but think on the bright side, how nice it is to be able to walk to work! The streets are far too dangerous for her liking and this just reinforces her belief!

With the sunlight streaming in, it is hard for Lauren to get caught up in the gloominess of all of her dreams. Instead, a real hunger comes over Lauren as she gets dressed and she decides to treat herself to some breakfast at the diner. Afterwards, Lauren plans on going to the market and getting some fresh fruit to try and gain her strength back.

Even though Lauren knows she should try to make a doctor's appointment, she wants to see if she is any better by Monday. Hopefully it is nothing but some sort of 24 hour thing or in this case a 72 hour thing.

Lauren rides the elevator down with a few people which is a nice distraction that helps her not to think about her dreams.

She is surprised that Mr. Akeru isn't at the door; however, it is the weekend. Perhaps he has the weekends off. A strange and unusual thought comes to her mind, one that she is not even sure is her own. Is it because Mr. Akeru is away that she feels better and is able to get up and out? Heading through the doors, Lauren shrugs her shoulders for her answer; however, the second she is through the door and out in the full sunlight she doesn't give it another thought.

Feeling a little guilty about treating Roxi the way she did last night, Lauren decides to invite her to breakfast. After the third ring Lauren hears a very sleepy Roxi answer the phone, "Hello?"

Lauren answers cheerfully, "Good morning Roxi!"

Roxi is not feeling the good cheer and mumbles, "What time is it?"

Lauren answers, "Time for me to treat you to breakfast since I was such bad company last night!"

Roxi appreciates it, “Very sweet but I can’t, remember I am going with my mom and sister to look at wedding dresses.”

Lauren instantly feels bad about forgetting Roxi’s sister is getting married. It had been a very touchy topic for Roxi, since it was her sister’s second wedding and Roxi had never come close to a proposal.

Lauren sympathizes, “I am so sorry, I did forget. Are you sure you don’t want me to go with you?”

Roxi struggles to get out of bed, “No, they told me it was supposed to be a bonding day for the family. Personally, I call bullshit. They know it will be easier to have two against one.”

Lauren has to giggle, “Honey, knowing you, two against one is still not nearly enough!”

Roxi smiles and begins to feel a little mischievous, “You know, you are right! I am going to milk this baby for all it’s worth!”

After a short walk Lauren arrives at the diner, “You plan on going back to your mom’s house and staying the weekend, right?”

Roxi nods, “That is the plan.”

Lauren understands, “Then we will touch base on Monday and you can tell me all the gory details!”

After their goodbyes Lauren has a huge breakfast. It is like she has not eaten for weeks! Lauren enjoys her morning out. Still feeling a bit weak she goes home after the market. By the time she gets up to her apartment she is exhausted, too exhausted to even put the groceries away.

Leaving the bags on the counter she starts undressing as she heads for the bedroom. This is ridiculous! Never in her life has she felt so fatigued!

Without thinking about it Lauren reaches over and turns the sound machine on. The bed feels so good. Within minutes she is fast asleep.

Home
Cooked
Dinner

Home Cooked Dinner

Tim and Lori enjoy the beautiful scenery as it passes them by in the car. They had decided to take a road trip into the mountains to enjoy the fall foliage; agreeing to stop whenever they want.

Tim glances at the gas gauge as he sees a sign telling them how far the next exit for gas would be, "Honey, we should stop at the next exit to fill up so we have plenty of gas to get through the mountains."

Lori agrees, "Ok, sounds good. Maybe we should start thinking about what we want to eat for dinner."

Tim cringes a little, knowing all too well how difficult it is for Lori to make up her mind when it comes to what she wants to eat, "You know me, anything will be fine."

Lori sighs, "I know dear, same old same old. We are on a road trip; I think we should try something new!"

Now it is Tim's turn to sigh, "Honey, you know that never works out. Why not just stick to something we know will be good?"

Tim takes the exit into a busy trendy town. Lori looks around disgusted, "Look at it all, it is no different than what we have back home. It is like we never left!"

Tim looks around at all the chain restaurants and admits, "You are right. Why don't you go online and see if there is something different we may not be seeing?"

Lori quickly pulls out her tablet, "Good idea!"

Tim parks the car and gets out to pump the gas. As he is pumping the gas he realizes that Lori is wrong, this fresh crisp mountain air is definitely something they did not have back home. In fact, Tim would have been perfectly content packing up some beef jerky, a couple of beers, and just parking the car in some wooded area to enjoy the scenery.

Tim goes inside to pay and looks longingly at the beef jerky and sees they even sell beer at the gas station! The cashier startles Tim, "Are you ready to pay Sir?"

Tim quickly pulls out his money, "Yes, I am. I was wondering if there were any nice restaurants, perhaps in the mountains with a view?"

The cashier shakes her head, "No Sir, with all the nice restaurants we have around here now, it was too hard for the mom and pop restaurants in the mountains to survive."

Tim looks out the window sadly, "That is a real shame."

The cashier disagrees, "Not really, everything is nice and convenient now and it has brought people into our town."

Tim understands but is still disappointed, "I suppose you are right. Have a good day."

The cashier smiles, "You too."

When Tim gets back in the car, he notices Lori is on the phone. She puts her finger up to him to tell him to wait a minute, "Yes, if there are no problems and you say it only takes a half hour from town, we can be there by 6:00."

Lori listens to the person on the other end of the phone and then finishes up, "That is awesome. We can't wait for a good home cooked dinner! See you soon, bye."

Tim starts the car, "I take it you found a place for us to eat?"

Lori, looking proud of herself, smiles, "I did and one I think you will even enjoy!"

Tim teases her, "As long as it is not that trendy fishy crap you made me eat last night I will be happy!"

Lori playfully punches him, "Am I ever going to live that down? No, since you had to endure that last night I geared the preference to more traditional food."

Tim looks around at the small town and is a little worried, "Traditional food around here could be road kill, you know!"

Lori laughs, "Well, it is up in the mountains so who knows?"

Tim begins to go to the highway but Lori stops him, "No honey, they said to get on 292 then we will be going on back roads all the way up."

Tim sees the signs for 292 and heads for it, "Did you get an address so we can put it in the navigation?"

Lori looks back down at her tablet, "That is strange. There is no address listed, just a phone number. But don't worry, the directions were very simple. We stay on 292 until we see Shadow

Lane. We take Shadow Lane for about ten miles and turn right onto Creek Road. We stay on Creek Road for fifteen miles and as soon as we go over a wooden bridge it is the first road on the left. That road is Willow and we just stay on it until the end."

Tim turns on to 292 and looks ahead, "Well, we wanted to see fall foliage and this is definitely going to put us right into it. After dinner we can always come back down to this town and get a hotel room for the night."

Lori sees a hotel up ahead, "Should we go ahead and get a room just in case?"

Tim thinks about it, "Nah, if the reservation is at 6:00, we take an hour to eat puts us at 7:00, another half hour to get back, give or take, it will be around 8:00. Even if they don't have a room we have plenty of time to get on the highway and go to the next town for a hotel."

Lori agrees, "Sounds like a plan."

Tim is curious, "How did you find this place anyway?"

Lori closes up her tablet, "I typed in 'local home cooked family restaurant'. It actually came up on Yelp as five stars, so it's gotta be good!"

Tim nods, "What is the name of it?"

Lori smiles a little, "Ma's Cooking."

Tim has to laugh, "Well, at least it is original."

Lori looks out at the beautiful scenery, "And popular, it required reservations. We are lucky they had a cancellation."

Tim visualizes a large wooden ski cabin in the middle of the woods with a big window overlooking the mountains. Large plates of home cooked food brought to them. His mouth begins to water, "Sounds great!"

They come up on Shadow Lane pretty quickly and make the turn easily. Shadow Lane quickly becomes a typical mountain road, narrower and not as nicely paved.

The scenery is breathtaking! They drive without talking, soaking in nature's beauty. Before they know it, they see Creek Road on the right. A little disappointed, they realize the road is not paved and far worse than Shadow Lane but their Land Rover easily maneuvers down the road.

As they bounce down the road, Tim tries to remain hopeful, "You know this reminds me of that road we took in Vermont to get up to the ski chateau."

Lori begins to get a little excited at the idea, "Maybe it is a chateau too and we can actually stay there after we eat. Wouldn't that be cool?"

Finally, after what seems like much longer than fifteen miles, they go across a wooden bridge. To the right is a crooked hand written sign that says "Ma's Cooking" with an arrow.

Suddenly both Lori and Tim are not so sure Ma's Cooking is going to be anything like they had imagined. However, Lori is not going to be defeated so easily, "Perhaps they are trying to appeal to a tourist's idea of Ma's Cooking?"

As Tim maneuvers the Land Rover onto nothing more than a dirt path he sighs, "I sure hope so. You would think if they needed reservations they could afford paving the road to their place!"

The once pretty scenery now seems to be closing in on them, almost suffocating them. The trees are so close together they hardly allow any sunlight down onto the road. In fact, Tim finds himself turning on his lights just to be able to see in front of them.

Lori starts getting nervous and finally admits, "Maybe we should just turn around and go back down towards town?"

Tim sighs, "I have been thinking the same thing but there is nowhere to turn around!"

Up ahead they finally see a clearing with sunlight and Tim turns his lights off, "Looks like we may be here, for better or for worse."

Once inside the clearing, Tim and Lori are shocked to see what is in front of them! An old decrepit house barely standing with junk all around it. In fact, so much junk it is going to be hard for Tim to turn the Land Rover around.

Lori can't help but giggle, "Oh my God! Yelp, what have you done to us?"

Tim laughs out loud, "Honey, somehow, some way, you had to have gotten the directions wrong!"

Before Lori can answer an old man in dirty jean overalls comes out to greet them, "Hi folks! You must be our 6:00 appointment. Just park this thing right here and come on in."

Tim smiles, “I guess we are, just let me get this turned around so we will be facing the right way when we are done with dinner.”

The old man looks a little perplexed, “There is no hurry friend, plenty of time for that later.”

Tim continues to roll the car forward so he can back it up to turn the right way, eventually the man has to move out of his way to do so. As he turns the car around he mumbles, “We are not staying are we?”

Just as Lori is about to speak an old woman with an apron comes out and goes up to Lori’s window, “Hi there honey. Dinner is almost finished. Been cooking nonstop since you called. Hope y’all are hungry, we got fried chicken, mash taters, biscuits, the works. And oh yes! My famous blue berry cobbler with home-made cream.”

The old man smiles lovingly over at the old lady, “Yea, ol’ Ma here cooks for the rich folk up at that ski place. She’s still the best cook in the county!”

Lori and Tim feel a great sense of guilt come over them. Lori makes the decision, “We can’t wait, I am sure it is everything Yelp said it was.”

Tim turns the car off but instead of taking the key he leaves it in a spot only he and Lori know about. They had always agreed that when in doubt, the key stays in the car at all times.

They both get out and timidly walk towards the house with the older couple. The old lady looks terribly ashamed, “I am so sorry we had to bring you to the old house. The ski resort is not open yet and the other place we use in the summer just recently burnt down.”

The old man holds the door open for them as the old lady continues, “We knew fall foliage was going to be upon us fast, but until we can get another set up this is the best we can do. Unfortunately, if we don’t work we don’t eat either.”

Tim and Lori step into the house and are pleasantly surprised at how clean it is; in fact one might go as far as charming. The smell throughout the house is simply heavenly! Tim and Lori find themselves beginning to relax. Tim offers, “By the way, my name is Tim and this is Lori.”

The old lady motions them into a fairly large dining room, "Just call us Ma and Pa, everyone else does."

Lori is impressed with the way the table is laid out, "My goodness what a beautiful set up. I can see you have been doing this quite some time!"

Pa motions for them to have a seat, "Yea, been a family business for as long as I can remember."

Ma nods as she goes around and fills the glasses with water, "Pa's right, before the ski place the family was cooking for miners and before that the pioneers. It is our lot in life."

Lori takes in a deep breath, "Well, it smells heavenly!"

Tim notices an extra place setting, "Is there anyone else that will be joining us?"

Ma answers as she goes into the kitchen to retrieve the food, "Our son might be joining us a little later. Never know with that kid, he seems to have an agenda all of his own."

Lori is a little surprised, their "kid" had to be close to their age! In a way, Lori hopes he shows up just to satisfy her curiosity.

Ma brings out plates upon plates full of delicious home cooked food. Throughout dinner Tim and Lori find themselves quietly eating, too involved with enjoying the food.

Finally finished, Tim admits, "Ma, that has to be the best food I have ever eaten!"

Lori wholeheartedly agrees, "He is right, it was awesome!"

Pa gets up and surprisingly brings them over a tablet, "Mind giving ol' Ma a rating on Yelp for us?"

Lori takes the tablet, a bit surprised, "Of course, actually I am a little surprised you two would even be interested in modern technology like this."

Pa watches as Lori gives them a good review and then hands the tablet back, "Andre, our son, introduced it to us."

Lori tries to help, "Maybe Andre should post a webpage with an address?"

Ma agrees, "In time we will, but for now since the cabin burned we are not sure where the new location will be."

Pa adds, "You two are the first we had come to the house. We weren't sure you would stay, but Ma here insisted the smell of her cooking would keep you here."

Tim smiles, “She was right and I am glad she was, it was a real treat. Thank you for everything!”

Ma gets up and starts clearing the table, “Can’t leave yet, we still have dessert a coming!”

Both Lori and Tim moan out loud, “Not sure if we have room!”

Pa shakes his head, “Always room for Ma’s desserts!”

Sure enough, as soon as Ma sits the cobbler down on the table with a pitcher of heavy cream Tim and Lori find themselves unable to resist. Afterwards, Tim and Lori lean back in their chairs and enjoy a cup of coffee. Tim shakes his head, “Ma, even your coffee is the best I have ever had!”

Ma blushes but before she can accept the compliment they hear heavy footsteps coming up from what must be the basement, “Ah looks like Andre might be joining us after all.”

The little house literally shakes as the footsteps get closer. A little frightened, Lori looks at Tim with big eyes. Tim tries to assure her with a calm look; however, he is already evaluating the area for an escape route for both him and Lori.

What Ma and Pa don’t know is that both Tim and Lori have participated in several survival type marathons. It is a passionate hobby of theirs and although Lori looks frightened, Tim can see her body is calm and ready for action.

A beast of a man appears in the doorway, his head misshapen and his body huge. A smile comes over his face as he eyes both Lori and Tim. In a loud childlike voice he asks, “Ma, is dinner ready yet?”

Before she can answer both Tim and Lori are up and dive through the window, it being the only avenue of escape they have. Shocked, Pa and Ma look at each other as Andre stomps towards the window.

Tim and Lori are already up and running and in the Land Rover before any of them can do anything. Pa pats Andre on the back. Andre begins to sob silently as he watches the Land Rover speed down the road.

Pa shakes his head and quietly says, “And that my son, is what they call fast food.”

Pa sees the disappointment on his son's face, "Not to worry, I am sure Ma is already on the phone with Uncle Rodney. He will meet up with them at the bridge and we all can go back to a nice dinner."

White Noise Stories Continued

This time Lauren finds herself fighting to wake up. The dream is long gone but Lauren seems to be in a void. A place of nothingness. Is this what made her lose so much time before? It would make sense; dreams are only supposed to last five to twenty minutes. And yet, she has a feeling she has been sleeping much longer than that!

Lauren looks around but there is nothing to see. In fact, her own body is not even here. Feeling frantic and claustrophobic, even though she has no idea how big the area she is in is, she tries to scream but finds she has no mouth or voice to scream with.

Feeling her eyes frantically dart back and forth Lauren concentrates on that motion. She increases the movement, making her eyes randomly flutter open. Concentrating on the light that streams in randomly, she is finally able to force herself awake. Once awake she suddenly sits up in bed.

Quickly looking at the clock she sees it is 6:00; however, she is not sure if that is AM or PM. Getting up to check, Lauren tries to tell herself it has to be only 6:00 in the afternoon. When she had gone to bed it was just after lunch and it was nothing more than a long nap.

In the living room Lauren finds her phone and to her dismay, she realizes it is morning. Not only that, but she had missed calls from her mom. Not wanting to concern her, Lauren texts her she is fine and getting some extra sleep.

Extra sleep? That is putting it mildly! Lauren goes to the kitchen and munches on a banana. Instead of coffee she opts for a class of orange juice.

Lauren tries to reason with herself that her body must be trying to fight an infection of some sort. Somehow, sleep is what her body is demanding.

A little concerned, Lauren thinks about how hard it had been to wake herself up. She reasons to herself, she had dreams before where she knew she was dreaming and tried to wake herself up.

Although Lauren would love to compare the dreams she is having to dreams she has had before, she can't. For one, these dreams she is having now never seem like a dream. They always seem very real to her. As for her not being able to wake from her dream earlier, that makes no sense either because in her mind she was not dreaming at the time. Or was she? Doesn't it stand to reason, if she is dreaming other people's dreams, eventually a dream of her own would factor in? Perhaps the dream of nothingness was her own dream.

Mr. Akeru had mentioned the others stopped dreaming these kinds of dreams once they had learned all of the incidents related to this building. Lauren can't help but wonder, how many more dreams are there? Hopefully she will come to the end of them by the time she needs to go back to work!

A little bored and still tired, Lauren figures there is nothing else to do today. Maybe going back to sleep so she can get through these dreams is not such a bad idea.

Once again Lauren finds herself in bed, anxiously awaiting the next dream.

Virtual
Death

Virtual Death

Luke looks proudly at his creation. To some it may look like nothing more than an advanced video game; however, "creation" is a better term for it. For you see, it truly is a creation!

The definition of creation is: The action or process of bringing something into existence. Or, the bringing of life into existence in the universe, especially when regarded as an act of God.

God, yes Luke does feel like God! Just as God, he will have the power over nature and human fortunes. He will be adored, admired and be an influential person. And like God, not only will he be able to give life but take it as well!

Luke looks lovingly at the program he created on the computer. The complicated design spread out over the computer screen in front of him is no different than the complication of DNA sequencing. In fact, Luke feels that he has surpassed DNA. For even God was not smart enough to put in random sequencing like Luke had done with his creation. Or perhaps He had? People die at random times, no different than what Luke plans on having his creation carry out.

Luke smiles at a different thought and wonders, what if God had put in random race scenarios? Could you imagine having a baby and it randomly is of a different race? More than likely that would have solved all the racial tensions we have today, and yet it is as if God wants the struggle to be real.

Luke thinks about all of the possibilities his program can have. If there is ever a day he feels the need to confess to his genius he will surely be called the greatest serial killer that ever lived. Luke thinks about how he would answer the inevitable question, why?

Because all his life gaming had been about destruction and the loss of life. His generation had grown up on the most realistic games any generation had seen. Through the massacres and battles, the dehumanization had been completed. The lack of real social interaction was replaced by virtual interaction. No one ever had to be their true self. Manners and grace had been replaced by emoji's. The touch of a real human is almost nonexistent.

Unlike most of his friends, Luke had moved out of his parents' basement by selling his programs to the gaming industry. It is great money and it gives him the opportunity to have a nice top floor apartment with a beautiful view overlooking the city.

The view is the only thing that interests Luke. He hardly ever leaves his apartment; take out is delivered on a daily basis. As for his family, they considered him a lost cause a long time ago. They are just thankful that Luke is self-sufficient and no longer a drain on them.

Luke first became obsessed with virtual reality when Nintendo came out with Virtual Boy. It was released in 1995 and was discontinued in 1996. Its design along with its marketing caused the new invention to fail.

Although easily creating new games for different systems is Luke's bread and butter, virtual reality is his passion. He had taken a long time perfecting his creation. Only recently had he finally finished his masterpiece.

The beauty of Luke's design is the program is compatible with all systems. When he presented his idea he could have demanded any amount of money. Money is not always the root of all evil. No, power is; and in his case the power is power of diversity.

After a long struggle with the legalities, Luke finally accomplished what he had intended. A program so state of the art that no matter what system you were faithful to, his program would be coveted by all.

Luke glances over at the boxes that were sent to him. In each one is a different system that is capable of handling his new gaming experience. Luke is pleased how each manufacture is handling the marketing. Nothing like Virtual Boy, it is being marketed to appease to all ages and genders. It will be the one game that everyone in the family will be fighting over, thus creating more sales so that everyone in the family, including mom and dad, will want one of their own.

The systems and game will be available for the public just in time for Christmas this year. Luke reaches over and picks up one of the more popular systems. Quickly he hooks it up and plops in the game he designed that comes with each purchase.

While the game is loading, Luke puts on the virtual glasses that is also his own patented prize and starts to do a series of button combinations. Something a true gamer would remember from back in the day when cheats were put in through a variation of hitting certain buttons in sequence. As soon as he hits the last combination, a friendly voice comes through the system, “Hello Creator, what game would you like to play today?”

Luke smiles at his success, “Bring up the race car.”

Luke finds himself in the seat of a car he has chosen and the game begins. All of his apartment surroundings disappear, in fact, he virtually drives the car right out of his apartment window and lands cleanly on the road below him.

His game is not only a race game but a way to see the world. He races down the highway only to turn off to enjoy the country scenery. The game allows him to go anywhere in the world without ever leaving his apartment. The game is so well designed you can actually get out of the car and walk around. The most amazing part of the game is Luke has figured out how to tap into the sensory part of the brain.

Because of his programming, if you get out of the car and walk up to a rose, your brain will trick you into thinking it is actually smelling a rose! This is where Luke had brought gaming to a whole new level. Not only did the visual give you a real sense of being a part of the game, but now smell will be a new sensory dimension no one has ever been able to use.

Once Luke had the incredible breakthrough of how to achieve such a feat, he of course created simple games that young children will enjoy. Then he created travel games that the older generation will enjoy, giving them the possibility of seeing places they missed out on earlier in their life.

More importantly, Luke’s application not only was an asset to gaming but to people with handicaps. People will feel like they are walking or running again, with a safety feature that will allow them to do only as much as their body can handle.

This was all accomplished by simply tapping into the sensory part of the brain that makes you feel, smell, and yes, even taste the things around you. Once Luke had found the key to tapping into the sensory part of the brain, all the senses became easily obtainable, although taste is a little tricky, especially if a person tries something they had never tasted before. And yet, even then, the brain will try and find something compatible to make it work.

Honestly, it is a page taken out of the Matrix. However, this is an individual choice. Luke likes to see it as an enhancement to life for those who wish to travel but have no desire to have human contact.

Of course the applications are endless and Luke is compared to a god in the gaming industry. All the challenges of gaming have been solved with his program. However, as God can create, He can destroy as well.

For Luke that is the ultimate gaming experience, to randomly chose anyone in the world to become his pawn. His toy, his trophy. More importantly, to be able to commit the perfect murder. Not only will Luke be able to actually kill, but he will be able to feel and smell the death. All the advantages of murder without the mess or the risk. This is the reason Luke had insisted on his program being launched on all systems. The murders will be random, without a trace.

For you see, when Luke discovered how to tap into the sensory part of the brain he realized it left an actual print on the system. If you are playing online with another person, their system automatically stores that print of your mind.

His poor gaming partner, Aaron, is how Luke discovered the print. Aaron used to beta test all of his games. In the early stages of the virtual game, he had only been concentrating on the sensory applications. However, never in a million years did he think that while playing the game, the mind would store not only the game itself but submit a print allowing accessibility to the mind at a later time.

One day Aaron and Luke had been playing the new game trying to discover any bugs. Aaron, not having any food in the house, decided to go out for something to eat. Annoyed, Luke agreed to wait and play more once Aaron came back home.

While Luke is waiting for Aaron to return, he realizes he can actually see Aaron walking to the store even though he doesn't have his headset on. For that matter, Aaron had turned his system off before leaving the house. How is this possible? Anxiously Luke speaks into the mike, "Aaron, can you hear me?"

Shocked, Aaron stops in the middle of the sidewalk and looks around, "Luke, where are you?"

Luke gasps, "I think I am inside your mind!"

Aaron begins to get nervous, "How can that be?"

Luke makes some notations as he watches the program running, "Aaron, it feels as if I am right next to you walking."

Luke takes a deep breath in through his nose and is happy with what he smells, "We are close to a pizza parlor, are we not?"

Aaron quickly answers, "Oh my God, yes! It is where I am going for lunch!"

Luke shakes his head, "I had pizza yesterday, let's go get some Chinese instead!"

Aaron finds himself changing directions, "That is weird!"

Luke needs to know, "What is it?"

Aaron tries to stop himself from walking but his mind is controlling his actions, "Because you want to have Chinese, my mind is making me walk to the Chinese restaurant. I have tried to stop walking but my brain will not allow it."

Aaron looks around nervously, "This is not good Luke, please just leave me alone until after lunch. Then we will talk about it when I get home."

Luke is frustrated, "Are you kidding me? This is a major breakthrough!"

Aaron starts shaking his head, "No dude, I don't like this! Please just get out of my head!"

Luke has always had to be careful with Aaron. Although long time gaming partners, in the back of Luke's mind he was worried that one day Aaron would sell him out, or worse, spill his secrets and this is too good of a secret to have others knowing.

Luke sees a bus coming and casually says, "Aaron, I think you need to step in front of that bus."

Shocked, Aaron suddenly has tears coming down his eyes, "No Luke, please! I will do anything you want, just please don't do this!"

As hard as he tries, Aaron can't stop his body obeying his mind. The witnesses later said that Aaron screamed over and over, "Please don't do this!" as he casually walked in front of the bus.

During Aaron's death, Luke had gotten such a high. Fortunately he did not feel what Aaron felt, but he was as close to death as a person could be. The sights, the smells and yes even the coppery taste of blood, all a fantastic experience!

After Aaron's death, Luke had feverishly worked on the program with a new agenda in mind. Not only was he able to perfect the experience he had with Aaron but Luke began to put in random sequencing.

The idea is for Luke's game to interact at will. It will select a random player online, then it will use a sequence he had installed for a particular death and initiate the idea into the player's mind. This gave the game a random choice all over the world, enabling Luke's game to kill without being detected. Luke had spent countless hours figuring out different methods to kill people in a way that would never tie it to the game.

The next part was to put in backdoors. This would allow only Luke to tap into the random sequence that was going on and then experience the particular death the game had chosen. This gave Luke the power of killing someone without ever leaving his apartment.

The next challenge was to make sure no one else would be able to experience what Luke did with Aaron. He enabled the computer to have the experience but only to share it with him and no one else.

Luke was clever enough to make the system hide the print from people's brain. If you did not know it existed you would never look for it. And if by chance you were smart enough to look for it, the system would never give you access to it unless it knew you were the Creator, which is Luke.

Even Luke will not know when or where the computer will choose its next victim. Luke's only ability will be to tap into the experience. The computer will store the deaths as they happen for his eyes only, giving him the opportunity to experience the kills any time he wishes.

With his visor on, Luke looks around his apartment, not seeing the apartment but a beautiful grassy field instead. He looks up at the sun and feels the warmth of it radiating down on him. Yes, life is good.

Soon the game and visor will be distributed around the world and then the true gaming will begin. Luke has not been able to test out the game's most devious actions during beta testing due to not wanting to risk the final outcome.

Luke could not risk his beta testers being involved in any deaths due to the possibility of the results becoming public and damaging the bigger picture. No, even though patience had been the hardest thing he had ever had to endure, he knew in the end it would be well worth it. In fact, he is not the least bit worried about if the random sequence will work. He had worked with computers interacting with humans most his life and his sequencing is solid. Luke smiles sinisterly, no everything he had put into place is going to work flawlessly. He is God after all.

As Luke sits in front of his very lavish and technical devices, he is completely unaware that the entire apartment complex just had a slight power surge. Not enough to completely darken the complex, but enough to make everyone reset all of their digital clocks.

The power surge doesn't affect the game Luke is playing, other than a slight glitch which happened so quick he is not even sure if it happened. The one thing it did do is reset his original settings. What that means is that it took away his cloak of safety.

Still not realizing his cloak of safety is gone, Luke returns to the car in the game. Once inside he instructs, "Computer, take me home."

A robot voice answers him, "Ok player, what is the address?"

Luke instantly knows when the computer doesn't answer him with 'Creator' something is seriously wrong! In the time it takes his mind to tell his hands to take the visor off, the computer has already flashed a scene to him.

Luke flings the visor off and focuses his eyes to look around his apartment. Sure enough he notices his microwave's clock flashing to be set. Luke shakes his head, "No! It can't be! How could I be so stupid?"

When the power surge caused Luke's system to revert back to normal settings, the system went into its random mode. The problem is, even though Luke was playing online, no one else has the game! So therefore there is no one else to be randomly selected for the murder sequence!

Luke is the random player! In disbelief, Luke finds himself getting up from his chair. Over and over he screams, "No! No! No! I am your Creator! This is not supposed to happen to me!"

With no response or control over his body, Luke finds himself running towards the big window of his apartment. Luke's body impacts it hard enough to shatter the glass and he finds himself falling towards the sidewalk below.

The only satisfaction Luke has is that everyone will think his death is simply a suicide and his visor and game will still be released.

Even though no one will ever know, Luke will still be the greatest serial killer of all time. His computer game will continue to randomly pick his victims, no matter the race, religion, gender or age. And in the end, is that not exactly like God?

White Noise Stories Continued

Lauren finds herself struggling to wake up from the void. This time though, it seems as if someone is trying to help her. A voice that is neither male nor female whispers to her to keep trying, she must wake up!

Lauren concentrates on the voice and slowly begins to see a faint light. Focusing on the light, she is finally able to open her eyes.

Terrified, Lauren has had enough! What if one of these times she doesn't wake up? Scared, she forcefully turns off the sound machine and makes herself go into the living room.

The dog and baby are at it again but Lauren finds comfort in hearing normal sounds. Looking at the clock she is relieved to see it is only 8:00 in the morning, two hours from when she was up the first time.

Lauren fixes a light breakfast and thinks about what she should do. There has to be a way for her to find out if any of these dreams are truly coming from someone else.

Lauren thinks about the most recent dream. After breakfast Lauren decides to do a search on the internet to see if she can find any information on a game designer that jumped to his death. Shocked, she finds it! Not only is the guy described exactly like the guy in her dream but he jumped from this building!

Lauren sits there trembling. What she should do? She needs to tell someone. What if his invention really kills people randomly?

Lauren looks at the forum and all the comments people have written about him. The man was considered a genius. A God in his own right.

Lauren thinks about how he thought of himself as being God. How is she going to convince people he was a vindictive God?

Lauren quickly looks to see if his program has been released yet. Apparently there had been a hold put on the patent due to his death; however, the companies felt confident that by the next Christmas it will be released. Lauren scratches her head, how can she convince someone there is something wrong with the program if it has not even been released yet?

Suddenly Lauren's head feels as if it is going to explode, the noises from outside are too much! Not wanting to, she goes into her bedroom to turn the sound machine on.

By the time Lauren takes some headache medicine, she finds herself drawn to the bed. Maybe just another quick nap. She takes her phone to bed so she won't miss any calls.

All of the frantic thoughts of telling someone about that game system have disappeared, it is as if nothing but white noise is on her mind.

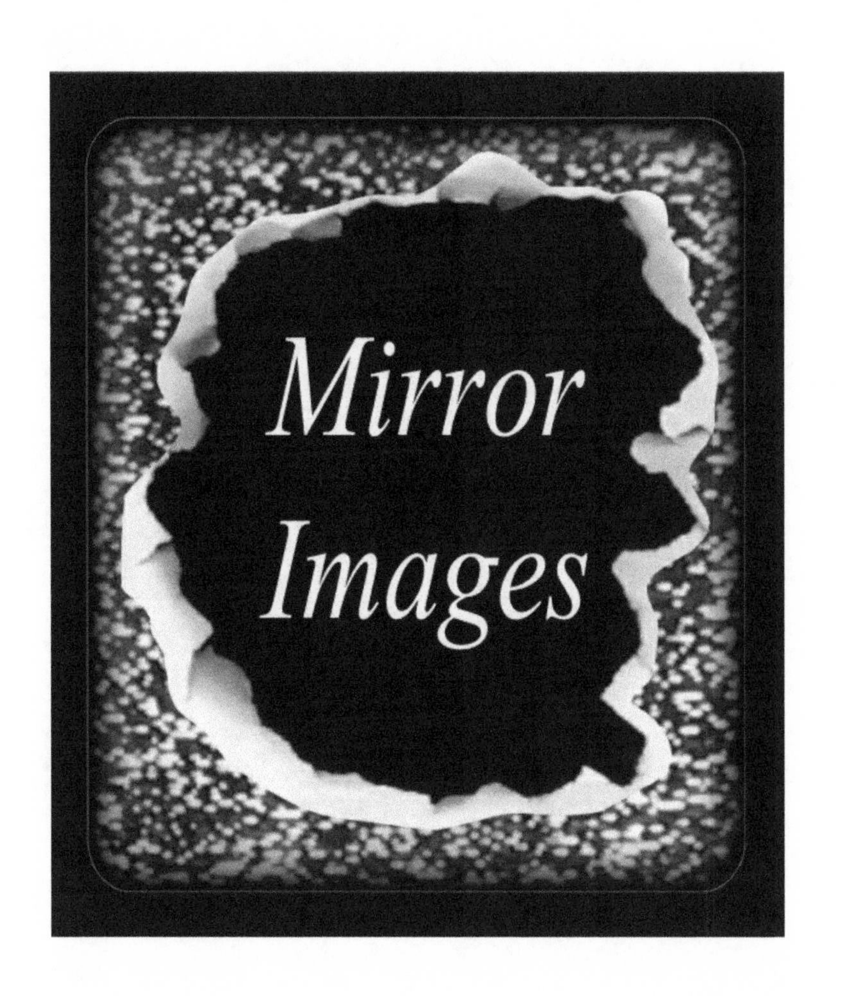
Mirror
Images

Mirror Images

Chapter One

Dr. Flynn comes to an apartment and stops before she enters. She looks at the two girls that are with her and sees their apre-hension, "Madison and Morgan, this is one of the apartments we have set up for your group therapy."

Dr. Flynn shows them her keys, "You will be given a key and will treat this place no different than your own apartments."

She is quite pleased with how her major project is coming along. When Dr. Flynn had heard this apartment complex would be available she had gone to the board and pitched her idea. The idea was simple, repair the apartment complex back to an apart-ment complex. The complex had a major explosion and the city had shut the complex down to the public. The owners were desperate to get rid of it due to the many lawsuits that were filed against them. The actual cost to repair the building was far less than building a new complex.

It was a great location for the research Dr. Flynn and her associates were trying to accomplish. The idea being each floor is dedicated to a doctor who specializes in phobia's or disorders. Those doctor's patients would continue their therapy with individ-uals with the same phobias. Meanwhile, they will be given the chance to learn how to live in an apartment in the city while they work through their phobias. The top floor were apartments designated for the doctors to have a place to stay, if they wished, along with a conference room to have meetings with the board to discuss their progress.

The city had agreed to the project only if the doctors could prove none of the residents were dangerous to society. So as not to alarm nearby residents, the city allowed the project to remain undercover. No where on the apartment complex was it identified as a clinic. The apartment complex was simply reopened as an apartment complex with no vacancies.

With most of the residents receiving some sort of disability or government assistance, the apartment complex was able to fund itself. In fact, it was not long before the board members began to see a return on the investment. For the residents that were not qualified for disability or government help, the doctors had resources in finding jobs for those who could work. The apartments then would be pro-rated based on what that individual would earn.

Dr. Flynn had certainly done her research before tackling such a project. With everything running smoothly, she could not be more pleased. Although in the beginning the project had taken a lot of time away from her own research, she is finally settled in enough to concentrate on her work.

Madison and Morgan are the last twins to fill the apartments on Dr. Flynn's floor. Her work involved twins that are in fear of their twins. Extreme cases where a twin is dominant over the other twin.

Dr. Flynn looks at Morgan as she nervously twirls her hair, "Morgan, there is nothing to worry about. Inside you will meet five sets of twins that have similar issues as you and Madison have."

Without even giving Morgan a chance to reply, Madison speaks up, "She will be fine! I don't even know why we are here!"

Dr. Flynn clears her throat, "Because Madison, it is a requirement the courts decided on after your little episode."

Fortunately for Dr. Flynn, she had been able to find twins that had juvenial records that were sealed. This allowed her to fly under the radar with the city when it came to the possiblity of the twins being a threat to society.

Normally they would have had to be detained in a lock down environment; however, Dr. Flynn had every intention of showing in her research that this is an unneccessary process.

Madison rolls her eyes, "So you say, and yet that situation happened several years ago. It was not until you showed up that miraculously this order had been put in place."

Dr. Flynn sighs, "As I told you before, the ruling had never been enforced. Once discovered, the court rectified it and then notified me."

The truth is, Dr. Flynn has a nice inside track with a friend of hers, Josh, that works with juvenial cases. Not only believing in her work but also enjoying the benefits, Josh has been instrumental in tracking down twins with juvenial offenses.

Having access to records that are sealed, Josh was able to get a list of twins for Dr. Flynn's research. In each case, he hacked into the court rulings adding the requirement that the twins fulfill a two year program of living in an apartment-like setting, overseen by the care of Dr. Flynn. This kept the city from knowing her patients had a record because they were sealed, plus it gave her the exact requirements she needed for her research. In each case, the twins were presented with legal looking documents which were convincing enough to look like they had no other choice but abide by the ruling.

With no way for officials or even the board members to question the list of Dr. Flynn's tenants, she was in the clear to do her research.

Dr. Flynn ignores Madison and puts her attention on Morgan, "Morgan, how do you feel about this situation?"

Morgan barely speaks above a whisper, "Honestly, I am nervous but a little excited."

Dr. Flynn smiles, "Of course you are! Living in your own apartment is supposed to be exciting! You can decorate it anyway you want!"

Madison glares at Morgan, "Sure, you say that now, but I don't even give you a day and you will be screaming for my company."

Even though Dr. Flynn is annoyed with Madison she has to agree, "You both will feel a bit of anxiety due to your separation but that is where group therapy will help. Come on, let's go inside and meet the others."

Chapter Two

Dr. Flynn enters the room with the twins. All the other twins are already there and seated in a circle of chairs. She smiles, "Good morning everyone!"

Moans and groans with only a couple of answering good mornings greet her. Dr. Flynn doesn't let it bother her. It's par for the course.

Dr. Flynn stands in front of the circle, "I would like to introduce Madison and Morgan."

Madison looks out into the group with her head held high, "Hi everyone."

Madison can tell instantly who are the dominate twins by the ones who look her back in the eye and answer. The rest of them answer just like Morgan, with their eyes down and softly spoken.

Dr. Flynn motions for Madison and Morgan to take a seat. Both of them are surprised that the seats are separated, even positioned so that there can be no eye contact between the two of them.

Dr. Flynn sees their hesitation and smiles, "Madison and Morgan you will see that our twins here are all separated. A simple step in getting you prepared to live lives on your own."

Dr. Flynn clears her throat, "Since Madison and Morgan are new to the program, I will review the goal the court has in mind."

Madison looks around and notices the dominate twins roll their eyes; however, the submissive twins seem to hang onto every word the dear doctor is saying. Pathetic!

Dr. Flynn watches Madison closely as she evaluates the other twins. Already she has seen a connection with not only the submissive twins among each other but the dominate twins as well. Now that she has a total of six sets of twins it will be interesting to see if any of the dominate twins become friends with any of the submissive twins. She highly doubts it.

She begins, "Each one of you are here today due to a crime you committed during your juvenile years. So, if anything, that should put all of you on the same playing field."

Dr. Flynn looks out into the room towards the submissive twins, "Unfortunately, some of you were nothing more than accomplices. In my opinion, when the court decided to give you all the same amount of time to serve, it was unfair."

Dr. Flynn wonders, "Is it not frustrating for all of you to constantly be considered as the two of you being as one and not as an individual? How many here had parents who insisted that you dress alike?"

Everyone in the class moans and all of them hold up their hands. Dr. Flynn shakes her head sadly, "This is where I am afraid environment is one of the causes for your disorders."

Dr. Flynn sees some of them surprised at her use of the word disorder. She clarifies, "Yes, I said disorder. It is not uncommon for a set of twins under the age of three to have separation anxiety. However, after the age of three doctors have determined if there is separation anxiety then there is a disorder."

Dr. Flynn smiles encouragingly, "This should explain a lot to all of you. It should make you feel that perhaps not all of this is your fault."

Dr. Flynn has to ask, "How many of you remember one of your parents separating the two of you and spending time alone with you?"

Dr. Flynn is not surprised that no one raises their hands, "How did that make you feel? Did you ever crave to do something alone with one of your parents?"

Paige raises her hand, "I remember I wanted to learn how to play baseball. My father had played in the minors and I was fascinated by it. You would think because I was a girl was the reason he did not want to teach me."

Paige leans forward so she can glare at her sister Payton, "However, the excuse was always that since my sister Payton did not like to play it would not be fair to her."

Paige looks back frustrated at Dr. Flynn, "What about fair to me?"

Dr. Flynn agrees, "You are absolutely right Paige, it was not fair to you. How did this make you feel towards Payton?"

Paige sighs, "I resented her."

Dr. Flynn looks out to the group, "I am sure many of you have similar stories."

Dr. Flynn is curious, "Do any of you ever wonder how other sets of twins always seem to be so happy while you and your twin do nothing but fight?"

London speaks up, "I think those twins never had to deal with a nitwit like my sister Paris!"

All of the dominate twins laugh meanly as Dr. Flynn tries to calm them down, "Ok London, let me ask you this; did it ever cross your mind that perhaps the two of you are not balanced?"

Dr. Flynn goes back to her previous argument, "In this discussion, we are talking about environment. In all of your cases you were treated as one when in fact all of you are quite different from your twin."

Dr. Flynn sees their confusion, "Perhaps, with the balanced twins they are more mirror images than simply in looks. There is a balance on the inside that you may not have with your twin."

Chloe chuckles, "Are you trying to say we are "Abby Normal" doc?"

Zoe, Chloe's twin whispers, "Chloe, must you?"

Chloe looks around at the other dominant twins for support, "What? It was funny!"

The dominant twins laugh in agreement and Dr. Flynn can't help but laugh herself, "No Zoe, it is ok. Chloe is right, it was funny."

Dr. Flynn knows it will be easy to gain the submissive twins' trust; however, she will have to tread lightly with the dominant twins. "I want group not only to be informative but interactive as well. In fact, I am very pleased at how many of you have spoken up."

Dr. Flynn smiles, "Madison and Morgan, you have only two sets left that you have not heard from. That would be Faith and Grace along with Mia and Sophia."

Madison smirks, "I feel like we are in a rhyming class."

Dr. Flynn can see Madison is really going to be her problem child, "I think even your names go back to the environment setting we were discussing. Although your parents may have thought it cute to name you your names how often did they confuse the names?"

Mia speaks up, "Honestly, I think to this day my parents would not know the difference between the two of us."

Faith is surprised, "Really? Our parents always knew the difference, they tended to favor their little Gracey."

Dr. Flynn is a little surprised too, "Mia, you really don't think your parents can tell you apart?"

Mia nods, "We had nannys raise us. We were only allowed to speak when spoken to. Sophia and I made a pact to never let them know who was who, since they really never cared to know."

Dr. Flynn is saddened by this, especially since she herself would give anything to have children. "That must have been very tough on the two of you."

Mia answers in a strange emotionless way, "Not really, you find other ways to cope."

Chapter Three

After the group session Dr. Flynn gathers London and Paris along with Madison and Morgan to the side, "London and Paris, your rooms are next to Madison and Morgan. I wondered if you could show them around and make sure they get settled in?"

London looks at Madison, "Not a problem."

Paris smiles shly to Morgan, "Of course."

Dr. Flynn is pleased, "I knew I could count on you two, thank you! And by the way, I wanted to say how nice it was that your father provided computers for the group."

Dr. Flynn explains, "Their father gave everyone, including you two, console computers. London here networked it so the group can communicate among themselves. Although, remember you are not to have any contact with your twin other than during group."

London smiles innocently, "Of course."

Dr. Flynn is not as stupid as London, or for that matter Madison, may think. Out of all the twins, she knows all too well these two are going to be a problem; however, she wants them to think they are smarter. It will be easier for them to make mistakes.

Dr. Flynn looks at her watch, "Ok, I have a board meeting to attend. I will see you all tomorrow in group."

The girls wait until Dr. Flynn leaves before they speak. London glares over at Paris, "Speaking of which, why have you not responded to my requests?"

Paris cowers a little, "You know why, it is against the rules."

Before they continue, Madison interupts by putting a finger over her mouth. She then signals someone may be listening. London agrees and follows along with a change in subject, "Paris, it is not against the rules for me to request some of my clothes back!"

Paris nods, following along, "I am sorry, I thought you meant going to get ice cream like we used to. I do miss that."

London softens a little, "I know, I do too. Could you just bring the clothes tomorrow?"

Paris smiles, “Of course. Morgan, come with me. We will see the two of you tomorrow.”

London and Madison watch as they leave. London speaks up, “Before we leave, let me introduce you to the others.”

Madison is not surprised to see all of the submissive twins had already left, scurrying back to their safe place. She realizes this may not be such a bad set up after all. In fact, now that they are in numbers it may be even more fun torturing the submissive twins.

Morgan follows Paris to their apartments in silence. Finally Paris speaks up, “I heard you moving in last night. I was going to come over but I did not want to bother you.”

Morgan nods, “I would have liked that. I really did not have that much to move in. With the apartments already furnished, it was only a matter of putting my clothes and little personal items away.”

Morgan adds, “I noticed the computer in the bedroom, it is a very nice set up. Make sure to thank your father for me.”

Arriving at Morgan’s door, Morgan unlocks it and invites Paris in.

Paris clears her throat and nods, “Thank you, there is something I need to show you on the computer.”

Morgan chuckles a little, “I am sure there will be a lot you will need to show me. I am afraid I am not very good with computers.”

Paris smiles, “Our father is a software engineer. We grew up around computers, although, London knows more than I do.”

Morgan takes Paris into the bedroom and is surprised as she closes the door behind her. Paris walks over to the computer as she pulls something out of her purse.

With big eyes Paris puts her finger to her mouth and hands a note to Morgan. Paris begins to talk randomly about how nice the bedroom is while Morgan reads the note.

The note is simple, “As you know, there are camaras in the living room but not in the bedroom; however, I believe they listen in on us in the bedroom. Don’t use the computer. London has hacked in for them to know our every move. Only use it to deflect suspicion. I will be giving you a prepaid phone, all of us submissive twins have one. It is a way for us to communicate without anyone knowing. The phone numbers are already entered in for you and we only text. I will explain more later."

Morgan looks at Paris and nods as Paris hands her a phone. Keeping up the ruse Morgan answers, "Thank you, my mother actually made that bedspread by hand."

Paris motions to the computer, "Very nice. Ok, this is where to turn the computer on."

Morgan laughs, "Ok smartass, I am not that bad!"

Paris and Morgan go over the computer. Morgan likes Paris, an instant bond is made. In fact, for the first time in her life Morgan feels there is hope.

Not only is she meeting friends besides Madison, living in her own apartment, starting her first job, but it also seems as if the submissive twins had found a way to bond into a stronger force against the dominant twins.

Morgan had not planned on that, but is very anxious to see what her texts will entail later on.

Chapter Four

Later in the evening both Madison and Morgan are able to finally communicate freely among the twins similar to themselves. London had shown Madison the computer and the private emails they would be using.

Madison, ready for bed, sits at her computer and logs on to the account London had set up for her.

Instantly she sees someone typing, "Hi Madison!"

Madison can see it is London, "Hi."

Madison is not used to a program where you can see someone actually typing in real time.

London types, "I was hoping you would try this tonight, how do you like it?"

Madison replies, "It is going to take some getting used to, a little weird seeing you type your response."

London answers, "I know right? But, pretty cool! Though it is unforgiving if you make mistakes or if you want to change your mind about what you want to say. The damage is already done."

Madison had not thought of that, "Or seen in this case."

London smiles, "Exactly! The others will be joining us soon. I wanted to thank you for this afternoon. Usually I am so careful! Of course they would be listening in on us. Why else would Dr. Flynn be so comfortable in leaving us alone with our twins when she is so adament about us not having contact without supervision."

Madison is curious, "And yet, you don't think they can see our conversation now?"

London chuckles, "Oh, they have tried! Several attempts have been made to hack us but they have never seen anything like my father's firewall. I have to give him credit, he is good at what he does."

Madison looks around the room, "What about cameras?"

London shakes her head, "Against the law to have them in the bedroom and with them being fairly new they are trying desparately to abide by those rules."

Madison is still not sure, "What about this conversation? Will they not be able to pull it up later?"

London types, "The beauty of real time. Another one of my father's babies. You will notice the moment you reply my previous sentence is gone."

Madison is surprised she had not noticed that, "Oh shit, it is! What is the time delay if I don't answer?"

London is happy that Madison seems impressed, "Two minutes."

Madison begins to relax and feel comfortable in asking questions now, "Do you really believe a court ordered all of us to be here?"

London answers, "It is a little hard to believe, given the age that Faith and Hope are."

Madison thinks about it, "You are right! Supposedly we all have juvenile records. With them being quite a bit older, if there was a court order it probably would have been null."

London agrees, "I am in the process of hacking into Dr. Flynn's files. Soon, we will be able to know what her real research is and also have something on her in case we need it."

Madison is surprised, "You know enough about computers to do that?"

London smiles, "You have no idea. I have also tapped into our twins' computers. You will be able to see what Morgan is up to when you want."

Madison begins to feel back in control, "That is awesome! You don't think Paris will know you have hacked in?"

London shakes her head confidently, "Paris is nothing but a shadow! No worries there. Now go to this link and you will be able to see if Morgan is on her computer."

Madison types in the link and is surprised to see a similar computer screen pop up on her screen. It looks as if someone is playing a game. Madison types London back, "It looks like she is playing a game."

London nods, "Yea, the submissive ones love their games."

Meanwhile, as Morgan does sit at her computer randomly playing a game she is also receiving texts from Paris on her prepaid phone.

The first text had been for Morgan to get on the computer and pull up a game. Next, turn the volume up a little so that no one can hear her receiving texts.

Paris proceeds to text Morgan on how London has hacked all the computers and to mainly use the computer for games only. Not a problem since Morgan really doesn't like computers to begin with.

Paris continue texting, "London is currently trying to hack into Dr. Flynn's files. I have beat her to it. The most important file, London doesn't know about nor will be able to find. I removed it from Dr. Flynn's computer."

Morgan texts back her concern, "Won't Dr. Flynn realize it is missing?"

Paris texts, "It is not a file she uses and not a file she should have had on her computer to begin with."

Morgan is curious, "What is it?"

Paris answers, "It shows how she maniupulated all of our files by creating fake court rulings."

Morgan is not surprised, "Madison was right! She had a feeling that the good old doctor was lying about the court ruling!"

Paris is not concerned, "I think she did all of us submissive twins a favor. Without her, none of us would be living alone."

Morgan agrees, "You are right. I feel very fortunate because of Dr. Flynn. But if you are not unhappy with what Dr. Flynn did, why take the file?"

Paris sighs, "To make sure the dominate twins can't get to it and use it against her."

Morgan understands, "How did you get the file before London?"

Paris smiles, "London would never believe I was capable of hacking into Dr. Flynn's computer or, for that matter, know our computers are hacked. She took her time and I simply beat her to it."

Morgan commends her, "Smart girl. Is there anything else you have found in Dr. Flynn's files?"

Paris's smile fades, "I have, but I have not gone through all of it to understand it enough to tell you. Maybe after group tomorrow we can go out for dinner and talk in public?"

Morgan nods, "Sounds good, what about the other girls?"

Paris texts, "They are up to speed but, honestly, you seem to be much stronger than them. You are like me, you have a quiet strength. Unfortunately, we are going to have to teach the others to be the same."

Morgan is concerned, "Why?"

Paris finishes for the night, "From the looks of it, it may mean their very life!"

Chapter Five

Paris and Morgan sit in a quiet café as they discuss the group meeting, "Morgan what were your thoughts about today's session?"

Morgan teases her, "You sound a lot like Dr. Flynn!"

Paris doesn't crack a smile, "I am serious."

Morgan shrugs her shoulders, "It seemed a little strange. I mean, yesterday she is talking about how our environment could be the reason for our strained twin relationships. And yet today she is wondering if any of us knew of complications during the pregnancy."

Paris agrees, "It is sort of odd that all of us in the group had never had twins in the family history. Or for that matter, none of our parents were on fertility drugs."

Morgan looks at her suspiciously, "Were you able to read through Dr. Flynn's research and figure it out?"

Paris looks around before answering, "I did but it is so far out there I am not sure you will believe it."

Morgan feels her heart beat faster, "The point is, do you think your sister will believe it."

Paris nods, "I do and I have a feeling tonight they will try and communicate with us in a most unusual way."

Morgan is confused, "What do you mean?"

Paris sighs, "First of all, let me throw some things at you so it will prepare you."

Paris pulls out a notebook from her purse, "I wrote some notes down so I would get the facts right when I try and explain this."

Paris looks down, "Did you know that all the dominate twins in our group are left handed?"

Morgan is a little surprised, "Really? That's kind of unusual isn't it?"

Paris agrees, "It is. Left handed people are only found in 10.8% of the poplulation. It is more common in twins at 17%. However, 21% in identical twins."

Morgan thinks about it, "Technically, only one or maybe two of us should be left handed in our group."

Paris nods, "I think it may have been one of the requirements for the group Dr. Flynn chose."

Morgan takes a drink of water, "That makes sense, a controlled group."

Paris smiles, "Exactly!"

Morgan sighs, "Ok, a strange requirement. What else?"

Paris flips through her notes, "Dr. Flynn has a lot of information about the 'Vanishing Twin'."

Morgan gets a slight shiver, "Sounds a bit ominous, what does it mean?"

Paris reads from her notes, "Fetal resorption is when one fetus dies and the other fetus absorbs it or it is absorbed in the womb."

Suddenly Morgan wishes she had not eaten such a big dinner, "That is quite apetizing."

Paris agrees, "I know, but get this, it has been hypothesized that left handed individuals may be the survivors of mirror image identical twins."

Morgan is confused, "Are you saying we may have had another fetus in the womb with us?"

Paris shakes her head, "No, we are just concentrating on twins right now. Not multiple fetesus."

Morgan is still not following her, "All of us in the group survived fetal resorption?"

Paris brings up their ealier conversation, "Remember when Dr. Flynn asked if any of us had complications in the early stages of the pregnancies?"

Morgan thinks about it, "Yea, and some of us remember our mothers saying it was a difficult pregnancy but none of us really knew why."

Paris looks back down at her notes, "Ok, when it comes to fetal resportion most women don't even know they are carrying twins to begin with; after the birth of their child there is no evidence of another child."

Morgan takes the thought a step further, "I am sure with the help of modern technology that has changed."

Paris agrees, "With modern technology they are now able to save more babies."

Morgan wonders, "Do you think Dr. Flynn's research is to show that all of us submissive twins were suppose to be reabsorbed by the dominant twins?"

Paris shakes her head, "I wish that were the case, but for some reason Dr. Flynn's research takes a darker twist."

Morgan doesn't like the sound of this, "What do you mean darker twist?"

Paris is not quite sure how to explain, "Have you ever heard of a doppleganger?"

Morgan nods, "It is the German word for double walker."

Paris is impressed, "That is correct. Do you know the folk tale of the doppleganger?"

Morgan answers, "There are quite a few different ones. The one my grandmother told us about always had me the most afraid."

Paris is curious, "I take it your grandmother was German?"

Morgan smiles, "She was and very old school. Madison and I only met her once before she died."

Morgan thinks back, "Our mother flew us back to Germany with her when my grandmother became sick. Madison and I were ten. We only went one time to the hospital but I will never forget it."

Paris is curious, "Why? Because it was the first time you had to deal with death?"

Morgan is honest, "I suppose, but there was something else. Instead of being overjoyed to finally meet her granddaughters the woman was terrified!"

Paris is surprised, "Terrified, why?"

Morgan shrugs her shoulder, "I don't know, mother told us it had to be because of the drugs they had her on."

Paris asks a strange question, "Was Madison scared?"

Morgan thinks back, "Actually yes, it was probably the one and only time I had to comfort her."

Morgan proceeds, "Mother left us in the room to retrieve the doctor. As soon as she left, Grandmother settled down and motioned us to the bed."

Morgan sighs, “Her voice was nothing more than a whisper. She asked us if we knew what a doppleganger was. We had heard mother say it before but did not really know what it meant.”

Morgan can still remember the conversation clearly, “She then told us that dopplegangers were double walkers. Her belief was that a soul can call on a doppleganger if it knows it is going to die before its time.”

Morgan can see the confusion on Paris’s face, “The soul would try and place the doppleganger in its place to fool the hand of death.”

Now it is Paris’s turn to have chills come over her, “What if the death doesn’t happen?”

Morgan is surprised by the question, “I do remember her saying right before the doctor came in that the two could not exist. One would have to die because they would have no soul. They would be nothing more than an empty husk.”

Chapter Six

In a restaurant not far from Paris and Morgan, London and Madison go over what London was able to hack from Dr. Flynn's files. Their conversation is very similar to Paris and Morgan.

London sighs, "I don't know if I can believe all of this weird speculation, what about you?"

Madison thinks about it, "Actually, I think it makes a lot of sense. Don't you ever feel like you are not complete? In fact, have you and Paris ever discussed one of you dying so the other one can live?"

London looks down at her notes, "Funny you should say that. In Dr. Flynn's notes there is a well known case called the 'Silent Twins'."

London explains, "The twins were June and Jennifer Gibbons, they grew up in Whales. They communicated only among themselves."

Madison thinks about their group, "A lot like Chloe and Zoe, remember they said they only communicated among themselves to keep their parents from telling them apart."

London nods, "Yes. But these two, June and Jennifer, took it to the extreme. They had their own language no one could understand but themselves."

London continues, "They were bullied in school and finally sent to separate boarding schools; however, that only made them go into a catonic state."

London glances down in her notes, "They were united only to be hospitalized for twelve years after an act of arson."

Madison raises her eyebrows, "And we thought we have it bad."

London smiles, "I know, right? Anyway, while in the hospital they started believing it was necessary for one twin to die."

Madison is curious, "Which one?"

London answers, "Jennifer agreed to be the sacrifice. Now, this is where it gets strange. After being transferred, Jennifer could not be roused. She had died of a sudden inflamation of the heart. No evidence of drugs or poison was found and to this day it remains a mystery."

Madison's eyes sparkle, "What happened to June after that?"

London shrugs her shoulders, "She went back to her home town and functioned as a normal person."

Madison sits back and looks around the restaurant, "I wonder how she did it?"

London takes a sip of her drink, "I think Dr. Flynn may have some speculation on that as well."

Madison sits up, "Really? Do tell!"

London is enjoying Madison's enthusiasm, "I am afraid it's another weird speculation, but one I am sure you may embrace."

Madison is hanging on to every word London is saying, "Go on."

London explains, "It has to do with mirrors. Dr. Flynn speculates that perhaps dopplegangers can use mirrors to travel. Her thinking is since they are from another dimension, a mirror could be used as a portal for them."

Madison's mind races, "Maybe that is how June killed Jennifer, through the mirror's reflection?"

London has to agree, "It sort of makes sense, since we seem to be a mirror image of our twin."

London reads from her notes, "Dr. Flynn had some interesting notes about mirrors. It seems many ancient cultures believed if a mirror was present in the room where a person died, their spirit could become trapped in the mirror."

Madison nods, "That is why they started covering the mirrors."

London continues, "Mirrors have also been viewed as portals to other realms, particularly the spirit realm. It is said that shadow people and demons use mirrors to freely enter and exit rooms."

Madison taps her fingers on the table, "This is all so very interesting!"

London agrees, "It is. Going back to ancient times, mirrors were used to scry, a way to see distant places, people and the future."

London glances back at her notes, "In the Asian art of feng shui and interior design, mirrors may extend space far beyond their physical depth in this reality."

Madison recaps what they have learned so far, "Let me get this straight. Dr. Flynn thinks that during the early stages of pregnancy there was only one fetus. This fetus foresaw its death and called on a doppleganger."

London nods as Madison continues, "For whatever reason, the death was not carried out. The doppleganger remains as a mirror image twin."

London adds, "And like anyone born, the doppleganger is born with no knowledge of its previous existance."

Madison agrees, "And yet, knows or feels not complete unless the other twin dies."

Madison finishes up, "To finish what should have happened the doppleganger could theoritically travel through a mirror to perhaps convince the other twin to die."

London nods, "And have the perfect alibi!"

Madison is excited, "When do we try it out?"

London looks back at her notes, "Dr. Flynn has speculated on that as well. It looks like three AM would be our strongest chance."

Madison is surprised, "Not at midnight?"

London shakes her head, "No, three AM is the demon hour. The number three representing many things such as the Holy Trinity; the number of man because he is composed of a body, soul and spirit; the three acts of existence: birth, life and death."

London gives some other examples, "For Egyptians, three is the number of elements: sky, earth and duat which is a zone surrounding intermediate worlds between the earth and celestial spirits."

London adds, "And of course, three AM is supposed to be exactly twelve hours when Jesus Christ died and his spirit descended into hell to preach to the spirits in prison until the third day. Three AM is the exact opposite when the evil spirits of hell are set free."

London finishes up, "Three AM is also known to be the darkest time of night. Darkness is power to demons and evil spirits."

Madison is impressed, "Then tonight at three AM we should try it out and see if it works!"

London agrees, "Yes, I think all of us should test the water; however, I think Faith may be able to push the envelope harder than any of us."

Madison is curious, "Why is that?"

London explains, "Grace has not been doing well with the separation. Since they are older, Grace has depended on Faith a lot longer than our twins have."

Madison understands, "Yea, I do remember that Faith thought Grace would crack soon. Grace is not happy interacting at work or socially. She has been a shadow for too long to even know how to interact without Faith."

London smiles, "I will explain everything to Grace. Do you mind contacting the others and getting them on board?"

Madison's eyes twinkle, "I look forward to it!"

Chapter Seven

After going over all of Dr. Flynn's research Morgan and Paris's conversation continues back at the café, "Paris, do you really think our twins will be contacting us through a mirror tonight?"

Paris nods sadly, "I do. If I can come up with that conclusion by the information I hacked from Dr. Flynn, I know it is only a matter of time for London to come up with the same."

Morgan looks defeated, "What are we to do?"

Paris smiles, "I have it already figured out and it will be in place tomorrow." She then explains what her plan is and how they will carry it out.

Morgan is surprised, "Tomorrow? But won't that be too late?"

Paris sighs, "It was the best I could do. There was not enough time to have it all done by today."

Morgan gives it some thought, "We will have to make sure all the submissive twins understand what is going on and to be on the look out."

Paris agrees, "Yes, the only one I am concerned about is Grace. She has become so withdrawn I am not sure if telling her this she will fight against it or simply embrace it."

Morgan pulls her phone out and types something. Paris is curious, "What are you trying to find out?"

Morgan waits for the answer, "I am curious if people can really die from fear."

Paris is now curious too, "What does it say?"

Morgan reads to her, "When a person is faced with fear they develop a fight-or-flight scenario. The rush of adrenaline is the involuntary response given."

Morgan continues, "A person will experience rapid heart rate, dilated pupils and increased blood flow to the muscles. Unfortunately, increased levels of adrenaline can damage the heart."

Paris thinks back to the research Dr. Flynn did on the Silent Twins and how Jennifer died of an enlarged heart. "Maybe that was the cause of death for Jennifer."

Morgan nods, "That idea is what made me look it up."

Paris agrees, "And of course with us being more submissive it would be easier for them to literally scare us to death."

Morgan puts her phone down, "I agree. I think the idea you have is brilliant, but how will we all survive until tomorrow? Should we cover our mirrors tonight?"

Paris forcefully says, "No! If we do that they will know we are on to them. We must make them feel they are in control until our plan is ready."

Morgan looks at her watch, "The other girls plan on meeting us for ice cream. We will tell them everything we know and what we plan on doing about it."

Morgan wonders, "Should we involve Dr. Flynn in any of this?"

Paris shakes her head, "No, I don't plan on being prodded and poked the rest of my life for research. Do you?"

Morgan sighs, "No, I would rather not."

Morgan and Paris pay their bill and go to the ice cream shop to meet with the others. Having just gone over all the information, it is easy for them to fill the rest of the girls in.

Zoe is most shocked about the June and Jennifer case, "You know Chloe is always teasing me that I should die so that she could become less burdened by me."

Throughout their conversation Paris has been keeping a close eye on Grace, "What about you Grace, has Faith said something like that to you?"

Grace doesn't even raise her head to answer, "I guess."

Morgan pats Grace on the hand, "Grace honey, you are not alone. You have us now and we will help you not be a shadow anymore."

Grace looks up and smiles; however, deep down she is so tired. The new apartment, the new job, it was all so overwhelming to her. Honestly, she missed the days when Faith took over and did everything.

The girls continue their conversation, confident that Grace is on board. Paris and Morgan agreed not tell the rest of the girls their plan on how they are going to protect themselves in case one of them mentions it to their twin before they can get it in place.

Both Paris and Morgan are hoping that all of this is nothing more than speculation. Only if anything truly happens are they willing to show their hand.

In fact, some of the girls are skeptical and rightfully so. It all is a lot to comprehend. They were stepping into a world of the unknown. Did this world really exist, and more importantly, were they really a part of it?

Chapter Eight

At three AM all of the dominant twins stand in their own bathroom looking intently into the mirror. None of them have a clue about how this is going to work; however, for some reason it seems natural. Each one of them find themselves looking into a mirror which is showing them a reflection of a bathroom that is different than their own.

All of them realize it must be the bathroom of their submissive twin. In an unnatural unison, they each call out to their twin in a soft haunting voice in hopes of waking the submissive twins.

Each submissive twin is awoken by the voice of their dominant twin coming from their bathroom. Even though each one of the submissive twins is prepared for this, knowing about the possiblity and actually dealing with the reality are two different things.

One by one the submissive twins hesitantly go to the bathroom. Paris and Morgan had insisted they all act terrified if there is contact; wasted words because all of them already are terrified.

Pleasantly surprised, the dominate twins finally see their submissive twins look quizically into the mirrors. To begin with, the dominate twins remain silent and mimic the movements of the submissive twins in the mirror. Growing bored they all finally reveal themselves. The reaction of the submissive twins gives the dominant twins confidence as they proceed to taunt and tease them.

Faith is far more meaner to Grace than the rest of them. Faith taunts Grace in the mirror, "You really thought you could get rid of me? How can you? Even when you look in the mirror you can't get away from me. Even your reflection has forsaken you!"

Faith can see Grace is truly terrified, "You are nothing but a shadow. You have always been a shadow and no matter what the good Dr. Flynn has in store for us, you know you will always be nothing more than a shadow."

Grace looks terrified at the reflection talking to her from the mirror. Slowly she begins to nod her head in agreement, "You are right. I can't do this any more!"

Faith is loving the power she holds over her sister, "We have talked several times of your sacrifice to me. Do you not think it is about time for you to follow through?"

Grace, big eyed, nods, "Yes, but how?"

Faith is a little annoyed that Grace is so easily maniupulated. She doesn't need her to be submissive now, but terrified instead. She suddenly gets mad and feels her eyes begin to burn.

Grace is shocked that Faith's eyes are burning red! What is this? This can't be real, this has to be a dream. Nothing more than a dream!

Faith can see that Grace is now physically scared. Feeding on that fear Faith finds herself reaching out of the mirror. Her mirror reflection arms easily reaching out towards Grace's body.

Grace stands there frozen with fear, her body pumping large amounts of adrenaline. And yet, her fight-or-flight response doesn't kick in.

Faith's arms extend out of the mirror and easily into Grace's body. Strangely, Faith can wrap her hand around Grace's fast beating heart.

Grace endures an icy pain she has never felt in her life. The pain is intense as Grace cries out, "Please! Make it stop!"

Faith's smile is nothing more than pure evil as she answers, "As you wish." Faith clamps down on Grace's heart and then releases it quickly.

The heart fills up too quickly with blood and Grace immediately collapses onto the floor.

Faith finds herself suddenly back in her own bathroom looking at her image in the mirror. Or is it? Faith is surprised to see her mirror image has a single tear sliding down her face whereas when she feels her face it is dry.

****

Early the next morning Paris decides to check on Grace. After knocking several times and not receiving an answer Paris decides to try the door. She is surprised it is unlocked.

Paris calls out quietly, “Grace, are you here?”

She proceeds to go towards the bedroom calling out for Grace, still no answer.

Paris is shocked to see poor Grace lying on the floor of her bathroom. It is apparent that Grace is dead. Holding onto her emotions, she quickly finds Grace’s prepaid phone and puts it in her purse.

Then, with little effort, Paris begins to scream over and over, the thing she had stopped herself from doing until she had found the phone.

It was bad enough to see Grace lying motionless on the floor with a slight hue of blue. However, it was far worse seeing her face twisted into such a horrified image.

There is no doubt in Paris’s mind that Faith had been the cause of it. Within minutes, men in lab coats arrive at Grace’s apartment. Paris realizes she is in for a long day.

Chapter Nine

At a local bar, the remaining submissive twins meet to discuss what had happened to each of them last night.

All of their stories were similar. Their twin's voice coming from the bathroom woke them. At first none of them were sure the reflection in the mirror was their own. After being mimicked, the reflection revealed itself as their dominant twin. Terrified, they interacted with the image as Madison had suggested. Each one of them denied the idea of the reflection being their twin out loud and that they merely were sleepwalking. They were able to walk away and turn the light off. Even though the reflection in the mirror kept calling out to them, they ignored it and it eventually went away.

Madison looks sadly down at her drink, "Poor Grace, I guess she did not have the strength to walk away."

Zoe agrees, "I have to say it was hard for me to walk away."

Everyone in the group agrees. Madison is curious, "Paris, what did you and Dr. Flynn talk about?"

Paris sighs, "I only told her that I was supposed to meet Grace for breakfast before work. I never mentioned the mirror incident. Did any of you?"

All of them shake their head no. Madison commends Paris, "I have to give you credit, being in the right frame of mind to find Grace's prepaid phone. That would have raised a lot of questions that would have been hard to answer."

Paris agrees, "I know, in fact I hate to do this, but just in case our plan doesn't work tonight I think we should all get rid of our prepaid phones. If we need to get in touch with each other just use your regular phone and be careful what you say."

Madison agrees, "Good idea."

Payton speaks up, "Here, put them in my gym bag and I will make sure to get rid of them for us." Everyone hands Payton their phones.

Zoe speaks up, "The worker came by and installed mine. Did everyone else get theirs?" They all nod.

Madison speaks up, "I have to say again Paris, a brilliant idea!"

Sophia is a little concerned, "How will we explain them to Dr. Flynn?"

Paris smiles, "Nothing more than a beauty trick I used and all of you were curious about."

Madison smiles, "And of course as generous as you are, you got Daddy to get us all one."

Paris raises her glass, "To Daddy!"

They all drink to Daddy. Afterwards Payton has to ask, "If tonight goes as planned, what next?"

Paris looks around before answering. With a lowered voice she says, "There will have to be an investagation which will take time. However, none of us are going to want to stay in that complex if this happens the way we want."

Zoe wonders, "Where will we go? How will we have money to go anywhere? I am not sure Daddy will want to take care of all of us!"

Paris shakes her head, "He won't have to. With the information I have on Dr. Flynn we will have Daddy's awesome lawyer file a lawsuit and he will make sure we are more than compensated!"

Payton raises her glass, "To Grace, I wish you could have found enough strength from us to fight the evil. May you have peace now."

Sadly, they all raise their glass in agreement. Each one of them desperately hopes that Paris's plan will work. If not, who is to say if one by one they will become like Grace?

****

In a different bar all of the dominant twins are having their own discussion; however, their mood is more of a celebrative mood than a somber one.

London has to know, "How does it feel Faith? Do you feel any different?"

Faith nods, "I don't even know how to explain it. I actually feel whole. I woke up this morning with no regrets."

Chloe is amazed, “I think that was the thing I worry about the most, that I will have regrets.”

Faith understands, “I know, it is all new to me now. You are probably wondering if after the newness wears off I will begin to feel regret.”

Faith looks at them all, “I really don’t think so. It is weird and hard to explain. It is like your twin never existed, that everything is as it should have been.”

Faith has a hard time grasping the right words, “Like your twin is now you. You are one again.”

To anyone listening in on their conversation they would have surely been confused, but the rest of the dominant twins understand.

Paige is a little skeptical, “We have all revealed the same events that happened last night except for Faith. Grace did not convince herself that you were nothing more than her sleepwalking, like all the other’s confessed.”

London cuts in, “I think that is because Grace was far more dependent on Faith than any of ours.”

Chloe wonders, “Then how will we be able to get our twins to the state that Grace was in?”

Madison smiles, “I think it is going to be easier than you think. We all saw the fear in their eyes, only by a little resistance did they leave us last night.”

Madison explains, “I am confident that each night we continue this, it will be harder and harder for them to resist.”

London suddenly comes up with an idea, “What if Faith stays overnight with one of us? Then she can act like she is Grace, giving our twin even something more to be afraid of.”

Paige giggles, “I love it!”

London is encouraged, “Ok then, so we do exactly what we did last night. Faith, why don’t you stay with Chloe, Zoe seems to be the most vulnerable one.”

Madison is a little concerned, “What if the twins are talking among themselves about what happened last night or worse, talk to Dr. Flynn about it?”

London had thought about that, “I think they would be too embarrassed to talk to Dr. Flynn about it, remember each one of them tried to convince themselves they were merely sleep-walking."

Paige wonders, "And what about among themselves? I know right now they are all together."

Chloe pipes in, "I think that is for support over the death of Grace. I don't think our submissive twins are smart enough to figure this all out and if they do, who would believe them?"

Madison nods, "You are right, without us they can barely function. Before long we all will be able to function as one!"

London is curious, "I wonder if the twin takes our place back from where we came from?"

Faith had been giving that a lot of thought, especially after Grace's reflection showed up in her bathroom with the tear coming down, "I think they do. After Grace died I was back in my own bathroom. While looking at the mirror, I did not see my reflection, but the reflection of Grace."

Everyone is shocked. London has to ask, "How did you know it was her and not you?"

Faith lowers her voice, "A single tear came down, I checked my face and it was dry."

Paige becomes a little concerned, "Do you think she will haunt you through the mirror?"

Faith shakes her head no, "I was afraid of that but this morning it was my own reflection and it was throughout the day. I think it was only right after she died that Grace was able to show up."

Faith finishes up, "It was not until I saw her last reflection that afterwards I suddenly felt whole. I think I had finally consumed her as it was supposed to have been in the beginning."

London smiles, "Aw yes, the consumption! How delicious it is that we were to be the ones sacrificed to the hand of death and yet now we have turned the tables."

Everyone raises their drinks in anticipation for the beginning of consuming their own twin. In unison they clink their glasses and say, "To consumption!"

Chapter Ten

As before, all the twins find themselves in their bathrooms that night at 3:00 AM. The dominant twins feel confident from the night before; not one of them have a clue that the submissive twins had come up with their own plan.

The submissive twins tremble with fear of what they have to do and yet an excitement from the thought of finally being rid of their dominate twin overrides the fear. They had agreed to try and fulfill their plan in unison so that none of the dominant twins could be alerted. Each submissive twins had left their watch on the bathroom counter.

At 3:15 they had planned on finalizing their plan, although those fifteen minutes seemed to be an eternity. In fact, Zoe had thought she would not make it since both Chloe and Faith kept taunting her.

Faith of course was trying to portray herself as Grace and convince Zoe that it was the right thing to do. That the dominant twin is the one who should live while the submissive twin gives over her life to them. Fortunately, Zoe is smart enough to realize it is Faith pretending to be Grace and, although she is allowing Chloe and Faith to believe she is almost ready to give herself over, she is not prepared for the red glowing eyes coming from the both of them! Let alone their arms literally coming out of the mirror to embrace her. Although Zoe's fear is all encompassing, she has mind enough to look at her watch. Relieved, she sees 3:15. Thank God! Time to enact the plan.

Zoe prays this will work as she reaches up to a mirror that is on a hinge above her. Paris had the mirrors installed in all of the submissive twins' bathrooms; all but Grace's of course.

The dominant twins looking through the mirror had not been able to see the mirror above their submissive twins. Through clenched teeth Zoe yells out to both Chloe and Faith, "Go back to the hell from whence you came!"

All of the submissive twins take a step to the side and lower the mirror on the hinge. Now, instead of their twin in front of them, the dominant twins are looking at another mirror which is course bouncing off their mirror shows them an infinity of mirrors.

Realizing what they had done, the dominant twins scream and try to get back to their own bathroom. The submissive twins can hear their dominant twins screams fade as the portal begins to close for the morning hour.

Suddenly all of the submissive twins feel renewed. Stronger, more alive, and more importantly, finally whole! Knowing they all will have a very long day, none of them mind because they honestly feel as if they now will survive.

One by one it is discovered that the dominant twins are missing. A true mystery, especially when all of the tapes show that each twin had gone to bed the night before and had never left the apartment through the front door.

Of course being distraught over their missing twins, Paris's daddy put all of the submissive twins up in a hotel. As promised, Paris contacted her father's lawyer and supplied him with Dr. Flynn's file that proved she had forged their court documents. A lawsuit occurred shortly afterwards. With the lawsuit and the case of the missing twins, the city had no choice but to close the research apartment complex down.

The apartment complex was once again up for sale to the public. The submissive twins won their lawsuit and were set up for life. Dr. Flynn tried contacting them several times, desperate to know the true story of her failed research; however, all of the twins turned her down. None of them even like thinking about their twin, in fact it was almost as if they never had one.

Even the parents seemed relieved. The fact that the dominant twins were still missing doesn't seem to be an issue, but rather a relief to all involved.

Only one problem exists. To this day when they look into a mirror they of course see their mirror image staring back. All of them had changed their appearance so that the mirror image would look more like them but no matter what, none of them dare look at a mirror at three AM.

White Noise Stories Continued

After the dream, Lauren finds herself walking down hallways covered with mirrors. She reasons with herself that it is nothing more than a continuation of the previous dream. Why else would she not be seeing her reflection in these mirrors?

No, the mirrors only allow her to see reflections of others. Others crying out to her for help. Lauren can't help but feel their desperation and yet she knows no way to help them.

Lauren looks around for something to break the mirrors but the hallways are sterile and empty. She, not able to stand their pleas anymore, even tries to pound at the mirrors with her hands. Unfortunately, this only makes her hands become bloody, yet strangely enough the mirrors remain undamaged. The blood from her hands doesn't even leave a simple smudge.

Lauren continues to walk helplessly around trying to find a way back to her own reality. For the first time, she realizes she is barefoot when her feet come across something other than a smooth floor.

She looks down and sees something like a bread crumb trail. If she had not felt it with her feet, Lauren would have never noticed it. The trail is very faint and almost invisible. Following her gut instinct, she literally lets her feet do the walking. Sure enough, she comes to a mirror that is lit up slightly more than the others. Lauren touches the mirror and feels her hand easily slide through.

Lauren finds herself waking up in bed, flat on her back with her hands straight up. Small rivers of blood trail down each arm. She quickly jumps out of bed, trying not to get blood on anything. Once in the bathroom, she carefully runs her poor bloody hands under cold water. Both hands are swollen from the intense way she had tried beating at the mirrors in her dream.

Confused, Lauren carefully wraps both hands. Finished, she looks into the mirror and sees a woman she barely recognizes. Her hair has even more gray, and now her face is not as young and vibrant as it should be. Lauren begins to cry. Once she has composed herself she reaches for her watch to see what time it is. Her eyes suddenly dry up and become wide with fear. It is 3:15 AM.

Trying to convince herself none of this is real and all of it is in her imagination, Lauren forces herself to look back at the bathroom mirror. Terrified, she sees two women staring back at her. She screams loudly as one of the women begins to reach through the mirror. Suddenly a voice in her ear screams, "Grab your hand mirror now and use it!"

Without thinking, Lauren reaches for her hand mirror and flashes it towards the bathroom mirror. The two women in the main mirror scream, "No!"

Lauren can hear the word "No" seem to bounce from one area to another until finally she hears it no more. Without looking at the main mirror, she carefully smashes her hand mirror into the sink and quickly grabs a towel and covers the main mirror.

Exhausted, Lauren comes out of the bedroom and looks at the bed. Although the desire is so strong to return to bed, Lauren fights it. Instead, she goes over and turns the sound machine off. Taking it a further step, Lauren flips the damn thing over and takes the batteries out.

Grabbing her pillow, blanket, and phone, Lauren heads to the couch. The minute she gets situated she finds herself fast asleep. Fortunately, this time there are no dreams.

Lauren is woken by her phone. Groggily she answers the phone, "Hello?"

A concerned Roxi replies, "Lauren! Are you ok?"

Lauren sits up and tries to get her bearings, "A little run down, but I will be fine."

Roxi sighs, "I was hoping by now you would be better! I think it is time for you to make a doctor's appointment!"

Lauren has a hard time holding the phone since both her hands are wrapped up. She clumsily hits the speaker button and then starts taking off the wraps on her hands, "What time is it?"

Roxi answers, "It is after six."

Lauren sits up confused, "I thought we were not going to talk until Monday night?"

Roxi is surprised, "Honey, it IS Monday night!"

Now Lauren is the concerned one, "Wow! I have been asleep since yesterday!"

Roxi is envious, "Must be nice, I am exhausted! Mind trading places?"

Lauren's mind is still in a fog and it is hard for her to follow the conversation, "Roxi honey, if you don't mind, I need to go to the bathroom. Take a shower. Shake myself out of this and then I will call you. Is that alright?"

Roxi understands, "Not a problem, I have some running around to do myself. Why don't we meet up on Wednesday night and then we can get all caught up."

Lauren is relieved, "That sounds perfect, see you then!"

Lauren looks down at her hands and is confused; both of her hands are perfectly fine, not swollen, bruised or bloody.

Lauren sighs, her dreams are now becoming so real she is having a hard time knowing when she is dreaming and when she is not.

Lauren goes to the bathroom. As she sits there she sees the hand mirror in the sink is broken. Obviously, that happened. Chills come over her, or did it? Perhaps she had been sleep-walking and during the sleepwalking she had broken the hand mirror. She likes that idea much better than the alternative.

Convincing herself that is all that happened, Lauren stands and takes the towel down from the mirror. Again she is shocked at the reflection of herself staring back. How could this have happened so fast? Scared, Lauren quickly takes a shower and gets dressed. She has every intention of going to a walk in clinic.

Feeling exhausted from getting ready, Lauren shuffles off the elevator. She sees Mr. Akeru at his post. His concern is displayed openly, "Ms. Lauren it has been a while! How have you been?"

Lauren musters up a weak smile, "Not good Mr. Akeru. Not sure what I have, but I plan on going to the doctor now."

Mr. Akeru sighs, "A lot of what you have is going around. In fact, one of the tenants said she went to the doctor and wished she had not."

Lauren looks concerned, "Why is that?"

Mr. Akeru explains, "There were so many like her at the doctor's she felt by going it made her have a relapse. Nothing the doctor gave her really helped. Time seems to be the only real cure."

Lauren begins to wonder if she even has the strength now to get to the doctor's office. Once she is there she will have to wait to see him, then make her way to a pharmacy and then home. Just thinking about it makes her tired.

Lauren hesitates, "Maybe I should wait."

Mr. Akeru agrees, "I think you should, or if anything, wait until someone can go with you."

Lauren suddenly feels a strong need to go back to bed, "I think you are right. Thank you Mr. Akeru."

Mr. Akeru smiles warmly, "You are welcome Ms. Lauren, feel better!"

Lauren rides the elevator up thinking. Wonder how Mr. Akeru knew she was going alone. Of course, it looked pretty obvious, but then again she could have been meeting someone there. Lauren thinks about Mr. Akeru. Ever since she met him, there was something about him she could not put her finger on. Nothing about him so much, but about his name. Akeru. Lauren is sure she had heard that name before, but where? Such a strange name.

Once Lauren is in her apartment she goes straight to her iPad and looks up Akeru. She now remembers as she reads what is in front of her. Of course! A class she took in college about Egyptian history. Aker was an earth god who was more or less a gatekeeper to the underworld. In fact, Akeru is the plural version of primeval deities more ancient than Geb.

Lauren closes her iPad in deep thought. What does this mean? Is she really trying to say that the little old man that is her doorman is a primeval gatekeeper deity? She is too exhausted to argue with herself and simply allows her mind to explore the impossible. What better way for a deity to openly carry out its duty? Trapping souls in this huge apartment complex would make for an easy task. Take it a step further, the souls trapped here could be dreaming. Dreams that she is experiencing herself! She vaguely remembers that Mr. Akeru was even in one of her dreams, almost as a clue.

Suddenly Lauren realizes that she hears her sound machine is on. She walks to the bedroom cautiously.

Lauren knows for a fact that not only had she turned the sound machine off but took the batteries out as well! And yet, here it is on! The white noise begins to have its effect on her even before she can make herself turn it off.

Her eyes become too heavy to bear and she crawls into bed without undressing. Lauren promises herself she will do something about all of this when she wakes up.

End
of the
Line

End of the Line

You find yourself waiting in line for a train. You are not sure how you got there or where you are going. There is a large crowd pushing to get on; many are anxious and excited but you are not, you take your time.

You look around and see all the seats are taken. A flash back to when you rode the school bus where there were no seats available and no one would let you sit with them.

You move from car to car. Finally towards the end you find cars of people standing, similar to a subway. You find an empty handle and grab it. As soon as you do the train starts to move.

You want to ask where the train is going but it is unusually quiet and no one will make eye contact with you. You look around to get your bearings.

There are large windows to see outside and you can see clearly things passing you by. At first, it is the countryside and the train slows as if to let you see more. You see a field of puppies and kittens, they look vaguely familiar.

Strangely, they grow from kittens and puppies to full size instantly. Once full size they look directly into your eyes before they disappear. They are all of the pets you have had during your life. Your heart breaks with each passing look, for you know you will never see that look again.

Your latest pet looks around as if not able to see you; however, in the last moment they lock eyes with yours. You see a combination of fear and sadness which leaves you with a great sense of guilt.

Reeling from the heartache you try to close your eyes but you can't, you are forced to keep them open. You look around and see others in immense sadness as well.

Sighing you look back out the window, the field is gone. This time you see a small town beginning to appear, it is the town you grew up in. A sense of hope begins to creep up on you.

Not wanting to turn your eyes from the window that surely will give you comfort, a persistent need fills you to look forward.

In front of you a large screen lowers. It shows you the cars in front of you with the people sitting down. You are allowed to see their reaction to outside first, before you have your own.

Every one of them is happy and joyful. They wave to their friends and neighbors. The friends and neighbors wave back. Some come on the train and sit for a while, embracing them, while the ones outside the train continue to laugh, wave and talk to them through the window.

The train slowly moves forward so that it is your turn. You see faces that you have not seen in many years and though you are happy to see them, they act as if they don't know you. Some who you thought of as your closest friends stand there and whisper about you, encouraging others to laugh at you instead of with you.

As with the emotion of sadness and guilt from your lost pets, this time the pain brings along new emotions; betrayal and humiliation.

The raw emotions leave you broken, anxious and yet so tired. Not knowing if you can deal with it, the train moves forward to a nearby station. You look at the large screen in front of you and watch the seated people react once again.

You can tell this is a stop for family. It is one big happy family reunion. Grandparents coming on the train, embracing their loved ones while other family members stay outside. You can literally see the love radiating warmth from them.

The time comes for your turn and you see your family on the platform. They sit there bored and uninterested. Your grandparents come on the train but walk right by you. A coldness like you have never felt before in your life envelopes you.

You look frantically back out at the platform for some sort of love that may warm you but the platform is empty. This time the emotion of abandonment not only adds to the other emotions but intensifies them.

The train slowly moves on but begins to pick up speed. The things you loved such as cars, games, even movies and books flash by you. They are nothing but empty memories. Nothing tangible gives you comfort or warmth now.

The big screen in front of you begins to show you that the train is emptying. You are not sure where the people have gone but you desperately want to move to where they were sitting; however, the train is moving too fast now.

Not wanting to, you look out your window because you can't resist. You see images now of what you know to be life continuing on without you.

You see your children moving easily on with their life. Embracing the things that would hurt you the most. A sense of disappointment and failure floods over you.

The pain is unbearable and yet there is hope of one. One that may have that flicker of heat and love you so desperately crave and need.

You finally see the love of your life and look! There IS a flame for you that burns brightly over his head.

Your shattered heart knows that the heat from that flame will mend all the broken pieces. You yearn for that flame and even try to reach out for it but the train doesn't allow it. You try to ignore the thought that nags at you as you watch his life quickly pass by.

Doesn't the flame seem to be getting dimmer? In fact, in time he seems almost content without you. Lives among friends, retires and enjoys his hobbies. A part of you yearns to be in front where you can sit and wait for him, but another part of you holds you back, knowing that rejection will be your ultimate demise.

Finally the train comes to what you know is the last stop. You see the love of your life about to board. Doubt becomes stronger and you find yourself even further back in the train. You can just barely see him. The fire above his head is quite dim now but you hope it is enough.

He steps onto the train and has a seat. As the doors close the slight breeze from the door blows out the flame. You can no longer see him.

You continue standing at the back of the train not knowing of anywhere to go. The final emotion has overcome you. One you have never experienced before. One with the combination of them all leaves you with no doubt what it is, for this must truly be death.

You look around at the people that are surrounding you and you are shocked to see they are transforming into demons.

Their humanity has finally been stripped from them. You look one more time out the window and a flash of all the people that ever hurt you and did you wrong were actually monsters like them in disguise.

It finally all makes sense, all of the hateful people in your life were nothing more than demons in disguise. Demons that continued to strip your own humanity.

The stronger people, like the love of your life, never had to worry about the demons. For you see, the demons only prey on the weak and fragile. The ones damaged from an early age.

Ones like you who attracted them like a magnet. They fed on you your whole life, your innocence and kindness was sweet and tasteful to them.

Bitterness begins to settle inside you towards the end which is the opening for you to become like them. You look back at the ones next to you and see they have embraced the bitterness and are ready to go out into the world to create more.

You look down at your hands and see them begin to transform, as silent tears begin to fall. However, the last bit of humanity still remains in your heart.

You concentrate on all the good things you accomplished. All the good people you met. On the one true love you were fortunate to find.

Suddenly you feel a change, you look down at your hands and they are normal. With a sense of urgency and determination, you will yourself to stand up and move forward in the train.

With each step you can hear the demons cry out in agony. To lose a fellow demon is a disgrace and rarely heard of and yet their screams give you even more strength.

Finally, you find yourself looking down at your one true love. At first he looks up at you, as if he doesn't know you. A quick pang to the heart comes over you and you begin to doubt yourself.

With one final act of hope you reach out and lay your hand on his. Suddenly a huge flame erupts from him. It envelopes you both in a protective cocoon.

All of the tender moments ever felt between the two of you heals all of the wounds ever done to you.

Never have you felt so safe. You know when it is time for you to get off the train to start to a whole new destination, things will be different.

You will be stronger, you will be able to see the demons for who they are and they will no longer be able to hurt you. You will never allow them to take your humanity.

Even though Lauren experienced the dream as the main character she now finds herself in place of the main character. Now she is on the train as herself. This is the first time Lauren is herself in her dream since she purchased the sound machine.

Lauren begins to be pushed towards the back of the train, no! She has family and friends who love her! She has never felt pain like the one whose dream she had tapped into. For that matter, the love either. She doesn't belong here! She is not dead!

However, the demons beckon her and she is getting closer to them. It doesn't matter how hard Lauren struggles, her destination is going to be with the demons. She will be the replacement for the one that got away.

Lauren's tired and weak mind can no longer handle the things she has seen or the things she is seeing. Just as she is about to give up, a voice tells her to concentrate on the fear. It will be her only escape.

White Noise Stories Continued

This time Lauren is not woken by her movements or by her phone. No, this time it is total abject fear! She jumps from the bed and flees her apartment. Not even bothering with the elevator she runs down the stairs. Slamming the door open, she enters the lobby like a mad woman.

Two people are at the front desk. One immediately starts making a call, while the other comes around the desk to offer his help. Slowly he goes up to Lauren and in a friendly voice asks, "Miss, may I help you?"

Lauren's eyes dart around and she screams, "Where is he? Where is Mr. Akeru?"

The man looks confused, "Mr. Akeru? I am not sure who you are talking about."

Lauren's frustration becomes heightened, "The doorman, the damn doorman, where is he?"

The man tries to assure her, "Miss, we have no doorman that works here."

Lauren's breathing is irregular as she looks around the lobby in complete fear, "What about the demons? You see them, right?"

A large group is now gathered in the lobby to watch the crazy woman's performance. Lauren looks into the group and can clearly see demons in their midst.

The demons smile back at her, knowing there is nothing she can do to them. The man helping her looks helplessly over to the other man behind the counter, "Jim, do you have something for me?"

Jim nods, "They are on their way, just try and keep her calm Dan."

Dan sighs, this was not how he had planned on ending his shift for the day, "Miss, there are no demons here, just normal everyday people. Can I get you something, perhaps a glass of water?"

Lauren tries to explain, "It is all in the dreams! Dreams I had from the dead dreaming! Unbelievable dreams!"

Dan offers, "Perhaps you would like to tell us about the dreams. Sometimes talking about them helps."

Lauren looks around at the people and thinks maybe he is right! She had never told anyone but Mr. Akeru about her dreams. She must tell them so they will talk about them, maybe even do some research on their own.

Lauren suddenly remembers, what if once they leave they forget about them? In fact, once she leaves she is going to forget all about this. She can't allow that to happen!

Lauren reaches for her pocket quickly, making Dan quite nervous, "Woa, what are you reaching for there sweetie?"

Lauren rolls her eyes, "My phone! I must record this so when after I leave I will have all the dreams down on tape."

Dan looks around at everyone and shrugs his shoulders, "Ok, sounds like a good idea to me."

Lauren pulls her phone out and starts to record. Knowing she doesn't have much time she quickly gives a short summary of each dream. Hopefully it will be enough to trigger her memories outside the complex.

Lauren begins, "There was a woman writer who lived here that died in a car accident. The accident happened on the way to the ferry. She missed the regular ferry and was placed on a different ferry."

Lauren looks down to make sure she is still recording, "Her body and car ended up on the island but no one knows how it got there. However, there is a story written about the mysterious ferry she was on. A story she had to have written after she was dead."

A couple of people in the lobby gasp. This encourages Lauren to go on, "Mrs. Anderson from apartment 1B died last week. She lived a very tragic and sad life. Her dream told of a place her soul would go every time it was abandoned, a lot like a pound. Each time she was there, people in her life would come and look at her but choose another. It stole the very life out of her soul." Lauren mumbles, "That one may be hard to prove but there are others!"

Lauren sees the disbelief on all of the people's faces. She continues to try and convince them, "Several years ago there was an explosion in this very building. In fact, it is why we all have electric stoves."

Even Lauren begins to get chills when she thinks about Sissy, "There was a new girl that just moved into the complex. She had grown up dealing with a dead sister who had not only been mean to her in life but even more so in death."

Lauren tries to stick to the facts, "This girl receives a phone call the same night as the explosion. Her parents had just died in a fire at the family home."

Lauren looks pleadingly out at the people, "After the girl gets off the phone, the dead sister shows up because now she no longer has anyone at the house to keep her company. The dead sister caused the explosion so the sisters would be together again."

Lauren hears the demons in the midst of the crowd chuckle and whisper how crazy she is. Lauren yells out at the crowd, "Look it up! This one would be easy to prove! You will see there was an explosion here and you will see that the girl lost her parents that same night!"

Lauren tries to explain, "How would I know these things if the dead were not dreaming about them?"

Lauren is surprised how easy it is for her to go to the next dream, "If you see shadows at night beware, they could be the hippies!"

Even Dan can't contain the smile on his face, "Seriously, did you just say hippies?"

Lauren realizes how crazy it all sounds but since she has an audience, she plans on using it to her advantage. Maybe someone in the crowd will recognize one of the dreams and back up her story.

Lauren pushes on, "Yes, hippies. There was a young couple that lived here who simply disappeared in their sleep one night."

Lauren must have hit a nerve because ol' Dan baby was not smiling anymore. Lauren pushes on, "When the girl was a teenager her parents bought a run-down house. The town folk stayed away from the house and had stories about the house."

Lauren explains, "The story about the house was there were hippies that lived in the house who had disappeared."

Lauren continues, "The hippies happened to be very intelligent, astrophysics intelligent. They must have found an alternate dimension. Their shadows are all that is left in this dimension."

Lauren finishes, “Since they had contact with the girl in her teens, they still had the connection when she moved into this complex.”

Lauren adds, “The girl would never sleep with the lights off but when her boyfriend moved in, he forced her to turn the lights off. That very night they both went missing.”

Dan has goose bumps rise up on him, how did this woman know that story? Not that he had ever had it told to him like this, but there was definitely a couple that disappeared from their bed in this complex and no one knows why.

Lauren realizes Dan must know about that story and it encourages her to go on, “A woman also died in this building due to an aneurism, the same night she found out she had been swapped at birth. Her brother was a serial killer and they had a connection due to the drugs their mother had taken. A lullaby a nurse sang to them kept them from doing drugs later in life.”

Lauren takes a deep breath, “Most of these dreams would be so easy for anyone of you to investigate them on your own!”

Lauren thinks about the next dream, “Especially this dream! A young man dies on a motorcycle. He was a donor. The person who received some of his body parts finds the dead man’s girlfriend and falls in love with her. Not because he loves her, but because the soul inside him still loves her.”

Lauren becomes even more agitated, “In fact, I ran into this poor couple recently at a bar. They need to be told what is happening to them!”

Lauren offers a solution, “This young man needs to get those damn cadaver parts out of him! This relationship is never going to work, the cadaver now may feel vindicated at being back with the love of his life but I know soon he will become bitter.”

Lauren continues, “His old habits will come back and his anger issues may go so far as to hurt the girl he loves.”

Lauren suddenly remembers and switches subjects, “Then, in my own apartment an artist died. His name was Bryan and he was given this cursed paintbrush that made his paintings come to life!”

Dan remembers Bryan and calmly answers, “I knew Bryan and he was what you would call a tortured artist. Bryan hit a rough patch and committed suicide. Very tragic but not uncommon."

Lauren shakes her head, "No! The paintings did come to life by taking the life of the subject! Bryan did not commit suicide, he tried to save himself!"

Dan tries to calm her, "Ma'am, you need to calm down, you are working yourself up into a frenzy."

Lauren can hear how crazy she sounds but she has to warn these people, "I forgot to tell you about the motorcycles! They have this special paint on them. They cause road rage and can get away with it because no one can see them!"

Lauren's mind quickly moves to the next dream, "Then there are these redneck killers that use that Yelp app online to help get their next victims."

Without pausing Lauren continues, "Oh yes! The game system! The man that created it lived here! He jumped from this very building! He had a God complex and designed the game to randomly kill people. We have to let as many people know about this as possible before they release it!"

Lauren catches a glimpse of herself in the mirror as she looks around the lobby. Lauren begins to tremble, "And for God's sake whatever you do, don't look in the mirror at 3:00 AM!"

Lauren continues, "A while back this apartment complex was a clinic and these dominant twins went missing. They are trapped in the mirrors here and are trying desperately to get out!"

Lauren's eyes bulge as she tries to explain, "You can't let them out because they are doppelgangers and they don't belong in our world!"

Lauren suddenly becomes quiet as she fearfully looks around the room. Dan gets a chill over him as he watches her, the woman is truly terrified.

Lauren calmly finishes, "The demons are the worst! They live among us as friends and family members. They feed on our misery and low self-esteem."

Lauren looks at several people in the group, "You don't understand, they are in disguise! They eat at our humanity until we have none!"

Lauren points at one man in particular, "Take him for example. He is a demon! In fact, Mr. Akeru opened the door for him and this man had a conversation with Mr. Akeru!"

The man Lauren is pointing to becomes very indignant, "First of all lady, I am no demon! How dare you to even imply that! And second of all, how stupid are you? Take a look, the doors open by themselves!"

Lauren looks at the doors in confusion. The man is right, they are automated doors. How can that be? Lauren's doubt begins to come over her until she sees her reflection.

Lauren looks back at the crowd, "I know all too well how crazy I look. I am a young woman, twenty-seven years old!"

One of the women puts her hand up to her mouth as she gasps; this woman standing in front of them has to easily be over fifty!

Lauren knows they don't believe her, "I know, but yet again this is something else very easy for any of you to research. My birthday is July 12, 1989."

Lauren's body can barely hold itself up, the pure exhaustion she feels is overwhelming. However, her stories are almost finished and the most important part of the story has not even been told.

Lauren sighs, "These dreams started when I bought a sound machine. I used the white noise sound to block out all the noises in this building."

Lauren admits, "It worked but then I started having these dreams I told you about. They started to consume me. Meanwhile, during the dreams I had interaction with a Mr. Akeru."

Lauren explains, "Mr. Akeru's last name is an Egyptian name for the gatekeeper. I believe Mr. Akeru is in charge of all of the souls in this complex."

Lauren hears the ambulance outside and quickly finishes up, "All of you are tied to this complex. When you die he keeps your souls here. These dreams have been from the souls trapped here."

Two paramedics come through the doors. They quickly evaluate the circumstances and instantly see who their patient is. They walk slowly towards her, "Miss, mind if we take you in to be checked out?"

Lauren offers no resistance, her body is simply too tired. As they walk her towards the doors, she stops and turns towards the crowd. Loudly she lectures, "Keep your humanity in check, for when you have lost it you become them!"

Lauren's eyes are wide with fear as she watches the demons in the group laughing. She can't help but scream out as they forcefully take her out, "PLEASE! FOR YOUR SOUL'S SAKE, DON'T BECOME LIKE THEM!"

Dan turns to the group apologetically, "Ok people, sorry for the scene. Let's try not to be too harsh on this poor woman. Obviously she has experienced a break of some sort."

The crowd begins to disperse as they mumble among themselves. Mr. Akeru comes out of the shadows and stands by the automated doors.

Most walk by him without seeing him, while the demons give him a slight nod as they go by. After the lobby is empty Mr. Akeru thinks about what happened. He sighs as he realizes he has lost yet another soul. Master Aker will not be pleased; however, Mr. Akeru is not concerned.

His numbers had been up for quite some time. Mr. Akeru admits it is not so much what he is doing as it is what society is doing.

More and more people are finding themselves lonelier than they have ever been. They think they have their social media to comfort them when in fact all it does is make them envious of what others have. It lowers their self-esteem and makes them even more vulnerable to his demons.

Mr. Akeru is quite pleased that white noise is making a comeback. Back in the day it had always been a handy tool for him. For who would be the ones to fall asleep in front of the TV, subconsciously hearing the hiss of the white noise when the station went off the air? Usually the loneliest miserable souls, opening themselves up for the dead around them to share their dreams with while they feed off their energy.

Mr. Akeru smiles. Yes, some may have escaped from this complex but for the most part he runs a tight ship. But one annoying thought does come over him.

Even though Lauren will most likely be committed and will be thought of as crazy, eventually he will have to take care of her. Mr. Akeru is never one for loose ends.

THE
FOLKS
TAMMY
VREELAND

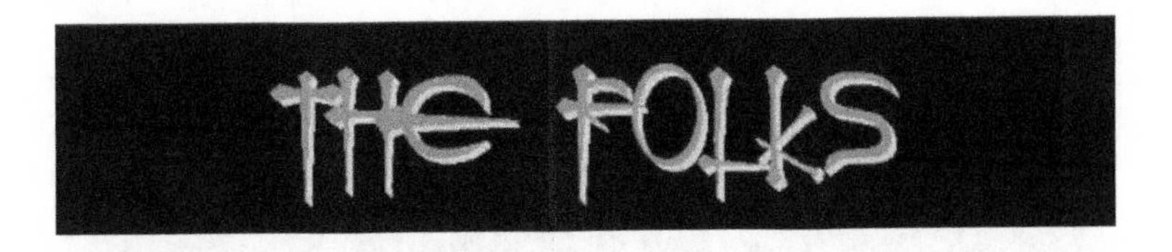

Moving into a new home can become quite stressful. For David, it is the matter of juggling a new job, a mistress and a family at home. For Terry, it is the matter of making her new house into a home and recovering from a nervous breakdown. For Tyler, it is the stress of a five-year-old trying to fit into a new neighborhood with no friends.

A move can be quite difficult on a child, so much so that a way for the child to cope is to have an imaginary friend. This is where *The Folks* come in. You see Tyler not only has one imaginary friend but a whole group of imaginary friends that call themselves *The Folks*. Tyler meets *The Folks* the very first day he moves into his new room.

When Terry, Tyler's mom, finds out about *The Folks* she becomes concerned. Terry's family, friends and even her own therapist tell her that it is a healthy way for Tyler to cope with the move.

However, when accidental deaths begin to occur and Tyler, with his imaginary *Folks,* happens to know more than they should, Terry begins to wonder that perhaps *The Folks* are not so healthy after all!

THE SEA
OF SOULS
SEQUEL TO
THE FOLKS
TAMMY
VREELAND

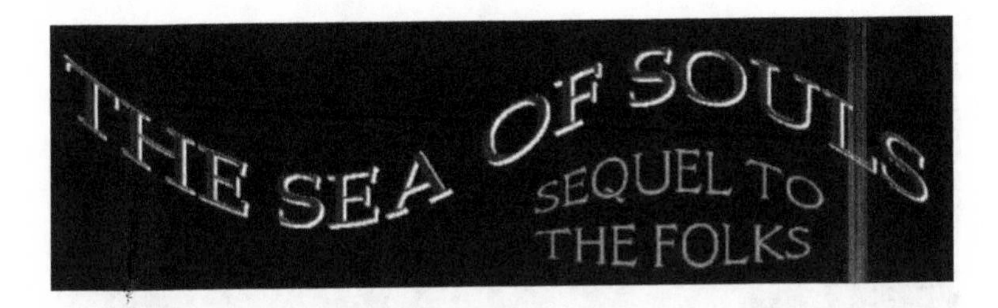

Tyler, the small boy with the imaginary friends called the Folks, is now grown up. Moving on with his life, he has entered the Coast Guard.

While at Boot Camp, Tyler endures a high fever which brings back flooding memories of the Folks. Memories he's not sure are his own.

Terry, Tyler's mom, ever watchful of the Folk's return, decides to help Tyler get settled in with his new orders. Travis, Tyler's brother, plans on sharing an apartment with Tyler making Tyler's transition even easier.

The two brothers are excited to start their new life in Galveston, Texas. Unfortunately, the island has a dark past of its own. Terry, Tyler and Travis find themselves re-living the past to ensure their future.

TAILOR
TAMMY
VREELAND

John is a small town reporter who has just been given the chance of a lifetime. The notorious serial killer, Taylor the Tailor, has requested him personally to write her life story. The catch is John has only three days before Taylor is to be electrocuted to interview her.

During those three days John unravels a story like no other. Overwhelmed in just the first interview, John turns to his young assistant Lauren for help. Lauren readily agrees and heads to Taylor's hometown to come up with cold hard facts to help make Taylor's story a credible one.

However, both Lauren and John quickly realize that Taylor's tale may not be that easy to prove. Although both of them are skeptics at heart, they are finding out that Taylor's story is not an easy one to understand or believe. Especially with its supernatural undertones.

John's interviews start off with Taylor's childhood and to his horror John realizes that Taylor had begun to kill as early as the age of four with her first victim being her father. As Taylor grows up her list of victims increases as her skills for being "The Tailor" sharpen.

Tim is Taylor's brother who had been institutionalized at a very young age; upon being released Tim had changed his name so as not to be connected with Taylor in any fashion. Unfortunately, due to Taylor's impending doom, Tim finds himself thrown back into Taylor's world.

Tim and Lauren team up to try and put a stop to Taylor's evil once and for all. Yet, all three of them question why Taylor wants her story to be told now? Is it to seek redemption for all the bad deeds she has done, knowing her time is limited? Maybe, it's to brag to the world how much she got away with and how she did it? Or is it something so much darker that none of them will find out until the third day at the stroke of midnight?

TRANSPORTER
OF
SOULS
TAMMY
VREELAND

Evan's boss John realizes that Evan has become burned out with Police Towing. The death and destruction that Evan sees on a daily basis has finally taken its toll. Not wanting to lose Evan, John proposes for Evan to start his own business in towing salvage cars.

John assures Evan that he can provide him with enough contacts to start the business up. And strangely enough, the money becomes available to Evan with the unexpected passing of his grandmother.

Now with a new business and a new love interest Evan begins his new life. But soon Evan quickly realizes that the horrors he has encountered at the scene of accidents may not be the end of life as he thought. That maybe souls are still trapped in the ruins of cars they perished in. A curse that began with the very first known automobile accident. A curse that continues to this day. And as with most curses, man has figured a way not to remove it but to profit from it.

CLASS
REUNION
TAMMY VREELAND

Tonya has just received a call from Darla, an old school mate, asking her to come to a class reunion.

Feeling guilty about leaving and never looking back Tonya decides to go.

The reunion is all about catching up with old friends. One friend though, is quite upset with the different paths people chose after graduation.

They feel it is their duty to keep the reputation of the class and school intact. Through the years they had done exactly that.

Now with the reunion coming up, it was the perfect time to deal with many of the classmates in one night.

It's a simple concept, they plan on using the different types of kills Tonya uses in her current horror book "Classmates" to make their own statement.

This will take the suspicion off them and place it on what may simply be a fan of Tonya's making a point.

Only the classmates themselves will know the true identity of the killer, but by then it will be too late!

THE FAMILY TREE
TAMMY
VREELAND

Katherine looks down at the book as she lightly runs her fingers over the cover. She can feel the raised insignia of the oak tree with mistletoe in the branches. The title is elegantly written with beautiful penmanship which spells out "The Family Tree".

She timidly opens the book and looks down at the familiar pages in front of her. Tears begin to form in her eyes as she subconsciously rubs her stomach.

Katherine thumbs through the pages. She had always been taught that through her past her future is determined. But, she did not like what her future was to bring.

Why were her ancestors allowed to decide the fate of her unborn twins? Why couldn't she have a choice? Didn't they know what the consequences were? Or were they so blind to the religion, they didn't see it for what it really is?

Again Katherine thinks about the title of the book. Her Family Tree had deep dark roots. Many branches filled the tree but all were tied to one dark secret.

Katherine realizes that she is the one that must cut this tree down. But, how and at what cost? She feels a kick from one of the twins and this gives her hope.

The key had to be the religion. What its origins were, why it was created and how to destroy it. The religion was so old and forgotten that only through tradition had it survived.

Katherine thinks to herself, maybe this generation needed to start a tradition of their own!

Visit me at:

www.tammyvreelandsfanpage.com

****

Also on Facebook:

Tammy Vreeland's Horror Books

CPSIA information can be obtained
at www.ICGtesting.com
Printed in the USA
BVHW072205160919
558621BV00004B/17/P